AN INNOCENT CLIENT

AN INNOCENT CLIENT

By

SCOTT PRATT

This book, along with every book I've written and every book I'll write, is dedicated to my darling Kristy, to her unconquerable spirit and to her inspirational courage. I loved her before I was born and I'll love her after I'm long gone.

PART I

APRIL 12
7:00 A.M.

I t was my fortieth birthday, and the first thing I had to do was deal with Johnny Wayne Neal. The forensic psychiatrist I'd hired to examine him said Johnny Wayne was a narcissist, a pathological liar, and a sociopath, and those were his good qualities. He called Johnny Wayne an "irredeemable monster." I'd asked the shrink not to write any of that down. I didn't want the district attorney to see it. Monster or not, Johnny Wayne was still my client.

Johnny Wayne Neal had hired two of his thug buddies to murder his beautiful, heavily insured young wife. She woke up at 3:00 a.m. on a Wednesday morning about a year ago to find two strangers standing over her bed. The men clumsily and brutally stabbed her to death while Johnny Wayne's three-year-old son, who'd been sleeping with his mother that night, crawled beneath the bed and listened to the sounds of his mother dying.

It took the Tennessee Bureau of Investigation and the Johnson City Police Department less than a week to figure out who was responsible for the murder. Johnny Wayne was arrested and charged with both first-degree murder and conspiracy to commit first-degree murder, and because of the heinous nature of the crime, the State of Tennessee was seeking the death penalty. A heartless judge appointed me to defend him. The hourly rate was a hundred bucks, about the same as a small-time prostitute's.

The prosecutor had offered to take the death penalty off the table if Johnny Wayne would plead guilty to first-degree murder and agree to go to prison for the rest of his life. When I told Johnny Wayne about the offer a week ago, he'd reluctantly agreed. We were supposed to be in court at 9:00 a.m. so that Johnny Wayne could enter his plea. I was at the jail to make sure he hadn't changed his mind.

Fifteen minutes after I sat down in the attorney's room, Johnny Wayne, in a sharply creased, unwrinkled orange jumpsuit, was escorted in. He was handcuffed, waist-chained, and shackled around the ankles.

"I wanted to make sure you're still willing to take this deal before we go to court," I said as soon as the uniformed escort stepped out and Johnny Wayne awkwardly made his way into the chair. "Once you enter the plea, there's no turning back."

Johnny Wayne stared at the tabletop. His short hair was the color of baled straw, wispy and perfectly combed. He was much smaller than me, well under six feet, thin and pale. His face and arms were covered with tiny, pinkish freckles. He started tapping his fingers on the table, and I noticed that his nails looked recently manicured. He smelled of shampoo.

"How do you manage to stay so well groomed in this place?" I said. "Every time I see you, you look like you just came out of a salon."

He rolled his eyes. They were pale green, sometimes flecked with red depending on angle and light. They were closely set, and the left eye had a tendency to wander. It made looking him in the eye uncomfortable. I never knew quite where to focus.

"The fact that I'm incarcerated doesn't require me to live like an animal," he said. "I'm able to procure certain services."

"You mean a barber?"

"I have a barber, one of the inmates, who comes to my cell once a week. He trims my beard and shampoos and cuts my hair."

"Does he give you a manicure too?" I glanced at his fingernails.

"I do that myself."

"Who does your laundry? All my other clients look like they sleep in their jail uniforms."

I could tell the questions were irritating him, so I kept on.

"My laundry is done along with everyone else's," he said. "I simply purchase commissary products for an individual who treats my laundry with special care." His speech was a tinny, nasal tenor, his diction perfect. I imagined shoving a turd into his mouth, just so he'd mispronounce a word.

"Why are you so interested in my personal hygiene?" Johnny Wayne said. "Does it offend you?"

"Nah," I said, "I was just curious."

His disdain for me was palpable. With each visit I could sense it growing like metastasizing cancer, but I didn't care. I disliked him as intensely as he disliked me. He'd lied to me dozens of times. He'd run me and my investigator all over east Tennessee following false leads and locating bogus witnesses. He whined constantly.

"So now that we have those incredibly important matters out of the way," Johnny Wayne said, "explain this *deal,* as you so eloquently put it, one more time."

"It's simple," I said. "A moron could understand it."

"Are you insinuating that I'm a moron?"

Answering the question truthfully would have served no useful purpose, so I ignored it.

"The deal is you plead guilty to first-degree murder. You agree to a sentence of life without the possibility of parole. You give up your right to appeal. In exchange, you get to live. No needle for Johnny Wayne. That's it, sweet and simple."

He snorted. "Doesn't sound like much of a deal to me."

"Depends on your point of view."

"Meaning?"

"It depends on whether you want to spend the rest of your life in the general prison population where you can at least get a blow job once in a while or spend the next fifteen years in isolation on death row, then die by lethal injection."

"But I'm innocent."

"Of course you are. Unfortunately, the evidence says otherwise."

"All circumstantial. Or lies."

"What about the cell phone records that match exactly with the statements Clive and Derek gave the police? The calls they say you made to check on them while they were on their way up here to kill Laura, and while they were on their way back."

The muscles in his jaw tightened. Johnny Wayne didn't like discussing facts.

"What about the four separate life insurance policies you took out on Laura over the past eighteen months? Three hundred and fifty grand, Johnny Wayne."

"Lots of people over-insure their spouses."

"Explain why Derek and Clive would say you hired them to kill Laura and promised to give them 10 percent of the insurance money."

"They're trying to save themselves."

"If you didn't hire them, why'd they do it? They didn't even know her."

"Why? Why? Why are you asking me all these stupid questions? You're supposed to be my lawyer."

I should have brought up the audio tape, but I decided to cut him some slack. Clive and Derek, the thugs he hired, had both caved immediately during the interrogation. They confessed and told the police Johnny Wayne had hired them. The police outfitted them with tape recorders and sent them to see Johnny Wayne, who talked freely about the murder and the money. The first time I played the tape for him his face turned an odd shade.

"Listen to me," I said. "Part of a lawyer's job is to give his client good advice. And my advice is that the prosecution could bring in a trained monkey and convict you of this murder. The evidence is overwhelming, the murder was especially cruel, and your little boy witnessed it. My advice is that your chances of getting the death penalty are better than excellent."

"I didn't kill anyone," he said.

"Maybe not, but she'd be alive if it weren't for you. The jury will hold you accountable."

"So I'm supposed to spend the rest of my life in prison for something I didn't do."

"You can either accept their offer and plead, or you can go to trial."

"With a lawyer who thinks I'm guilty."

"Don't put this on me. I'm just giving you an honest opinion as to what I think the outcome will be. You should be thankful. Your mother- and father-in-law don't believe in the death penalty any more than I do. They think if you're convicted and sentenced to death, your blood will somehow be on their hands. They're the ones who talked the district attorney into making this offer."

"They're hypocritical fools," Johnny Wayne said.

I wanted to backhand him. James and Rita Miller, the parents of his murdered, beautiful, innocent young wife, were two of the nicest people I'd ever met. I interviewed them as I was preparing for the trial. One of the questions I asked was how a nice young lady like Laura had ever become involved with Johnny Wayne. James Miller told me Laura met Johnny Wayne while she was attending college at Carson-Newman, a small school in Jefferson City only sixty miles away. Johnny Wayne, who lived in Jefferson City and was a part-time student, had made himself a fixture at the Baptist Student Union, a gathering place for students of the Baptist faith. It was there that he ran his con on Laura, convincing her that he held deep convictions about Christianity. James and Rita said they had concerns, but they trusted Laura's judgment. Johnny Wayne seemed intelligent and acted as though he loved Laura. They never imagined a monster lurked beneath the careful grooming and easy smile. But the marriage began to show serious cracks soon after the wedding and steadily broke down. Not long after their third anniversary, Johnny Wayne left Laura for another woman and moved to North Carolina. He was in Charlotte at a bar with his newly pregnant girlfriend the night Laura was murdered.

I looked at Johnny Wayne and envisioned my knuckles cracking into his teeth. It was an image I found soothing.

"What's it going to be?" I said. "I need an answer. We're supposed to be in court in two hours."

"I need more time to consider it."

"No, you don't. It's a gift. Take it or leave it."

His hands went to his nose, and he began his obnoxious habit of squeezing his nostrils together with his thumb and index finger. Squeeze and hold. Release. Squeeze and hold. Release.

After three squeeze-and-holds, he said, "Screw it. I'll do it. Throw me to the wolves."

"Good decision," I said. "First one you've made in a while."

"Are we done here?"

"I suppose. You in a hurry?"

"I have to take a crap. It's the bologna they serve in this dump." His voice, like his face, was devoid of emotion. He hadn't bothered to ask how his son would be affected. He hadn't mentioned the boy in months.

I got up and pushed the button on the wall to summon the guards. Johnny Wayne remained seated while I leaned on the wall and stared at the ceiling. I didn't want to sit back down. I wanted to be as far away from him as possible. After three or four minutes, I could hear the thump of heavy boots as the guards made their way down the hallway toward the door.

"Hey, Dillard," Johnny Wayne said suddenly.

"What?"

"Everybody thinks she was such a saint. She was a stupid whore. All she had to do was give me a divorce on my terms, which weren't that complicated. She brought this on herself."

"Don't say another word," I said. The vision of flying teeth was acquiring details.

The door clanged, and the guards pushed their way through and gathered him up. One of them, a skin-headed, thick-necked youngster, looked me up and down.

"You only do criminal defense, ain't that right?" he said.

"That's right."

"Then I reckon you'll be glad to know that an old lady called into dispatch a little while ago and reported that her cat found a human pecker out near the lake. A body'll probably turn up soon."

"A pecker? Do you mean a penis?"

"Penis to you. Pecker to me."

"So?"

"Thought you'd like to know. A dead body means business for you, don't it? Sort of like an undertaker."

He winked at his partner and they shared a laugh. Even Johnny Wayne smiled. After they left, I stayed on the wall for a few minutes, their laughter and Johnny Wayne's vulgar confession replaying in my head. The rattle of the chains faded as they led him away.

My head started to pound and my stomach tightened as I made my way back through the labyrinth of steel and concrete. I was sick of defending the Johnny Wayne Neals of this world, and I was sick of being mocked and laughed at by pricks like the two guards. I reminded myself that I was getting out of the legal profession. In less than a year, I'd be free of it. No more Johnny Waynes. No more pricks.

As I made my way toward the entrance, I tried to tell myself to take it easy. *Don't let it get to you. You did your job.* I forced myself to think about something more pleasant. My birthday. Celebrating with my wife Caroline and the kids, the most important and beautiful people in my life. Chocolate cake. What would I wish for this year?

It came to me as I stepped out the front door into the rain, and the thought made me smile. The chances of the wish coming true were about a million to one, but what the hell? Why not?

This year, I'd make my birthday wish simple and selfish. This year, before I gave up the practice of law, I'd wish for one—just *one*—innocent client.

APRIL 12
8:45 A.M.

An hour later, I was sitting in my truck in the parking lot at the Washington County Courthouse in downtown Jonesborough. It's a postcard-pretty little town, the oldest in Tennessee, nestled in the rolling hills ninety miles northeast of Knoxville. I looked across the street at the National Storytelling Center, which was built a few years ago and brings Jonesborough a limited amount of national acclaim. Every October, thousands of people gather for a huge storytelling festival. I smiled as I thought about the irony of having a storytelling center so near the courthouse. There were whoppers being told in both places.

As the raindrops patted against the windshield, I opened the console, took out a bottle of mouthwash, and gargled. I'd gotten in the habit of carrying the mouthwash with me because my mouth seemed to stay dry and bitter during the day, especially when I had to go in front of a judge or jury. The dryness was accompanied by a hollow feeling in the pit of my stomach and a nagging sense of impending doom. It would disappear sometimes when I was with my family, but it was never far away. At night, I kept having a dream where I was on a makeshift raft without a paddle, floating down the middle of a wide, raging river that was rushing me toward a deadly waterfall. I couldn't get to the side of the river, and I couldn't go back upstream. I'd wake up just as I went over the falls.

I put the cap back on the bottle and took a deep breath. Showtime. I climbed out of the truck and walked up the courthouse steps, through the foyer, and up to the security station.

The security officer was John Allen "Sarge" Hurley, a gruff but good-natured old coot with whom I traded friendly insults every chance I got. Sarge was legendary around the sheriff's department for his bravery and machismo. My favorite story about him was the time Sarge single-handedly apprehended a notorious armed robber named Dewey Davis after Davis held up a grocery store on the outskirts of Jonesborough. A much younger Sarge, responding to a robbery-in-progress call, showed up just as Dewey was walking out the front door of the Winn-Dixie carrying a shotgun. As the story goes, Sarge jumped out of his cruiser oblivious of the shotgun, ran Dewey down in the parking lot, and knocked him unconscious with one punch before he hauled him off to jail.

Sarge had to be in his early seventies now. He was still tall and lean, but Mother Nature was beginning to bend him like an old poplar in a stiff wind. There were dark liver spots on his huge hands, and his upper lip had retreated until it was tight across his dentures, giving him a permanent snarl. The buckle on his gun belt was notched two inches above his navel, but he had no holster and no gun. He carried only a nightstick and a small can of pepper spray.

"What's up, Sarge?" I said as I walked through the metal detector.

"The rent," he growled. "I hear your boy Johnny Wayne is throwin' in the towel today." The sheriff's department was a more efficient gossip pipeline than a sewing circle. Sarge always knew what was happening, sometimes *before* it happened.

"Good news travels fast," I said.

"Can't believe they ain't gonna give him the needle."

"Hell, Sarge, he's innocent. He's just being railroaded by the system."

"Innocent, my ass. Nobody you represent is innocent."

As I started to walk past Sarge toward the elevator, he grabbed me by the arm. His gnarled fingers dug deep into my bicep.

"You know what I'd like to see?" he said. "I'd like to see that sorry SOB hanged on a flatbed truck right out here in front of the courthouse. That's what I'd like to see. I'd buy a goddanged ticket."

It was a sentiment prevalent in the community. Laura Neal, Johnny Wayne's wife and victim, was guilty of nothing more than picking a bad husband. She was a third-grade teacher with a wonderful reputation, her parents were solid and hardworking, and her brother was a college professor. People wanted to see Johnny

Wayne burned at the stake, and I had the feeling most of them wouldn't have minded seeing his lawyer go up in flames with him.

I pulled away from Sarge and headed up the side stairwell to the second floor. There were about a dozen people milling around in the hallway outside the courtroom, speaking in hushed tones. The hallway was dimly lit and narrow. I never noticed any color in the corridor outside the courtroom. Everything always seemed black and white, like I was walking onto the set of "Twelve Angry Men."

I stepped into Judge Ivan Glass's courtroom and looked around. No judge. No bailiff. No clerk.

"Where's His Holiness?" I asked Lisa Mayes, the assistant district attorney who had been assigned to prosecute Johnny Wayne. She was sitting at the prosecution table contemplating her fingernails.

"Back in chambers. He's not in a good mood."

Glass had been a notorious drinker and womanizer for more than three decades. He'd been divorced twice, primarily because of his affinity for younger women, but the good people of the First Judicial District didn't seem to mind. They elected him every eight years. Glass's father had been a judge, and his father before him. To hear Glass tell it, the bench was his birthright.

He was known among the defense bar as Ivan the Terrible because of his complete lack of compassion for criminal defendants and because he treated defense attorneys almost as badly as he treated their clients. I got off on the wrong foot with him right out of law school. The first day I was in his courtroom he put an old man in jail because the man couldn't afford to pay his court costs. I knew what the judge was doing was illegal—debtor's prisons were outlawed a long time ago—but he seemed to do whatever he wanted regardless of the law. I did some research and found Glass had been doing it for years. I wrote him a letter and asked him to stop. He wrote back and told me young lawyers ought to mind their own business. So I sued the county for allowing one of their employees, the judge, to commit constitutional violations during the course of his employment. By the time I was done, the county had to pay out nearly a million dollars to people Glass had jailed illegally, and Glass was seriously embarrassed in the process. He hated me for it, and one of the ways he exacted vengeance was by appointing me to cases like Johnny Wayne Neal's.

The courtroom was tense and somber. The media vultures had already filled the jury box. James and Rita Miller, Johnny Wayne's in-laws, were sitting in the front row. Rita was crying. James looked away when I tried to catch his eye.

I walked over to the defense table to wait for the judge, who finally teetered through the door in his black robe a half hour later. His hair was snow white, medium length and chaotic. He wore tinted reading glasses that made it difficult to see his eyes. His clerk helped him up the steps and into his chair. The clerk called the case, and the bailiffs brought Johnny Wayne in through a door to my right and led him to the podium ten feet in front of the judge.

I stood at the podium next to my client while the judge went through a lengthy question-and-answer session to ensure that Johnny Wayne was competent to enter a guilty plea, that he understood what was going on, and that he wasn't under the influence of alcohol or drugs. Lisa Mayes, the prosecutor, then stood and read the litany of evidence that would have been presented had Johnny Wayne gone to trial. I could hear Rita Miller sobbing uncontrollably behind me as she was forced, one last time, to listen to a detailed description of her daughter's brutal murder while her grandson hid beneath the bed. I felt ashamed to be representing the man who had caused her such misery.

When Lisa was finished, Judge Glass stiffened. "Johnny Wayne Neal," he said in a voice made gravelly from booze and tobacco, "how do you plead to the charge of first-degree murder?"

The moment of truth. The point of no return.

"Guilty," came the answer, barely audible. I breathed a sigh of relief.

"On your plea of guilty, the court finds you guilty and sentences you to life in prison without the possibility of parole."

Glass then lowered his glasses to the end of his nose and leaned forward. His eyes bored into Johnny Wayne.

"Just for the record," the judge said, "I want to tell you something before they trot you off to the penitentiary for the rest of your miserable existence. In all my years on the bench, you are, without question, the most disgusting, the most cowardly, the most pitiful excuse for a human being that has ever set foot in my court. There isn't an ounce of remorse in you, and I want you to know that it would have been my distinct pleasure to sentence you to death if you'd had the courage to go to trial. I hope you rot in hell."

Johnny Wayne's head rose slowly, and he met the judge's gaze.

"Screw you," he said quietly.

Glass's eyes widened. "What did you say?"

"I said screw you, and the district attorney, and the Tennessee Bureau of Investigation, and this pathetic excuse for a lawyer you dumped on me, and everybody else who had a hand in framing me." The words spilled out in a crescendo. By the time he finished, his voice was echoing off the walls.

There was a stunned silence. The judge surprised me by smiling. He turned his head to me.

"Not only is your client a coward, Mr. Dillard, he's a stupid coward."

"Screw you!" Johnny Wayne yelled.

"Bailiffs!" Judge Glass roared. He half rose from his seat, like a jockey on a thoroughbred, and pointed his gavel at Johnny Wayne.

"Take him out and gag him!"

They were on him in a second. Two of them took him down and another two jumped into the fray. I could hear the cameras clicking and people gasping as I moved out of the way. Johnny Wayne was screaming obscenities as they punched and kicked at him. The bailiffs finally got enough control so that they could drag Johnny Wayne across the floor by his feet and out the door. I sat down at the defense table and wondered briefly whether I should be offended that Johnny Wayne had called me a pathetic excuse for a lawyer. I was a pathetic excuse for a human being, maybe, but I was a pretty damned good lawyer.

Everybody sat around stupidly for a few minutes until finally the bailiffs, now in a tight phalanx, dragged Johnny Wayne back into the room. They'd stuffed something into his mouth and covered it with duct tape. I wondered how it was going to feel when they ripped the tape off his neatly trimmed beard. They pulled him upright at the podium in front of the judge.

"Mr. Neal," Judge Glass said, "your little outburst caused me to briefly consider rescinding your plea agreement and forcing you to go to trial. But I think this punishment is more appropriate for a man like you. You're going to die in jail, but before you die, I think you have plenty to look forward to. A handsome young man like you, with a pretty potty mouth like yours, will undoubtedly enjoy tremendous popularity in the general population at the penitentiary. I'm sure you'll be a favorite among the sodomites. The sentence stands. Life without parole. Get him out of here."

My last image of Johnny Wayne was of his being dragged backwards across the floor, refusing to walk, tears streaming down his face and onto the silver tape stretched across his mouth. The worst part of it for him, though, had to be the fact that his jumpsuit had become terribly wrinkled during the fight with the guards.

I ducked out through a side door to avoid the media, went down the stairs, and headed back through the security station. Sarge was going through a woman's purse. As I walked by, he handed her the purse and headed straight for me.

"Hey, Dillard, you hear about the murder?"

"What murder?"

"They found some guy in a room up at the Budget Inn stabbed to death. Somebody cut his dick off. A cat found it this morning out by the lake."

"I didn't do it, Sarge." I kept on walking, but I could hear him laughing.

"Maybe you'll get to defend the killer," I heard him say. "Yeah, maybe the killer'll be just like ol' Johnny Wayne. Innocent. Railroaded by the system."

APRIL 12
10:00 A.M.

Special Agent Phillip Landers's cell phone rang a little before 10:00 a.m., just as he was wrapping his mouth around a breakfast burrito at Sonic. Bill Wright, the special agent in charge of the Tennessee Bureau of Investigation office in Johnson City, was calling. Bill was Landers's boss. Not that the brownnosing jerk should have been the boss. Landers should have been the boss. By his own account, he was, by far, the smartest, hardest-working, best-looking TBI agent in the office. He knew he'd get his chance soon though. Wright was about to retire.

"There's a body at the Budget Inn," Wright said as Landers chewed slowly and stared at a teenage waitress on a pair of roller skates. "Male. Stabbed to death. That's about all I know. I already called forensics. They're on the way."

The Johnson City police didn't have any forensics people on the payroll, so murders were often passed along to the TBI. Landers took his time finishing his burrito. No big rush. The guy was already dead.

There were six city cruisers in the Budget Inn parking lot when Landers pulled in a half hour after he got the call. All the cruisers had their emergency lights on, as though the cops who drove them were actually *doing* something. The patrol guys never ceased to amaze Landers. They'd stand around for hours at a crime scene, screwing off, trading gossip, and hoping for some little tidbit of information they could share with each other. If they were really lucky, maybe they'd get a glimpse of the body and could go home and tell their wives or girlfriends the gory details.

Landers opened the trunk, lifted out a couple pairs of latex gloves, and walked up the stairs to Room 201. It was overcast and drizzling outside, but it still took his eyes a second to adjust to the dim light in the room. As soon as he cleared the door, he could smell blood. His eyes moved to the left. Jimmy Brown, a big, dim cracker with a butch haircut who had worked his way up through patrol and was finally, after twenty years, an investigator with the Johnson City police, was leaning over the bed. Beneath him was the body of what appeared to be a male whale. A very pale male whale. He was buck naked, lying flat on his back. His legs were splayed, and his arms went straight out from his shoulders. Spread-eagled. He was covered in dark, dried blood.

"So much for death with dignity, huh?" Landers said.

Brown looked at him deadpan. He didn't even smile. How could he not smile? That was pretty funny. Landers chalked it up to petty jealousy.

"Where's the forensics team?" Brown said.

"On the way. Should be here in an hour or so." The TBI's east Tennessee forensics guys and girls scrambled out of Knoxville, ninety miles to the west. They were responsible for covering the entire eastern half of the state. Landers knew they'd show up in their fancy, modern, mobile crime-scene van dressed in their cute little white uniforms. Thanks to the CSI television shows, they all thought they were stars.

"Who's the pretty boy?" Landers said.

Brown stepped back away from the body and pulled out his notepad.

"Signed in as John Paul Tester and gave a Newport address, confirmed by registration in the glove compartment of his car. His wallet's gone, if he had one. Manager says he checked in late yesterday afternoon, said he was here to preach at a revival, and asked where he could get a good hamburger. The manager told him to go to the Purple Pig. We're getting a driver's license photo from the Department of Safety so we can take it down there and ask around."

Landers wondered why Brown needed the notepad to impart such a brief summary. The guy was really thick. Landers began to walk around the bed, looking at the dead whale. There were dozens of stab wounds, most of them concentrated around the neck and chest.

"Preacher, huh? Looks like somebody didn't like the sermon,"

"That's the least of it," Brown said. "His dick's gone."

"Jesus! Really?" Landers hadn't noticed with all the blood. He looked between the whale's legs, and there was nothing but a mess of dark red goo. Whoever cut it off had to work for it. Landers figured it had been quite a while since the whale had seen his own dick.

"And get this," Brown said. "Some woman called the sheriff's department this morning. She lives out by Pickens Bridge, and her cat brought her a little gift. Turned out to be a human penis. Probably belongs to this guy."

His logic was astounding. "Any idea how long he's been dead?" Landers said.

"He's cold and stiff. I'd say more than eight hours."

"Security cameras?"

"Just at the front desk. Nothing in the parking lot or anywhere else."

A patrol officer knocked and walked in. He was carrying an eight-by-ten photo of the dead guy. He handed it to Brown, who handed it to Landers.

"Are you here to help or are you just sightseeing?" Brown said.

"Your wish is my command, at least until the case officially gets dropped in my lap."

Brown gave him a shove-it look. "Why don't you take this down to the Purple Pig and ask around?"

"Done," Landers said. "Anything else?"

"I don't think so. I've got people running down the woman who was on duty last night, canvassing the rooms, and working the Newport angle. You say forensics is on the way. I think we've got it under control for now."

"Cool. I'm off to the Pig."

Landers walked down the steps, past the patrol guys, and got into his car. He recognized a reporter from the

Johnson City paper loitering outside the entrance. Her name was Sylvia something. She wasn't gorgeous, but she wasn't hideous, so Landers got back out of the car and went over to chat with her for a couple minutes. He leaked her a little tidbit about the missing penis, thinking it might be worth a blow job somewhere down the line.

As he made his way south down Roan Street, Landers kept glancing at the photo of the dead preacher. He had reddish hair, semi-decent features, and wide sideburns that ran to the bottom of his ear lobes, *á la* Elvis Presley. Not a bad-looking dude, but damn sure not in the same league as Landers.

"What'd you do to get yourself killed, Rev?" Landers said to the photo as he turned into the parking lot at the Purple Pig. "Dip the old wick in a vat of bad wax?"

APRIL 12
10:20 A.M.

Caroline Dillard, wearing a sharp, dark blue Calvin Klein knock-off suit, took a deep breath, straightened her back, and strode up to the reception area. Behind the bulletproof window sat a dour, pudgy, middle-aged man with a dark widow's-peak crew cut and a jaw full of tobacco. He was seated, wearing a black pullover shirt with a stitched badge on the chest. Beneath the badge, also stitched, were the words "Washington County Corrections." As Caroline approached, he spit brown tobacco juice into a Styrofoam cup.

Caroline picked up the sign-in sheet and smiled. "I need to see inmate number 7740," she said. No one at the Washington County Detention Center seemed to have a name. Everything was tracked by number.

The officer leered. "Got an ID, pretty lady?"

"My name is Caroline Dillard," she said. It was only Caroline's third visit to the detention center, and she hadn't encountered this particular officer on either of the other two occasions. She reached into her purse, pulled out a driver's license, and slid it into the metal tray at the bottom of the window.

"You a lawyer?" he said.

"I'm a paralegal for Joe Dillard."

"You his wife?"

"I am."

"You're too pretty to be married to him."

Caroline sighed. "If you'll check the approved list, you'll find my name."

The officer opened a spiral notebook next to him and took his time searching the pages.

"I can smell you through the window," he said. "You smell good."

"I'll be sure to tell your boss you like the way I smell." Caroline looked at the name stitched opposite his badge. "Officer Cagle? The sheriff comes to our house every year for a Christmas party. He and I have gotten to be pretty good friends." It was a lie. The sheriff had never set foot in Caroline's home, but it seemed to have the desired effect.

Officer Cagle looked down and slid the ID back through the window.

"You know the way to the attorney's room, ma'am?"

Caroline nodded and smiled.

"I'll buzz you through."

Caroline quickly made her way through the maze of gates and steel doors. She was a little anxious about the visit because she never knew what kind of mood the inmate she was about to see would be in. The woman had been in jail for nine months, by far the longest stretch she'd ever done. She'd lifted her own mother's checkbook, forged a check, and used the money to buy cocaine. Caroline's husband Joe had represented her. He'd talked the prosecutor into reducing the charge from a felony to a misdemeanor, but because of the woman's long history of problems with the law, in exchange for the reduction the prosecutor had insisted that she forego probation and agree to serve her sentence in the county jail.

Five minutes after Caroline sat down in the attorney's room, a female guard opened the door and stepped back to let the inmate inside. There were no handcuffs, waist chains, or shackles. The inmate wasn't dangerous. There was no risk of escape because she was getting out in a few hours. She smiled slightly and nodded when she saw Caroline.

Caroline rose from her seat and opened her arms. "How are you?" she said.

"I'm fine," the woman said, guardedly returning the hug.

"You look great."

"You look pretty darn pretty yourself."

They both sat down, and Caroline smiled at her sister-in-law, Sarah Dillard.

Caroline was always struck by the features her husband and his older sister shared. Both of them had thick dark hair, green eyes, pristine white teeth, and lean, sturdy bodies. Sarah's only visible flaw was a tiny pink scar that cut like a lightning bolt through her left eyebrow, the result of a punch from a drug dealer the last time she was on the street. She had high cheekbones, a strong jaw, and a cleft chin. Joe had told Caroline that he and Sarah were often mistaken for twins when they were kids. The comparisons stopped when Joe began to grow to six foot three and over two hundred pounds. Caroline also marveled at the resilience of Sarah's appearance. She had a fresh beauty that made it hard to believe she'd been abusing herself with drugs and alcohol for years.

"I was wondering if you'd made a decision on what we talked about last week," Caroline said.

Sarah looked down at the table. "I'm not too hot on it if you want to know the truth."

"Why not?"

"I'm too old to live with my brother, Caroline. I'm too old to be living with you. I appreciate what you're trying to do, but I think I'd be better off making my own way."

Caroline looked hard into the green eyes for a long moment. Finally she spoke.

"So you're going to make your own way. Like you have for the past twenty years?"

"Oh, now, that hurt. Please tell me you didn't come all the way down here just to screw with me."

"I came all the way down here to try to talk some sense into that thick head of yours. If you don't come stay with us, where are you going to go? What are you going to do?"

"I have friends."

"What kind of friends? Dealers and users? You need to stay away from those people."

"Yeah?" The green eyes flashed, but Caroline held her gaze. "What I *don't* need is a lecture from my brother's wife. Why are you doing this, anyway? Why isn't Joe here?"

Caroline leaned forward on her elbows. "I'm doing this because I care about you. We both care about you. We just want to try to help. And Joe isn't here because he can't stand to see you in this place again. It tears him up."

"Seeing me in here tears him up? He ought to try living in here for a while. It'd give him some compassion for his clients."

"He has plenty of compassion for his clients, especially you. He's done everything he could possibly do for you, including sending you money every month."

"I'll be sure to send him a thank-you note when I get out."

"God*dammit*, Sarah, why do you have to be so cynical? Why can't you believe that somebody could care enough about you to want to help? That's all it is. There aren't any strings attached."

"No strings? What if I feel like getting high tomorrow night?"

"I said there weren't any strings. But there will be rules. If any of us sees one sign of drugs or booze, you're out the door."

Sarah smiled. "And there it is. We'll love you Sarah unless you do what you've always done. If you do that, we won't love you any more."

"We'll still love you. We just won't help you destroy yourself."

"No thanks." Sarah rose from the chair and moved to the wall to push the button that summoned the guard.

"So that's it? No thanks?"

"That's it."

"Fine." Caroline got up from her chair and moved to the opposite door. Both women stood in uncomfortable silence, facing away from each other, until the guard appeared.

"The offer stays open," Caroline said as Sarah walked out of the room. "All you have to do is show up."

APRIL 12
11:15 A.M.

Agent Landers knew there'd be some added pressure to make an arrest because the dead guy was a preacher. Not that there wouldn't have been pressure to find out who killed him if he'd been a plumber or a bartender. But preachers still had a special place in the hearts and minds of most upper east Tennesseans. Killing a man of God was an insult to the Almighty Himself.

The Purple Pig was a small, popular burger and beer joint about a mile from East Tennessee State University. It was like one of those English pubs—same people, sitting in the same places, telling the same old jokes, drinking the same kind of beer.

Landers ate lunch there two or three times a month. Every now and then he'd stop in and have a beer after work. He went to high school with the owners, and he knew several of the regulars and the waitresses. Especially the waitresses. Landers had phone numbers for all of them, even the ones who were married. "Skilled with the ladies," was how he referred to himself.

He parked his Ford in the lot, picked up the photo of Tester, and jogged up to the door. He could smell the grease as soon as he got out of the car. The Pig wasn't open for breakfast, but there were cars in the lot. He knew the employees were prepping for the lunch rush, so he knocked on the locked front door. Patti Gillespie opened it. Patti was a cute little brunette, barely over five feet tall. She and her brother Sonny owned the place. Landers had banged Patti once in the girl's bathroom during a basketball game back in high school. He wanted to know what a small girl felt like.

"I need to talk to you," Landers said, and she led him inside. He plunked down on the first bar stool he came to. The place was dark and smelled of stale cigarette smoke and animal fat. A mirror ran the length of a long wall opposite the bar. Landers checked himself out as Patti walked around the bar and back toward him. He liked what he saw.

"What's the difference between a sperm cell and a TBI agent?" she said. Patti loved to bust his chops.

"Go ahead, slay me," Landers said. "What's the difference between a sperm cell and a TBI agent?"

"A sperm cell has a one in a million chance of becoming a human being. Can I get you something to drink?"

"A Pepsi, and I have a photograph I want you to look at. Do you mind?"

"Are you doing real police work?"

"I am."

"Hey, Lottie," Patti called toward the kitchen. "Special Agent Phillip Landers here is doing real police work in my little old bar. He wants me to help him. What should I do?"

"Deny everything," a voice called back. "Ask for a lawyer."

"She doesn't like you," Patti said. "She says you have a small penis."

"You know better than that," Landers said with a wink.

"I was drunk, dickhead. I don't remember your penis."

Landers slid the photo of Tester onto the bar. "Any chance this guy was in here yesterday evening?"

Patti nodded. "Came in about six, sat right over there in that booth." She pointed behind Landers. "I waited on him. Ordered a cheeseburger and fries. Drank two Blue Ribbons. Nobody drinks Blue Ribbon anymore. I remember thinking he wouldn't have looked too bad if he lost some weight and shaved those goofy sideburns."

"I don't think he'll be shaving anytime soon. He's dead."

Patti gasped. "You kidding me?"

"Dead as dirt. Got himself killed last night. Any chance he hooked up with somebody in here? Did you see him leave?"

"Sonny was working the register when he left. He didn't leave with anybody, but he asked Sonny about the Mouse's Tail."

"Really? Tell me more."

"He was a little creepy, you know? A little too cocky for his own good with that big belly and that cheap suit. When he paid his bill, he asked Sonny where he could find some adult entertainment, a place where they showed it all. Sonny told me about it after he left. He thought it was funny. He said the *only* way that dude would get any was to pay for it."

"Mouse's Tail, huh? Thanks, Patti. After all these years, I'm finally gonna put you on my Christmas card list."

"Whoa, now, wait just one minute," Patti said. "I need details. Tell me something juicy."

"Sorry, can't do it right now. I'm sure you'll hear all about it on the news."

"Just like a man. Always wanting something for nothing."

Landers turned to leave without offering to pay. "Thanks for the Pepsi," he said, "and thanks for the information. I'll come back and tell you about it later."

"I'm holding you to that," she said. Landers looked in the mirror as he started out the door and saw Patti blow him a kiss. "That man has a fine ass, Lottie," he heard her say.

"Screw him," Lottie said. "He's a fag."

Lottie was pretty good, but once Landers did her a few times, he dumped her. He had to. There were a lot of other women out there who wanted to be with him. He figured he owed it to them to stay unattached.

APRIL 12
11:45 A.M.

A horny preacher. A man after Landers's own heart. Landers called Jimmy Brown, told him about the lead and that he was going out to the Mouse's Tail. Brown said they'd found one witness, the night clerk at the motel, who said she thought she saw a woman go up toward Tester's room around midnight. The forensics van had showed up. Maybe they'd find something.

Brown said Tester was an evangelist, a traveling preacher from Newport, which was located in Cocke County about sixty miles southwest of Johnson City. Newport was infamous in the law enforcement community for three things: chop shops, marijuana production, and especially cock fighting. Landers had also heard some of the preachers down there were snake-handlers, religious extremists who proved their faith by waving copperheads and rattlesnakes around while they delivered their sermons. He wondered whether the dead rev liked to play with slimy serpents.

He pulled into the parking lot at the Mouse's Tail just before noon and circled the building. There was only one vehicle in the back, a black BMW convertible. A redheaded woman was just getting out. She was wearing black leather pants and a tight, cheetah-print top and was having a hard time walking through the gravel in her three-inch spiked heels. The outfit was definitely on the outrageous side, but her body was good enough to pull it off.

Landers pulled up beside the BMW, got out, introduced himself, and showed the woman his identification. She shook his hand and said her name was Erlene Barlowe. She owned the place. Said her husband passed away a while back, and she took over after he died. She had a pretty face and was wearing a push-up bra that pushed up plenty. But she had to be at least fifty, so Landers figured the bright red hair was bottle-fed.

"What can I do for you, honey?" she said after a little small talk.

"What time do you open?" Landers was disappointed that the place was closed since he wanted to talk to some of the employees. Actually, he was hoping to get to see some of her employees in action. He'd heard the Mouse's Tail was a pretty steamy place, but he'd never been in there. When Landers wanted to go to a strip club, he went to the beach or Atlanta. As much as he liked to look at tits, he knew the TBI would probably fire him if they heard he was hanging out at the local titty bar. Those kinds of places were notorious for drugs.

"Five," the woman said. "We're open five to two, six days a week. Closed on Sundays." Her voice was kind of Southern belle-ish, not exactly what he expected to hear from a woman who looked like her, with a syrupy

Tennessee drawl. Landers thought it was nice that the titty bar observed the Sabbath.

"So you were open last night?"

"Wednesday's usually a pretty good night for us. It's hump day, you know."

She had a little smile on her face when she said "hump day." Landers wondered how much humping went on in there on hump day.

"Was it crowded last night?"

"Wasn't anything special, sugar. Do you mind if I ask why you're asking?"

As she talked, Landers noticed her mouth. Nice teeth, and candy-apple red lipstick. Looked like a color you'd paint a '56 Chevy. Landers briefly envisioned those red lips wrapped around his pole.

"Just doing my job, Ms. Barlowe," he said. "Obviously, I wouldn't be here unless I was working some kind of an investigation."

"I understand completely," she said, "but I'm sure *you* can understand that I'm concerned when a police officer, even one as handsome as yourself, shows up at my place of business asking questions. Maybe I could help you a little more if you'd let me in on what you're investigating."

Landers stepped back over to his car, reached in, and picked the photograph of Tester up off the front seat.

"Were you here last night?" he said.

"I'm here every night, sweetie."

"Recognize this guy?" Landers handed the photo to her. She looked at it for a few seconds, then shook her head and handed it back.

"I don't believe I do."

"I think he was here last night."

"Really? What would make you think that?"

"Just some information I picked up. He was killed last night."

She gasped and covered her mouth. "Oh, my goodness. That's terrible!"

Landers held the photo up in front of her face again. "You're absolutely certain you didn't see him in your club last night?"

"Well, now, I don't believe I could say for *certain*. Lots and lots of men come and go. I don't notice all of them."

"I'm going to need to interview the employees who were working last night and as many of your customers as I can."

"Well, I swan," she said. "You'll scare my girls to death. And the customers? Honey, they'd run from you like scared rabbits. Most of them don't even want their wives to know they've been here, let alone the police. If you were to come in here and start asking them about a murder, why, I just don't know what would happen to my business."

"I didn't say anything about a murder."

The phony smile she was wearing stayed frozen on her face, but her eyes tightened the slightest bit. At that moment, Landers knew she realized she'd fallen face-first into a dungheap. It didn't surprise Landers. Any woman who dressed like that had to be a moron.

"I thought you said the man was killed," she said.

"I did, but I didn't say he was murdered. I didn't say anything about how he was killed. He might have been run over by a train or gotten killed in a car wreck. He could have jumped off a building or blown his brains out. What makes you think he was murdered?"

"I don't claim to know a whole lot, honey, but I didn't think the TBI got involved with car wrecks. I thought they only sent you boys in for the bad stuff."

Nice try. She knew something, and now that she'd screwed up, she was trying to backpedal. Landers decided to try to get her out of her element and into his, get her to a place where she'd be less comfortable.

"Ms. Barlowe, let's you and I go down to my office where we can sit down, have a cup of coffee, and talk. You can give me a list of your employees and the names of as many customers from last night as you can remember, and I'll have you back here in a couple hours."

The smile vanished.

"Honey, did I mention to you that my late husband, God rest his soul, used to be the sheriff of McNairy County? I was his personal secretary for almost a year before he resigned, and then we got married about a year after that. It was a long time ago, but I remember a few things about the law. Now, I don't mean to be rude to you, sugar, but one of the things I remember is that unless you have some kind of warrant or unless you arrest me, I don't believe I even have to talk to you. I've tried to be nice up to this point, but you've made it clear that you think I've done something wrong. So you know what? I think I'm just going to go on inside and get to work now, okay? You have yourself a wonderful day."

She turned around and sashayed off. It was the only word to describe the way her hips swayed as she headed into the Mouse's Tail on her spike heels. Landers stood there watching her for a minute, then turned and got back into his car.

Most people cringe when they talk to TBI agents, and damned near all of them cooperate unless they have something to hide. This woman had something to hide. Landers decided to stick a flashlight up her skirt until he found out what it was.

APRIL 12
12:10 P.M.

I went up to see my mother after Johnny Wayne was carted off. It was lunchtime, and walking down the hall in the long-term-care wing at the nursing home was like running a wheelchair gauntlet. I knocked gently on the door and walked in. She was awake. It seemed she was always awake. The doctors told me that Alzheimer's, as it progresses, interferes with sleep patterns. She was sitting up in bed, watching *Sportscenter*. Baseball season had started, which meant her beloved Atlanta Braves were back on the field.

"Hi, Ma. How're you feeling today?"

"Like I've been hit by a train."

"Good. At least you're with us."

The disease was steadily running its course. One day I'd walk in, and she'd say "Hi, Joe," and we'd talk for a little while, and the next day she wouldn't even know my name. It was painful to watch. She was only sixty years old, and she'd always been strong and vital. But her skin had lost its elasticity and was the color of bleached bone. Her weight had dropped to ninety pounds, and she seemed to have shrunk by at least two inches. Her cheeks were hollow, her hazel eyes dull, and her hair gray and stringy. Her teeth were in a jar on the bedside table. As I sat down in the chair next to her bed, I knew it wouldn't be long before she wouldn't be able to talk at all.

Ma was born in 1947 in a small town called Erwin, Tennessee, which sits nestled in the Appalachians not far from the North Carolina border and is surrounded by the Cherokee National Forest. She fell in love with a football star from nearby Johnson City and married him in 1964, a month after they graduated from high school. She had Sarah in 1966 and me in 1967, after my father was drafted and went off to Vietnam. I never laid eyes on my father; he was shipped home in a body bag by the time I was born.

Ma provided for my sister and me as best she could by working as a bookkeeper for a small roofing company and taking in other people's laundry. She didn't talk much, and when she did, it was usually a bitter tirade against Lyndon Johnson or Richard Nixon. She never dated another man and hardly ever left the house. Her only real requirement of me was: "Get an education, Joey."

"Sarah's getting out of jail today," I said. "I hope she's going to stay at my house for a while. Caroline was supposed to go down and talk to her sometime this morning."

Her eyes dropped at the mention of Sarah, and she began to shake her head.

"My own flesh and blood in jail," she said. "Tell me where I went wrong."

"No sense in beating yourself up over it. She is what she is. It isn't your fault."

"You better lock up your valuables, Joey. She'll haul the whole house off if you give her the chance."

"Sarah wouldn't steal from me, Ma." In fact, Sarah *had* stolen from me in the past, but I'd never told Ma about it.

"Well, she's stole from me, plenty of times."

"Maybe she's changed. You looked sad when I came in. What's the matter?"

"I was thinking about Raymond." She reached for a tissue beside the bed and dabbed at her eyes. Raymond was Ma's younger brother. He drowned at the age of seventeen. "Such a waste."

"No it wasn't," I said before I realized what was coming out of my mouth. "Don't spend any tears on him, Ma. *That's* a waste."

"Joey, you've never had a kind word to say about your uncle. What did Raymond ever do to you?"

I shook my head, not wanting to get into it. She hadn't mentioned him in years. "He wasn't a good person."

"He just needed—"

"Ma, could we please not talk about Raymond? You're entitled to your opinion. I'm entitled to mine."

I wanted to tell her what my opinion was based on, but I didn't see the point. It had happened so long ago, and Ma was dying. I didn't see the sense in sullying whatever pleasant memories she had of her only brother.

I managed to get her mind off Raymond and onto my son Jack's baseball prospects for a little while, but then, like a sudden change in the weather, she looked at me as though she'd never seen me before.

"What are you doing here?" she said. "Who are you?" It was a fast transformation, even for her, like some inner switch had been flipped. Even the pitch in her voice changed.

"It's me, Ma. I'm Joe. Your son."

"Why are you wearing that tie? You some kind of big cheese or something?"

"No, Ma. I'm not a big cheese."

"Where's Raymond?"

"Raymond's dead."

She let out a long sigh and stared at the ceiling.

"Ma? Can you hear me?"

She didn't respond. She lay motionless, almost catatonic. I looked over at the bedside dresser. On top of it were several photos of our fractured family. There was one of my grandfather, wearing bib overalls and following a plow pulled by a mule through a cornfield. There was a framed photograph of me walking across the stage at my law school graduation ceremony. Next to it, in a smaller frame, was a black-and-white of Sarah and me when I was seven years old. We were standing on a plank raft in the middle of a half-acre pond out back of my grandparents' home. Both of us were grinning from ear to ear. Two of my front teeth were missing.

Just to the right of that photo was a slightly larger one of Uncle Raymond, taken about six months before he died. He was seventeen years old, standing next to a doe that had been shot, hung from a tree limb, and gutted. He held a rifle in his left hand and a cigarette in his right. I walked over and picked up the photo. I looked at it for a minute, then turned back toward the bed. Ma was still staring at the ceiling.

"Can you hear me?" I said.

Nothing.

I sat back down on the chair next to the bed and began to dismantle the picture frame. I pried the small staples loose on the back of the frame, pulled the photo out, and tore it into little pieces.

"Hope you don't mind too much, Ma, but I'm going to put Raymond where he belongs." I walked to the bathroom, dropped the pieces in the toilet, flushed it, and watched them swirl around the bowl and disappear.

I went to her bedside and sat down again. I leaned back, closed my eyes, and tried to compose myself, the mention of Raymond's name still ringing in my ears. Finally, I sat up straight.

"Since you can't hear me anyway, I'm going to tell you what he did," I said. "At least it'll give me the chance to finally get it off my chest."

I leaned forward, rested my elbows on my knees, and clasped my hands.

"I was eight years old. Sarah was nine. You and Grandma and Grandpa had gone out—it was a Friday evening—and you left Sarah and me at Grandma's house with Raymond. He was sixteen, I think.

"I remember watching a baseball game on TV. I must have dozed off because when I woke up, it was dark. The only light in the house was the light from the television. I remember sitting up and rubbing my eyes, and then I heard this noise. It scared me because it sounded like a cry for help, but I got up off the couch and started walking toward the noise, more scared every step I took. I was tiptoeing.

"As I got closer, I could make out some words, something like 'No! Stop it!' I knew it was Sarah's voice, coming from Uncle Raymond's bedroom. I pushed the door open just a little, and I could make out Uncle Raymond in the lamplight. He was naked on his knees in the bed with his back to me. Sarah's voice was coming from underneath him."

I stopped and took a deep breath, the image of my naked uncle looming over my sister burning in my mind's eye. "Can you hear me, Ma?" I said. "Are you getting this?" I noticed my voice was shaky. Ma was still staring at the ceiling.

"Sarah kept saying, 'It hurts. Stop it!' I didn't know what was going on. I didn't know anything about sex. But there was so much pain, so much fear in Sarah's voice that I knew it was bad. I finally managed to say, 'What's going on?' I remember being surprised that my voice worked.

"Raymond's head snapped around, and he looked at me like he was going to kill me. He said, 'Get out of here, you little twerp.' I asked him what he was doing to Sarah. And then, Ma, right then, Sarah said something that haunts me to this day. I'll never forget that little voice. She said, 'Get him off me, Joey. He's hurting me.'"

I had to stop for a minute. The rape of my sister had haunted me, and her, for more than three decades. When I started talking to Ma, I thought it might somehow help to finally describe to another human being— even a human being who couldn't take it in—what had happened to Sarah. But talking about it was transporting me back to that tiny bedroom. I could feel my heart pounding inside my chest, and my hands had become cold and clammy.

"I stood there like an idiot for a second, trying to figure out what to do, but Raymond didn't give me a chance. He jumped off the bed and grabbed me by the throat. He slammed my head so hard against the wall that it made me dizzy. Then he picked me up by the collar and threw me out the door. I remember skidding along down the hallway on my stomach. He slammed the door, and I froze. I thought about going out to the garage to get a baseball bat or a shovel or an axe, anything. I could hear Sarah crying on the other side of the door, but it was like one of those nightmares where your arms and legs won't work. I was too scared to move.

"Finally, after what seemed like forever, they came out of the room. I remember Sarah sniffling and wiping her nose with the back of her hand. Raymond grabbed both of us by the back of the neck, dragged us into the living room, and pushed us onto the couch. He bent down close to us and pointed his finger within an inch of my nose. And then your brother, the one you loved so much, said to me, 'If you say one word about this to anybody, I'll kill your sister.' Then he turns to Sarah and says, 'And if you say anything, I'll kill your brother. Got it?'

"Neither one of us ever said a word to anyone, including each other. When that sorry SOB drowned a year later, it was one of the best days of my life. I tried to get him out of my mind after that, but I couldn't do it. Obviously, neither could Sarah."

I sat back in the chair and let out a deep sigh. "So now you know."

She hadn't moved since I started talking. She lay there, barely breathing, staring at nothing, blinking occasionally.

"I can't believe you didn't notice the changes after that day. I can't believe you never even bothered to ask what was wrong. I might have told you about it, and maybe you could have done something to help Sarah. But you were too busy feeling sorry for yourself, weren't you? You've spent your whole life being miserable, and now it's over."

I looked for some telltale sign that she understood. Nothing.

"Did you hear a word I just said? *Did you hear? Ma?*"

There was a knock and the door opened. A nurse's aide stepped tentatively into the room.

"Is everything all right?" she said. "I thought I heard someone shouting."

It took a few seconds before I understood what she was saying. I suddenly realized where I was, like I'd just been awakened from a deep sleep.

"Everything's fine," I said. "Please close the door."

She turned and left. I got up from the chair and looked down at Ma.

"I guess I better go now. I'm glad we had this little talk."

APRIL 12
4:00 P.M.

Shitdammit. Erlene Barlowe missed Gus more than ever. He'd have been better than her at handling the TBI agent. As soon as she got away from him in the parking lot, she sat down at the bar and asked herself what Gus would do. She was worried. The TBI man didn't strike her as the type she could hold off for long. She knew he'd be back, and she knew it would probably be soon.

Like she told the agent, Gus had been elected high sheriff of McNairy County when he was only twenty-six years old. It was nearly thirty years ago. Erlene wasn't much more than a baby, only twenty-two and didn't know the first thing about the world. Her uncle on the McNairy County Commission helped her get a job as a dispatcher at the sheriff's department. She and Gus were sweet on each other right from the get-go.

What she hadn't told the agent was that Gus was married to another woman at the time, and his wife Bashie caught Erlene and Gus in a motel room in Gatlinburg on a Friday night. Bashie divorced Gus a few months later, and he resigned from the sheriff's department. There was also some talk that Gus was selling protection to gamblers and marijuana smugglers, but Erlene didn't believe a word of it.

Gus met some people while he was sheriff who helped him get into the adult entertainment business in Hamilton County after he resigned. He asked Erlene to go with him, and she did. She was love struck, and it went deep down. Gus was big and strong and handsome, a real man's man. He treated her like a princess. They weren't able to have children—a botched abortion had left Erlene barren—but they had a wonderful life together for almost thirty years. She and Gus owned four clubs in four different counties during their marriage. They'd either buy a club that wasn't making a profit or build one on the cheap and start up. Gus ran the business and dealt with the customers; Erlene handled the girls. They'd make the club profitable, ride it for a while, then sell it. They took in tons of money. Along the way, they helped a lot of young girls who were in bad situations.

Erlene and Gus were planning to run the Mouse's Tail for another five years and then move to the South Carolina coast and retire. But late last September, he'd been mowing the yard on a Sunday afternoon, keeled over, and was already dead of a coronary when Erlene found him. Her heart broke into a million tiny pieces. Her sweet Gus—he was there one minute, smiling and waving on the riding mower when she looked out the kitchen window, and then poof! Just like that. Gone. The only thing that kept her going was the knowledge that the two of them would be together again someday. Her Gus would be waiting on the other side.

After the agent left and she thought for a while, she called the bartender and all the girls who worked the night before and told them to meet her at the bar at four o'clock, an hour before the place opened. Ronnie was the bartender. Mitzi, Elizabeth, Julie, Trisha, Heather, and Debbie were dancers. The other two were waitresses, April and Alexandra. They were all beautiful, with *wonderful* bodies. The older Erlene got, the more she loved being around them. She tried to teach them to respect themselves and to stay away from bad men and drugs. It was a challenge, but she did the best she could.

Angel had waited tables the night the man was killed, but Erlene didn't want Angel to be at the meeting. The man who was killed had behaved shamefully toward Angel, and Erlene was afraid that if the TBI man found out about it, he might suspect Angel of something. Besides, Erlene felt guilty for even having Angel working at the club. She didn't have any way of knowing it when they first met, but Angel wasn't the type of girl who could handle herself in a place like the Mouse's Tail. She was just too tender.

Erlene knew some of the girls thought it was a little strange that Erlene took such a shine to Angel right from the beginning, but they didn't understand. A lot of it was because of Gus. He had a daughter from his first marriage, a beautiful brunette named Alyse. After Gus and Erlene ran off together, Gus's ex-wife Bashie hated him so much that he never got to see Alyse again, but he talked about wanting to see her all the time, and he sent money for her every month. He'd always tell Erlene, "She'll come some day. You wait and see."

Sure enough, about a week after Alyse's seventeenth birthday, Gus got a framed photograph of his daughter in the mail. There was a little note with it that said, "I miss you, Daddy. I'll see you next year after I turn eighteen." Gus hung the photograph up right next to the kitchen door, and every time he left the house, he blew a kiss at it.

Then the most terrible thing happened. Alyse and two other teenagers were killed in a car accident on New Year's Eve, just a few months after Gus got the picture in the mail. Gus went down to her funeral, but Erlene stayed home. She didn't think it would be proper for her to go. Gus was the saddest man Erlene had ever seen for the next few months, though he eventually came out of it and got back to being his old self again. But he never took the picture down, and he never stopped blowing kisses to Alyse. After he died, Erlene left the photograph hanging right where it was. She even started blowing kisses herself.

When Angel showed up on the bus with Julie Hayes, Erlene's teeth near fell out of her mouth. Angel looked so much like Alyse that Erlene swore they could've been sisters, maybe even twins. When she first laid eyes on Angel, she heard Gus's voice: *"She'll come some day. You wait and see."* Erlene knew she had to take Angel home with her. It was like having a piece of Gus back in the house all over again, like Gus himself had sent Angel to comfort her. And doing for Angel, helping her, did comfort Erlene. It was healing, that's what it was. It helped heal some of the pain of losing Gus and a lot of what she'd carried around ever since the doctor told her she'd never be a mother.

After Angel had been with Erlene only a little while, during some of those moments when they'd curl up on the couch in front of the fireplace and watch a movie, Angel started to open up a little and told Erlene some of the terrible things that had happened to her. That's when Erlene knew she was right. She knew Gus—or God—had sent Angel to her. She didn't really care which. Angel was the daughter she never had. She was meant to take care of her.

The girls showed up between four and four fifteen. Erlene told them to sit at the bar. As soon as Julie dragged in—late, as usual—Erlene stood on the other side of the bar and gave them a little speech.

"There was a detective from the Tennessee Bureau of Investigation here around noon. He was asking about a murder. He had a picture of the man who was killed, and he thinks the man was here last night. He may even think one of us had something to do with it."

Erlene paused for a skinny minute and looked at their faces. She set such high standards for her girls. They had to dress a certain way when they came into the club, and Erlene was real particular about their makeup and the way they wore their hair. When Erlene mentioned murder, the girls' mouths dropped open, and they started looking at one another.

"Is that the murder they've been talking about on the radio?" Heather said. "They're saying the man was a preacher. It made me think of that guy last night who was spouting—"

Erlene held up her hand.

"I haven't heard anything on the radio," she said, "but I want all of you to forget about that man last night. He wasn't here. I want every one of you to look at me, right now, and listen real carefully to what I'm saying. He wasn't here. When the TBI man comes back here, or if he comes to your place and starts asking you questions, he's going to show you a picture. And you're going to tell him that the man in the picture was *not here*. Do all of you understand that?"

Everybody but Julie nodded. Julie looked at Erlene and said, "So you're telling us to *lie* to a cop about a murder? Isn't that illegal or something?"

Julie had become a problem again. A gorgeous green-eyed redhead was great for business, but she was back on the cocaine, and she was getting worse by the day. She was always late, always distracted, and she did outrageous, vulgar things sometimes when she danced.

Julie had also had a huge crush on Gus, even though he was old enough to be her granddaddy, and she was jealous. Erlene finally had to fire her last year after she caught her snorting cocaine in one of the storage rooms. Julie made a huge, ugly scene and was hollering at the top of her lungs when she stormed out of the club. Erlene didn't hear a word from her for eight months, and then maybe two months ago she called Erlene up, all sweet and apologetic. Julie told Erlene how sorry she was about Gus and said she was clean as a whistle and wanted to come back to work. She was in Texas at the time, and Erlene's head told her to let Julie stay in Texas, but her heart said Julie was just a lost young girl who needed a job. And she was good for business.

"Nothing will happen if we stick together," Erlene told them. "Do you girls have any idea what getting caught up in a big murder would do to this business? People would stay away from this place in droves. We'd all wind up on the street, including you, Miss Julie. All that money you've been making? Gone.

"Besides, I'm sure nobody in this room killed that gentleman, and I doubt very seriously if any of you has any information that would help the police. The man was a drunken fool. Every one of you saw the way he acted. He probably went somewhere else after he left here and ran into somebody who wasn't as tolerant of his behavior as we were. So why do we need to get involved in it? If the detective asks you, just tell him the man wasn't here and let him move on to people who can help."

"Where's Angel?" Julie said. "She's the one who waited on him."

"Angel's at home. She and I have decided that she's not really cut out for this business. Don't worry about Angel. She won't say a word." Erlene paused for a minute and looked at all of them again. "Girls, are we all on the same page?"

They all sat quietly, but they were nodding. Erlene knew mentioning the money they were making would get their attention, and besides, she treated them good. She expected a little loyalty in return.

"Julie?"

Julie popped her gum and shrugged her shoulders.

"All right, then, let's get ready to go to work."

APRIL 12
6:00 P.M.

After I left the nursing home, I spent the next hour driving to Mountain City to stand next to a client who was entering a guilty plea to a reduced charge of negligent homicide in what had originally been a second-degree murder case. My client, a thirty-year-old man named Lester Hancock, had come home unexpectedly one evening to discover his best friend in bed with his wife. Lester had initially handled the dispute admirably. He simply told his buddy to get the hell out of his house and never come back. His friend left but returned fifteen minutes later and began yelling insults at Lester from the road in front of Lester's house. Lester yelled back. His friend grabbed a baseball bat from the bed of his pickup and started toward the house. Lester stepped out on the front porch and blew a hole in him with a black powder rifle. He probably would never have been charged had he not dragged the man inside his house and then lied to the police about the way things really happened.

The drive was spectacular in April. The mountain peaks reflected off the shimmering water of Watauga Lake, and the mountains themselves were coming to life. Dogwood, redbud, Bradford pear, and azalea blossoms dotted the slopes with pink and white. As I wound slowly through the beautiful countryside, I thought about the question Ma had asked me earlier: *"What did Raymond ever do to you?"*

Almost immediately following the rape, I started over-reacting to anyone who I perceived was trying to bully me. Over the next year, I got myself thrown out of school three times for fighting, and I was only in the third grade. I was afraid of being left alone and had nightmares all the time.

The nightmares eased after a while, but then, when I was in the eighth grade and just starting to hit puberty, I threw my helmet at a football coach who grabbed my face mask and screamed at me when I made a mistake on a play during practice. The helmet hit him in the head. They threw me off the team and out of school for a month.

My freshman year in high school, during the time when the hormones were pouring and I felt like I wasn't in control of anything, including my own body, I went days without sleep and fell into deep depressions. It was the first time I remember having the dream of floating down the turbulent river toward the waterfall.

And then, during my sophomore year, I met Caroline. She was beautiful, smart, funny, and opti-mistic, and at first, I had a lot of trouble believing she wanted to have anything to do with me. But she did. She saw something in me that I didn't see, and while I didn't understand, I was grateful. She'd flash a smile at me or give me a sideways glance and wink, and my heart would melt. Gradually, the nightmares stopped, and for the next few years, I actually started to enjoy life.

Caroline and I were inseparable all through high school. We both worked hard. I was an athlete, she was a dancer, and we were both good students. We both had part-time jobs. I worked on the weekends stocking groceries at a supermarket, and she taught dance to kids at the studio where she took lessons. Caroline's father was a long-haul truck driver who was hardly ever home, and her mother was almost as emotionless as mine, but she never complained about either one of them. We had each other, and that seemed to be enough.

The only serious problem we had was around graduation time. Caroline wanted to get married—and so did I—but I had something else I wanted to do first. I had trouble explaining it to her, but I wanted to join the army. Caroline said I was crazy, that I was somehow trying to forge a bond with my dead father. She was probably right, but it didn't matter. I'd made up my mind. I enlisted a month after I graduated from high school and left for boot camp the same week Caroline entered college at the University of Tennessee in Knoxville. She said she'd wait for me, and she did. I wrote to her almost every day, and I came home to see her every time I went on leave, but it was the longest three years of my life.

By the time I got out of the army, Caroline had earned an undergraduate degree in liberal arts. We were married in her mother's Methodist church in Johnson City the same weekend I got back, and I enrolled in school at U.T. in the fall. Caroline went to work at a dance studio owned by a former Dallas Cowboy cheerleader. She taught jazz and tap and acrobatics and choreographed routines for the dance recitals. I majored in political science and knew what I wanted to be. I was going to be a prosecutor. I was going to put people like my uncle Raymond in jail.

Marrying Caroline was the best decision I ever made. She was so beautiful, so full of life, and she taught me the most important lesson I'd ever learned—how to love. Over the next two years, we had two healthy children, and Caroline helped me learn how to raise them. She nudged me when I needed nudging, held me back when I needed holding back, and did her best to keep my outlook optimistic.

Unfortunately, I brought more than my duffel bag home with me from the army. The Rangers are gungho, small-unit specialists who pride themselves on being able to fight in virtually any environment on a moment's notice. I trained all over the world for three years, but I didn't see any combat until two months before my enlistment expired when my unit was sent to Grenada. Terrible images from the short but bloody battles I fought there haunted me through college and law school. I'd wake up in the middle of the night screaming, covered in sweat, with my wife talking softly to me, trying to calm me down.

As with Sarah's rape, I eventually managed to suppress the memories, at least most of the time. I even managed to make excellent grades and graduate from both college and law school, despite the fact that I always held a part-time job and was doing my best to be a good husband and father along the way. I kept myself so busy I didn't have time to think about the past. I don't think I slept for seven years.

By the time I graduated from law school, my son Jack was just entering kindergarten. When I interviewed for a job at the district attorney's office back in Washington County, I was disappointed to find that the starting salary for rookie prosecutors was less than $25,000 a year and that it would take me at least ten years to get to the $50,000 range. It seemed like such a waste to have spent all that time and effort for so paltry a salary. Caroline was starting up her own dance studio, and we knew she wouldn't make much money. I figured I could make at least twice what the D.A. was offering by practicing on my own, even as a rookie, so I set up shop in Johnson City. I told myself that after I'd made some serious money and gained some experience, I'd close down the office and go to work for the district attorney.

I immediately started taking criminal defense cases, reasoning that the experience would help me later when I went to the D.A.'s office. I put the same amount of sweat and effort into my law practice as I'd put into being an athlete, a soldier, and a student, and I soon became very good at it. I found that the law offered a great deal of leeway to an astute and enterprising mind, and I learned to take on even the most damning evidence and spin it to suit my arguments. Within a couple years, I started to win jury trials. The trial victories translated into publicity, and I soon became the busiest criminal defense lawyer around. The money started rolling in.

I defended murderers, thieves, drug dealers, prostitutes, white-collar embezzlers, wife beaters, and drunk drivers. The only cases I refused to take were sex crimes. I convinced myself that I was some kind of white knight, a trial lawyer who defended the rights of the accused against an oppressive government. And along the way, I made an unfortunate discovery. I learned that many of the police officers and prosecutors who were on the other side weren't much different from the criminals I was defending. They didn't give a crap about the truth—all they cared about was winning.

Still, the thought of moving to the prosecutor's office was always on my mind. But the money kept me from it. I was taking good care of my wife and my kids. I took pride in being a provider. I took pride in being able to give my children things and opportunities I never had. Before I knew it, ten years had passed.

And then along came Billy Dockery.

Billy was a thirty-year-old mama's boy charged with killing an elderly woman after he broke into her house in the middle of the night. He was long-haired, skinny, stupid, and arrogant, and I didn't like him from the moment I met him. But he swore he was innocent, the case against him was weak, and his mother was willing to pony up a big fee, so I took it on. A year later, a jury found him not guilty after a three-day trial.

Billy showed up drunk at my office the next afternoon and tossed an envelope onto my desk. When I asked him what was in it, he said it was a cash bonus, five thousand dollars. I told him his mother had already paid my fee. He was giddy and insistent. I knew he didn't have a job, so I asked him where he got the money.

"Off'n that woman," he said.

"What woman?"

"That woman I killed. I got a bunch more'n this. I figger you earned a piece of it."

I threw him and his money out onto the street. There wasn't any use in telling the police about it. Double jeopardy prevented Billy from being tried again, and the rules about client confidentiality meant I couldn't divulge his dirty little secret anyway.

Prior to Billy, I did what all criminal defense lawyers do—I avoided discussions with my clients about what *really* happened. I concerned myself only with evidence and procedure. But when Billy slapped me in the face with the truth, I realized I'd been fooling myself for years. I realized that my profession, my reputation, my entire perception of myself was nothing more than a facade. I was a whore, selling my services to the highest bidder. I wasn't interested in truth. I was interested in winning because winning led to money. I'd completely lost my sense of honor.

When that realization hit me, I wanted to quit practicing law altogether. But my children were in high school and would soon be going off to college. Caroline had managed our money well, but we didn't have enough stashed away to allow me to quit outright. So Caroline and I talked it over, and we decided I'd keep going until the kids had graduated and gone on to college. After that, we'd figure out what I was going to do for the rest of my life.

I immediately began to cut back on the number of cases I took. The death-penalty cases I was doing were all appointed, payback from judges for the days when I was spinning facts and helping people like Billy Dockery walk out the door. My son was in college, and my daughter was a senior in high school. In less than a year, I hoped to finish up the cases I had and walk away from the profession that Uncle Raymond, at least indirectly, had led me to.

By the time I got back from Mountain City, it was almost dark. So far, my birthday had been a bust. Johnny Wayne had been gagged, I'd practically fallen apart in Ma's room, and the flashback of Sarah's rape kept playing over and over in my head. And I couldn't reach Caroline or either of the kids on my cell phone. I'd called ten times on the way back down the mountain.

I finally pulled into the driveway and pushed the garage door opener. There wasn't another car in sight. Rio, my young German shepherd, came bounding out of the garage and started his daily ritual of running around the truck. I'd rescued Rio from a bad situation when he was only two months old. I was his hero. When he saw me pull into the driveway every day, the excitement was too much for his young bladder. As soon as I got out of the truck, he peed on my shoe.

Where could they be? I didn't see my son's car. When I'd talked to Jack on the phone last week, he promised to come to dinner with us on my birthday. I thought seriously about backing out and going somewhere to drown my sorrows, but I decided I'd go in and see if they left me a note. Surely they wouldn't forget my birthday. These were the people I loved more than anything else in the world. They'd never forgotten my birthday. They always made a big deal out of it.

Caroline hadn't said anything that morning, but I'd left at 5:30 a.m. and showered at the gym after I worked out. She and Lilly were still asleep when I walked out the door. Maybe they did forget.

Or maybe something was wrong. Something had to be wrong. I rubbed Rio's ears for a minute and walked up and opened the door that led to the kitchen. It was dark inside. I let the dog go in ahead of me. It was quiet.

"Hello! Anybody home?" I flipped on the light in the kitchen.

A huge poster had been hung from the kitchen ceiling. It stretched all the way to the floor and was at least six feet wide. It looked like something a high school football team would run through when they took the field for a game. The poster, in bright blue letters, said:

Happy Birthday Dad!
WE LOVE YOU!

I laughed as the three of them came around the corner from the den into the kitchen singing "Happy Birthday." All three were wearing striped pajamas and grinning like monkeys. They'd tied their wrists together. The Dillard family chain gang. My self-pity vanished, and I opened my arms for a group hug.

Caroline announced that they were taking me to dinner, and they changed out of their striped pajamas. I chose Café Pacific, a quiet little place on the outskirts of Johnson City that served the best seafood in town. As I sat there eating prawns and scallops in an incredible Thai sauce, I looked at their faces, settling finally on Caroline's. I'd fallen in love with the most beautiful girl in school all those years ago, and she was even more beautiful now. Her wavy auburn hair shimmered in the candlelight. Her smooth, fair skin and deep brown eyes glowed, and when she caught me looking at her, I got a coy smile that brought out the dimple in her right cheek.

Caroline has the firm, lithe body of a dancer, but it's soft and curvy where it matters. She's studied dance all her life and still operates a small dance studio. Lilly is Caroline's clone, with the exception that her hair runs to a lighter shade and her eyes are hazel. Lilly is seventeen and in her senior year of high school. She wants to be a dancer, or a photographer, or an artist, or a Broadway actress.

Jack looks a lot like me. He just turned nineteen and is tall and muscular, with dark hair and brooding eyes that are nearly black. Jack is a top student and a highly competitive athlete whose goal is to play professional baseball, and he works at it with the intensity of a fanatic. He and I have spent countless hours together practicing on a baseball field. He'll hit until his hands blister, throw until his arm aches, lift weights until his muscles burn, and run until his legs give out. The work paid off in the form of a scholarship to Vanderbilt, but the scholarship paid only half his tuition. I still had to come up with $20,000 a year.

When the waiter brought me a piece of chocolate cake, Caroline reached into her purse and produced a candle. She stuck it in the cake and lit it.

"Make a wish," she said.

"And don't tell us what it is," Lilly said. She says that every year.

I made a silent wish for an innocent client. And the sooner the better.

Jack reached under the table and pulled out a small, flat, gift-wrapped box.

"This is from all of us," he said.

I opened the card. There was a message in Caroline's handwriting: "Follow your heart. Follow your dreams. We'll all be there, wherever it leads. We love you." She's as eager as I am to get me out of the legal profession. She thinks my work keeps me at war with myself—she's told me more than once that she's never seen anybody so conflicted. She's been encouraging me to go to night school and get certified as a high school teacher and a coach.

Inside the package were box-seat tickets to an Atlanta Braves game in July.

"I cleared your calendar," Caroline said. "We're all going. Don't you dare schedule anything for that weekend."

"Not a chance," I said. It was perfect.

We finished dessert and drove back home around nine. As I pulled into the driveway, the headlights swept over the front porch about thirty feet to the left of the garage. I saw something move. We lived on ten isolated acres on a bluff overlooking Boone Lake. We'd left Rio in the house when we went to the restaurant. I stopped just outside the garage and got out of the car. I could hear Rio raising hell inside.

"Go in and turn on the porch light," I said to Caroline. "You guys stay in the car."

"No way," Jack said as he got out of the backseat.

I walked around the corner toward the front with Jack right beside me. Someone stood on the porch.

"Who's there?" I said.

Silence. And then the porch light came on. Standing next to the porch swing in a pair of ratty khaki shorts and a green T-shirt that said, "Do me, I'm Irish," was my sister Sarah.

APRIL 12
11:00 P.M.

By the time Landers returned to his office, the Johnson City dicks had managed to gather more information on the murder victim. John Paul Tester was a widower with one grown kid, a son who was a deputy sheriff and a chaplain at the Cocke County sheriff's department. Tester had come up to Johnson City to preach at a revival at a little church near Boone's Creek. He delivered the sermon, collected almost three hundred dollars from the offering plate for his trouble, left the church around nine, and nobody had seen him since. His bank records showed that he withdrew two hundred dollars in cash from an automatic teller machine at 11:45 p.m. The machine was at the Mouse's Tail. If Tester ran through three hundred dollars there and needed more money around midnight, the Barlowe woman had to have noticed him.

She lied.

Landers spent the afternoon drafting an affidavit for a search warrant and running down a judge. All he had to do was tell the judge that the owner of the club where the murder victim was last seen lied and was refusing to cooperate. The warrant the judge signed authorized the TBI to search the Mouse's Tail for any evidence relevant to the murder of John Paul Tester. And since it was a strip club, the judge didn't have any qualms about Landers executing the warrant during business hours.

Landers planned the raid himself. About an hour before the SWAT guys were supposed to hit the front door, he'd go in to check things out, then at the appointed time he'd signal the start of the raid. Landers was looking forward to it, especially the part about checking things out.

A little after nine, he stopped by his place to shower and change. He put on a pair of jeans, a collared black pullover, and a jacket, stuck his .38 in an ankle holster, and drove out to the Mouse's Tail around 10:15. It was a tacky joint, built of concrete block and painted powder blue. The front entrance was covered by a bright blue awning trimmed in black. A big gray mouse, grinning from ear to ear and with a tail that curled up into what looked like an erect penis, had been air-brushed on the side of the building that faced the road.

There were twenty or thirty cars in the parking lot out front. Landers had to pay a ten-dollar cover to get past the blonde in the foyer. She looked like a high-end hooker, elaborate makeup and black spandex. Huge tits. The ATM machine the murder victim withdrew the money from was sitting right beside the counter in front.

Blondie buzzed Landers through into the main part of the club. It was a large, open room, about a hundred feet long and forty feet wide. On each side of the main room were what appeared to be small anterooms, the entrances covered by black curtains.

There were three stages, each about the size of a boxing ring, set in a triangle and complete with brass poles. Each stage was framed by mirrors and occupied by a naked, gyrating lady. Cigarette smoke hung in a cloud about ten feet off the floor, and a mirror ball was throwing light around the room. The music was loud. Landers had heard the bass buzzing off the walls from the parking lot. He didn't recognize the song that was playing, but it was one of those idiot black rappers.

Landers did a quick head count. There were six people, all men, at the bar to his right and another thirty or so sitting at counters and tables around the stages. Besides the dancers and two waitresses, who were wearing *extremely* attractive tight white nurse's outfits, there wasn't a woman in the place. Landers didn't see Erlene Barlowe anywhere.

He took a seat at a table toward the back. The redhead on stage was magnificent. She had a gorgeous face, and she kept throwing her head around and making her hair fly. Her legs were long, her ass was tight, her tits were small and firm, and she could *move*. Landers was sitting there fantasizing about his balls slapping off her cheeks when one of the nurses stopped by the table. Her little top was a zip-up that hadn't been zipped up very far. Her tits were falling out all over the place.

"What can I get you, honey?" she said.

"Club soda. Twist of lime." The nurse gave Landers a dirty look when he ordered the club soda. He would much rather have had a whiskey, but he never knew what might happen in a raid. He needed to stay sharp.

Nurse Betty brought his club soda a couple minutes later. Cost him five fifty. She gave him an even dirtier look when he didn't give her a tip. Landers called Jimmy Brown at 10:45. The raid was supposed to start at eleven straight up. Landers could barely hear him over the music. Brown said they were just pulling off the interstate. They'd be in position in five minutes.

That's when he saw Erlene Barlowe, still wearing the leather pants and cheetah top. She was standing by the bar. Nurse Betty was talking in her ear and pointing in Landers's direction. The music had stopped, and the disc jockey was telling the customers that touching the girls wasn't allowed. Erlene spotted Landers and headed straight for him.

"Are you here to arrest me, handsome?" she said when she got to the table. "Or are you just a bad boy looking for a good time?"

"You remember the guy I was asking you about? The dead guy who wasn't here? He withdrew some money out of your ATM machine out there in the lobby last night."

"Well, I swan, honey, I must have just missed him somehow."

"My name isn't honey. It's Landers. *Special Agent* Landers. And you're about to find out how much I hate it when sluts lie to me." Landers took out his phone and dialed Jimmy Brown. "You guys ready?"

"All set. Standing outside the front door."

"Go."

There was a scream from the lobby, and the door banged open. SWAT guys in black combat gear and helmets came rushing in. They looked like Navy SEALs. They had their weapons up and were yelling.

"Police! Get on the floor! Get on the floor!"

Landers stood up and pointed his .38 at Erlene Barlowe's face.

"This is a raid, sweetie," he said. "Get your hands up against that wall and don't move until I tell you to."

The look on her face was priceless.

APRIL 26
11:00 A.M.

Two weeks after my birthday, I finished up a hearing on a drug case in federal court in Greeneville and had just gotten in my truck to drive back to Johnson City when I looked at my cell phone and saw a text message from Caroline: "Call me. Urgent."

Caroline had taken on the job as my secretary/paralegal two years earlier, after we made the decision that I was getting out. Since I was taking fewer cases, I needed to cut down on my overhead. The classes Caroline taught at her dance studio were held in the evenings, so she volunteered. When the lease was up on my office downtown, I found my secretary a job at another law firm and moved the essentials out to my house. The move saved me almost sixty thousand dollars a year, and Caroline took an online course and got herself certified as a paralegal. She turned out to be a quick study. I still had a small conference room downtown where I met clients, but it cost me only two hundred a month.

"What's up?" I said when she answered the phone.

"Could be good, could be bad," she said. "A woman named Erlene Barlowe called early this morning. She was frantic. She said the police barged into her house and arrested a young friend of hers for murder and that she needed to hire a lawyer. She kept saying the girl couldn't have done it."

Right.

"She wants to meet with you. It's been a long time since you've been hired privately on a murder case."

"Billy Dockery's mother hired me." I'd never told anyone about Billy's confession. Not even Caroline.

"You made a lot of money on that case, didn't you?"

"Fifty thousand."

"We could use it."

"I thought we were in good shape."

"We are, but a murder case? And this one could be big money, babe. It's the case where the preacher was murdered. The one who was found in the motel room."

"I don't want to take on a murder case, high profile or not, Caroline. It could go on for years."

"That's why I didn't make her an appointment." She sounded disappointed.

I thought about it for a minute, weighing the pros and the cons. Curiosity finally got the best of me.

"Ah, what the heck, it won't hurt to talk to her. Call her back and have her meet me downtown at one."

It took me an hour to drive back to Johnson City. I ate a quick lunch at a café about two blocks from my conference room and walked in the door about ten minutes before one. There was a woman sitting at the table waiting for me. She stood when I came in. It was all I could do to keep my jaw from dropping. She was dressed in tight, black spandex pants and an orange and black tiger-striped top that nearly exposed the nipples on her very substantial breasts. Her hair was a shade of red I'd never seen before, on or off a woman's head.

"Joe Dillard," I said as I shook her hand. Her fingernails were at least an inch long and painted the same design as her shirt.

"Erlene Barlowe. You're even better-looking in person than you are on television." She smiled, and when I looked her in the eye, I saw that despite the shocking outfit, she was an attractive woman. I motioned toward the chair.

"What can I do for you, Ms. Barlowe?"

"Oh, honey, I have the most terrible problem. It's just awful. A very close young lady friend of mine has been arrested for a crime she didn't commit."

"Close friend?"

"More like a daughter. I sort of took her in about a month ago."

"Start from the beginning, Ms. Barlowe. Tell me everything you want me to know."

"Please, sugar, call me Erlene. I suppose I should start by telling you that I own the Mouse's Tail Gentlemen's Club. My husband and I owned it together, but he passed away last year and now I'm running it. I don't believe I've ever seen you out there."

I laughed. "Haven't had the pleasure. I've heard a lot about it though."

"Doesn't surprise me. We've had several lawyers come and go over the years. A couple judges, too."

Which judges, I wondered. I considered asking her, but then I decided I didn't want to know. Screw them. Before long, I'd be moving on.

"Tell me about your friend."

"Have you heard they made an arrest in the murder of that pastor from Newport? The one who was stabbed?"

"I think everybody's heard."

"She didn't do it, Mr. Dillard. I'd swear it on a stack of Bibles. I want to hire you to represent her."

"How do you know she didn't do it?"

"Because I was *with* her all night. I drove her home from the club after her shift ended. She lives at my place and she never went out. She *couldn't* have done it. And besides that, she's the sweetest, kindest little thing you'll ever meet. She wouldn't so much as step on a bug, let alone kill a human being."

Erlene Barlowe had an almost mesmerizing Southern drawl and a sweet kind of charm about her. The fact that she was easy to look at, even in those wild clothes, made the conversation even more pleasant. I got the sense a few times that there might be more to Erlene than she wanted me to see, but there was something about her— maybe danger—that held my interest.

After a half hour, I glanced back over my notes. She said she'd taken Angel Christian, the girl who was arrested, into her home after Angel showed up here on a bus with another girl, a dancer named Julie Hayes, a little over a month ago. She said Angel reminded her of her dead husband's beautiful young daughter who'd been killed in a car accident. I got the distinct impression she'd convinced herself that Angel was the reincarnation of the daughter. She said Angel had suffered some serious abuse at home and was a runaway. She mentioned something about Angel's hands.

I was more than a little concerned about a few things. Erlene told me that she'd initially lied to a TBI agent I knew named Phil Landers. She said Angel Christian wasn't the girl's real name. She said the police had obtained a warrant to take a hair sample from Angel, or whatever her name was, and one from Erlene. That meant DNA evidence would probably be involved, and DNA almost always proved to be devastating to defendants. The police obviously had witnesses or some other evidence or they wouldn't have been able to get the warrants. And she said something about the police searching for a missing Corvette.

But Erlene was adamant about the girl's innocence, and if she was telling the truth, it certainly didn't sound like Angel had either the motive or the opportunity to commit a murder. I was tempted, but not so tempted that I was willing to take on a murder case that would probably wind up going to trial. I didn't want to waste any more of her time, and I didn't want to just flat-out refuse her, so I decided to set the bar so high she'd either be unable or unwilling to jump it.

"Erlene, do you have any idea how much it would cost you to hire me on a case like this? A first-degree murder. I heard something about the death penalty on the radio, you know. And it'll most likely go to trial."

"Mr. Dillard, my husband provided well for me, both while he was alive and after he passed. Money isn't something I'm concerned about."

She shouldn't have said that. The price I had in mind immediately doubled.

"I'm going to be honest with you, ma'am," I said. "I'm planning to get out of this business sometime in the next year. If I took on this case, it would mean I might have to stay a lot longer than I want to."

"Please, Mr. Dillard. I'll pay you whatever you want. You're the best lawyer around here. I've been hearing about you and reading about you for years. You've even represented some of my girls—just piddly stuff years ago—but they all spoke so highly of you. I wouldn't want anyone else to defend my sweet little Angel. Why don't you look at it as your last hurrah? You can go out with a great big bang."

I took a deep breath. "You've only known this girl a month. Are you telling me you'd be willing to put up a quarter million dollars for her defense?"

She didn't bat an eye. "Angel didn't kill anybody, Mr. Dillard. I swear it. I'll do whatever I have to do."

"That's the only way I'll do it. Two hundred fifty thousand, cash, up front, nonrefundable. And that's just for me. You'll also have to pay the expenses. We'll need an investigator, and we may need experts. They're not cheap."

"Tell you what, sweetie," she said, "why don't you go down to the jail and meet Angel. When you get finished, you give me a call and I'll have your money."

APRIL 26
3:00 P.M.

O n the way to the jail, I seriously considered not taking the case. I'd made up my mind to get out, and the time had come. Lilly would be graduating in a month, and I only had a couple cases left. But the money ... my God! A quarter million? Would she really pay it? That kind of money would go a long way toward giving Caroline and me some peace of mind, especially with the extra expense of Ma being in the nursing home. Her care was costing me more than a thousand dollars a month. I decided to wait and make up my mind after I talked to the girl.

As soon as the door to the attorney's room opened, I realized Erlene Barlowe had been telling the truth about at least one thing. The girl was beautiful. I stood up while two guards held her elbow as she shuffled into the room, shackled at the ankles. They helped her into the chair as though they were seating her for a gourmet dinner, then backed out the door. For a second, I thought they might bow. The door closed, and I sat back down.

"Well, I've never seen that before," I said.

She smiled absently.

"Guards aren't polite to inmates, male or female. I've never seen a guard help an inmate with a chair."

Her hair was the color of polished mahogany and flowed like a mountain waterfall from her head to just beneath her shoulders. Her nose was small and thin and turned up slightly. She had almond-shaped eyes that were a rich brown. Her left eyebrow was slightly higher than her right, giving the impression that she was perpetually interested, or maybe perpetually perplexed. Her lips were full and protruded ever so slightly, and even in the standard-issue orange jumpsuit, I could see that her body was magnificent.

"My name is Joe Dillard," I said. "I'm a lawyer. Erlene Barlowe asked me to come and talk to you."

"I'm Angel," she said, "Angel Christian." Her voice was a gentle soprano.

"Do you understand why you're here, Miss Christian?"

"Yes." There was a slight pause. "Murder."

She put her elbows on the table and began to cry softly. I'd seen hundreds of clients cry, male and female. I'd grown hardened to tears and the accompanying sounds, but the crying of this beautiful young girl touched me. I stood up and knocked on the door. A guard opened it immediately.

"Do you guys have any tissue around here?" I said.

The guard glanced over my shoulder at Angel, then scowled at me. "What'd you do to her?"

"Nothing. Do you have any tissue or not?"

"Hang on, I'll find something."

He disappeared briefly, returned with a roll of toilet paper, and gave it to me with another scowl. I closed the door and handed the roll to Angel.

"Best we can do, I'm afraid."

"Thank you," she said. "I'm sorry I'm crying."

"Don't worry about it. I see it a lot."

"I can't believe this," she said through a sob. "Do I have to stay here? Can't I go home to Miss Erlene's house?"

"I'm sorry. I'm afraid you're going to be here for a while. Do you want to talk about what happened?"

"Nothing happened." She sniffled and blew her nose.

"Are you telling me you didn't have *anything* to do with Reverend Tester's murder?"

"I didn't kill him. I didn't do a thing to him."

"Did you know him?"

"I never saw him before he came into the club that night. I was waiting tables. I waited on him."

"Tell me about it."

She bit her lower lip and gathered herself. "He ordered a double scotch on the rocks. He started flirting with me right away. A couple times he yelled all the way across the bar at me, you know, making a scene. Then, as he got drunker, he started quoting the Bible and acting really strange. Every time I got near him, he would try to rub up against me. He finally tried to kiss me and asked me to leave with him. That's when Miss Erlene and Ronnie came over and asked him to leave."

"So that's it? You didn't see him again after he left, and he was alive and well when he walked out the door?"

"That's it, I swear. They told him to leave. I didn't see him again. Then a couple days later, a bunch of policemen came to Miss Erlene's house. She told me not to talk to any of them, so I didn't, but one of them had a piece of paper that said I had to give him some of my hair. They tore Miss Erlene's house all to pieces. Then they came back this morning and put me in the car and brought me down here."

As she spoke, something kept nagging at me. It took me a few minutes to realize what it was, and when I did, I could only wonder. Sitting in front of me was one of the most beautiful young women I'd ever seen, with a body so sexy that under normal circumstances I'd have either been aroused or, at the very least, distracted. But despite the incredible packaging, Angel didn't emit even a whiff of sexuality. Talking to her was very much like talking to a child.

"Did the police officer ask you any questions when he arrested you?" I said.

"He tried after we got here. He took me into a room like this. But Miss Erlene told me not to say a word to him, so I didn't. I think that policeman is pretty mad at me."

Either Angel and Erlene were two of the best liars I'd ever met, or the police had made a monumental blunder. I had no love for Agent Landers—he was a dishonest, womanizing sleaze with the biggest ego I'd ever encountered—but the TBI was known as a top-flight investigative agency. I found it hard to believe they'd arrest someone for first-degree murder unless they had a solid case.

"Have you ever been in any kind of trouble with the law, Miss Christian? Ever been arrested for anything?"

"No."

"Not even a traffic ticket?"

"I don't even know how to drive."

She started sobbing again. She seemed so helpless, so utterly incapable of violence. My heart went out to her, and I kept asking myself why. Why would she murder some stranger? What could possibly have happened that would have turned this young girl into a killer?

As I sat there wondering, she looked over the tissue at me, her eyes shining with tears, and she said, "Help me, Mr. Dillard. Please, help me."

Suddenly, the voice I was hearing wasn't hers. It was a voice from the past, the voice of a defenseless little girl ... *"Get him off of me, Joey. He's hurting me."*

I looked at her and nodded my head.

"Okay, Miss Christian," I said. "I'll help you. You've got yourself a lawyer."

PART II

APRIL 26
5:05 P.M.

When I called Erlene Barlowe and told her I was in, she asked me to meet her in the parking lot behind her club. I'd never been in the place, but I'd driven by it dozens of times. I got there a little after five and backed into a spot next to a black BMW. It had been a beautiful afternoon, clear and in the low seventies. The sun was starting to drop in the western sky, but as I looked to the northeast, I could see a massive dark thundercloud rolling across the tops of the mountains. I put the window down and could smell rain.

About five minutes later, I saw Erlene come out the back door of the club carrying a gym bag. She had changed into a zebra-striped jumpsuit that was so tight I could see every crevice in her body. She walked carefully in her heels across the gravel lot, glancing from left to right, and stopped at the window. She leaned over and dropped the gym bag in my lap.

"Everything all right?" I said. "You look a little nervous."

"Those TBI men have been following me around for a week. Makes me kind of jumpy. Your money's in the bag, sugar. How's Angel?"

"Scared."

"Poor thing. I hate the thought of her being locked up in that terrible place. You have to promise me you'll get her out of this."

"I'll do everything I can."

"It would probably be best if you leave now. You need to get that money someplace safe. We'll talk more later."

She blew me a kiss and I pulled out. As I drove down the road, I started thinking about what I was carrying. I'd taken some big cash fees from people accused of dealing drugs in the past, but never anything near a quarter million. I kept looking in the rearview mirror to make sure nobody was following me. If Landers had any idea what was going on, it would be just like him to make up a reason to stop me, search my truck, and seize the money.

About a mile from my house, I pulled into the parking lot of a small shopping strip, locked up the truck, and went into a liquor store to buy a bottle of good champagne. I didn't take my eyes off the truck the entire time I was in the store. After I finished, I drove toward home and pulled onto a dirt road that led into the woods just across the street from my house. I wanted to count the money, and I knew if I pulled in the driveway Rio would make such a racket that Caroline was likely to come out. With the light just beginning to fade, I started to count—fifty bundles of hundred-dollar bills, fifty in each bundle. It took me almost an hour, and it was all there. I couldn't believe it. I stuffed the cash in my own gym bag and headed for the house.

I found Caroline in the kitchen emptying the dishwasher. I walked up behind her and kissed her on the ear.

"Hi, baby," she said. "Did Rio pee on your shoe?"

"I was too quick for him today."

"I haven't heard from you all afternoon. How did it go with Ms. Barlowe?"

Caroline had called, but I hadn't returned the call. At first I wasn't sure I was going to take Angel's case, and later I was afraid I wouldn't be able to resist spilling the beans. I set the bottle of champagne down on the counter.

"Where's Lilly?" I said.

Caroline looked at me slyly. "At rehearsal. Mother's going to pick her up and take her out to eat. She won't be back for a couple hours."

"Sarah?"

"A friend of hers took her to an NA meeting."

"Good. At least she's trying."

Caroline looked over at the champagne. "What's the occasion?"

"Let's go out to the deck. We need to talk."

"Be there in a second."

I took a couple champagne glasses out of the cabinet, opened the bottle, and walked out onto the deck. I put the bottle and glasses on the table and stuck the gym bag underneath. The storm was moving closer and the wind had freshened, but we still had some time. It was just getting dark. The Big Dipper was creeping over the horizon to the northeast. The moon hadn't quite cleared the large hill to the northwest, and the reflection of running lights twinkled off the lake like fireflies as pontoon and bass boats made their way up and down the channel.

I lit the two oil lamps that flanked the deck and sat down just as Caroline came out. She sat across from me. I poured the champagne and looked intently at her.

"What?" she said.

"I was just lusting," I said. "Can't help it."

"I'm sure you can't." The dimple high in her right cheek showed only when she smiled a certain way. She was smiling that way now.

"So it went okay," I said, "with Ms. Barlowe."

"I saw the girl's picture on television. She sure is pretty."

"She's also very nice. And there's a very strong possibility that she's innocent. I talked to her today."

Caroline gasped. "You *talked* to her? Oh my God, is that where you've been all day? Are you going to represent her?"

"I don't think I have much choice."

Caroline's eyes lit up. I knew exactly what she was thinking.

"How much?" she said.

"What do you think a first-degree murder, maybe a death-penalty case, probably my last case, is worth?"

"I don't *know*." She took a sip of champagne and leaned forward. "How much is it worth?"

"Guess."

"Fifty?"

"Higher."

"Eeeeeh," she said. "Sixty?"

"You're way low. Jack it on up."

"Oh my God, Joe. Seventy-five? No, you look smug. I don't even know if I can say it. A hundred?"

"You're almost halfway."

Her jaw dropped. "You're not serious," she said. I don't think she knew it, but she was bouncing in her chair like a schoolgirl.

"Dead serious. *Half* way."

"T-t-two twenty?"

"Almost there. Add thirty more."

"Two fifty?" She said the words as though she were dreaming.

"Bingo! And what do we have for the lady who guessed a quarter million dollars, Don Pardo?" I reached down, grabbed the bag, and slammed it on the table. Champagne spewed from Caroline's mouth.

"Is that what I think it ...? No, it couldn't possibly. ..." She reached out and opened the bag. "Joe! Is this real?"

"Scout's honor," I said, holding my hand across my heart.

She began jumping around the deck like a cheerleader. She ran around the table and grabbed me by the neck. She hugged me so hard I almost choked.

"Damn, Caroline. Ease up a little. I'd like to live to spend it."

She stopped in her tracks, walked back to her seat, and took a deep breath.

"I'm going to hyperventilate. I'm going to pee my pants. Tell me how this happened."

"There isn't that much to tell. The woman came in and I talked to her for a while, then I went down to the jail and talked to the girl for a while. I actually said the words, Caroline. I actually said, 'A quarter million dollars, cash, up front,' and she didn't flinch. I called her after I went to the jail and she paid me."

"I want to kiss your whole face right now," Caroline said. "I want to gobble you up. I want to have your babies."

"We've got enough babies."

"Oh, Joe, this is unbelievable. This takes so much pressure off us."

"It's a double-edged sword. You know that."

She was on me before I got the last syllable out of my mouth. She kissed my forehead, my lips, my eyebrows, my ears.

"I have to tell someone," she said when she stopped kissing my whole face. "Where's the phone? I have to tell my mother."

"Don't do that, you'll be on the phone for an hour. Drink your champagne and let's just enjoy it for a minute. I have a feeling I'm going to earn every dime of it."

I watched her as she sat grinning in the flickering light of the lamps. She peeked into the bag again.

"Can I touch it?"

"Knock yourself out. It's your money now."

She was as pleased as I'd ever seen her, and nothing could have given me more satisfaction.

"My God, Joe, what a relief. Now ... what are we going to buy?"

"What are you talking about? You're supposed to be the miser. We're not buying anything. We have everything we need."

"Let's splurge just a little. We have to buy something."

"No, we don't."

"Yes, we do." Her eyes were bright with mischief. "Then we have to go somewhere."

"No."

"We have to go to the Caymans or something when the trial's over. You've always wanted to go there. Stop being such a killjoy."

"Why don't we worry about what we're going to do with it tonight?"

"I know exactly what we're going to do with it. We're sleeping with it. It doesn't leave my sight until I get it in the safety-deposit box tomorrow morning. Then I'll figure out what to do from there. Tell me about the girl. What's she like?"

"She's ... sweet," I said. "She seems like a really sweet kid."

"Is she as pretty as me?"

"Not even close."

"Good answer."

She held out her empty champagne glass, and I refilled it. She raised the glass.

"Here's to pretty girls with rich friends."

"Cheers." I took a big swallow of the champagne.

"When's the arraignment?"

"Monday. Nine o'clock in Jonesborough. Let's talk about something else. It's a beautiful evening. I'm sitting on a candlelit deck overlooking the water with a beautiful, slightly intoxicated woman. I've just made more money in one day than most people make in five years. Law and disorder and murder do not seem to be appropriate topics of conversation."

"You're right." Caroline rose from the table and reached for my hand. "Come with me."

She led me inside to the bedroom.

"This is heavy," she said, nodding toward the bag in her hand. "Delightfully heavy."

She tossed the bag of money into a corner, pushed me onto the bed, and began to slowly unbutton her blouse. Caroline is the only woman I've ever slept with. We've been together for so long that when it comes to making love, she knows exactly which buttons to push.

And for the next hour, she pushed every one of them.

APRIL 27
6:00 P.M.

Agent Landers ran three miles a day, at least five days a week. It kept his body tight and helped with the hangovers. The day after he arrested the girl, he was running along Watauga Avenue in Johnson City thinking he would've much rather nailed that kid than arrested her. She was hot.

She was also smart enough not to talk. Landers spent an hour in the interrogation room with her after he arrested her. All she'd say was that she wanted to talk to a lawyer.

Deacon Baker, the district attorney, had called Landers down to his office a couple days before the arrest. Baker was nothing but a fat, stupid little prude, but he'd somehow managed to get himself elected, so he was calling the shots. Deacon told Landers he was getting a lot of pressure to make an arrest. The victim's son was a chaplain and deputy sheriff in another county, and he'd been calling three times a day. The victim also had a cousin who lived in Carter County and was active in the

Republican women's group over there, and she'd been calling. Big deal, Landers told Deacon, let them call.

Landers didn't have much evidence. The night they raided the Mouse's Tail, they'd interviewed forty people. Nine of them were employees; the rest were customers. Only one person said she recognized Tester, a stripper named Julie Hayes. She said Tester came in around nine, stayed until almost midnight, and got plastered in between. She said he was quoting scripture one minute and getting lap dances the next, and that he took a special interest in a waitress named Angel Christian. Hayes said the preacher and Erlene Barlowe had about a five-minute conversation around eleven thirty. As soon as they were done talking, she said the preacher went out the front door, and Barlowe and Angel went out the back. None of them came back to the club that night. She also said that up until the day the preacher was murdered, Barlowe drove a red Corvette. The next day, she was driving the black BMW.

Nobody else in the place gave them anything they could use, which made Landers wonder whether Julie Hayes was telling the truth. Maybe she had some kind of grudge against Barlowe, or the girl, or both. But Landers wrote out her statement and she signed it. She said she was willing to testify.

The forensics team found some hair on Tester's shirt, so Landers took the Hayes girl's statement and parlayed it into a search warrant for Erlene Barlowe's house the next day. He also persuaded the judge to sign an order saying that both Erlene Barlowe and Angel Christian had to give him hair samples. They hadn't found a thing in Barlowe's house, not even so much as a porn video. Landers took a photograph of the girl though. She had a nasty bruise on her face.

There was no sign of a red Corvette. Landers ran Erlene Barlowe's name through every database the TBI had. No Corvette registered to her anywhere.

He got a call from the lab a few days later. Two hairs that were found on Tester's shirt matched the girl. That was the best evidence they had, and as far as Landers was concerned, it wasn't much. The lab also said the preacher had a date-rape drug in his system—GHB, otherwise known as Georgia Home Boy. Whoever killed him drugged him. Everybody knows you can get drugs at a strip bar, but Landers couldn't prove the drug in the preacher's body came from the Mouse's Tail.

So when he went down to the D.A.'s office, Landers laid the case out for Deacon Baker: Two witnesses, the stripper who might have a grudge, and a clerk from the motel who saw a Corvette pull in behind Tester around midnight and *thought* she saw a woman go up the stairs toward Tester's room. All the other employees at the club denied Tester was there, or at least said they didn't notice him, but he'd definitely withdrawn money from an ATM machine at the bar just after eleven thirty. Erlene Barlowe had lied—Landers was sure about that—and the others were probably lying. He had a DNA match from the Christian girl, a nasty bruise on her face, a shriveled penis (the medical examiner said it had been removed postmortem), no murder weapon, and a missing car. That was it. Oh yeah, they also had a gem of a victim. Preacher at a strip club. An east Tennessee jury would love that.

"Let me keep our surveillance on Erlene Barlowe for a while longer, see if she makes a mistake," Landers said.

"Here's the *real* deal, Phil," Deacon said, "just between you and me, all right? I don't care about the victim's son calling, and I don't care about that old hag over in Carter County. Hell, my secretary takes the calls anyway. It's no skin off my butt. But eight years ago, when I was running for D.A. for the first time against a powerful incumbent and I needed money the way a fat kid needs cake, that sorry SOB that owned the Mouse's Tail gave my opponent five thousand in cash as a campaign contribution. Didn't give me the first dime."

"So?"

"I've been after him ever since. There have always been rumors that Gus Barlowe was running drugs out of the club, but we haven't been able to catch them."

"He's dead, Deacon."

"I know that, but his wife isn't dead, is she?"

"We don't have any evidence against her."

Deacon waved his hand dismissively. "You know how these things go, Phil. You've got a pretty strong circumstantial case. We'll take it in front of the grand jury, get an indictment, and go arrest the girl. She'll most likely confess or roll on the Barlowe woman. If she doesn't, I'll file a death-penalty notice and up the pressure on her. Don't worry about it. Let's go ahead and shake this tree and see what falls out. Hell, this is an election year. It'd be a real feather in my cap to put that glorified hooker out of business before August."

Before August. Election year. Put that hooker out of business. None of this has anything to do with getting a murder conviction. What Deacon was really saying was that they needed to make an *arrest.* Didn't matter whether the girl was guilty, as long as somebody got locked up for the murder. No way it would go to trial before the election, and if it turned out she didn't do it, so what? At least Deacon would be assured of eating at the taxpayer's trough for another eight years. Moron. Him and his damned tree.

Landers finished his run and headed inside for a shower. He had a date at eight.

APRIL 30
8:45 A.M.

I smiled at Tammy Lewis, a pretty, green-eyed blonde with a sharp sense of humor and a sharper tongue. She'd worked for the circuit court clerk for twelve years. Her primary responsibility was to sit at Judge Leonard Green's side during proceedings and ensure that his court ran smoothly. There were two criminal court judges that presided over the four-county circuit where I did most of my work. Ivan the Terrible and Leonard Green the dancing machine. I called Green that because he'd gotten drunk at a Christmas party a few years back and started dancing on a table. Cases were assigned by number. Odd numbers went to Glass, even numbers went to Green. Angel's case was an even number.

"Good morning, Tammy," I said. "Ready for the circus?"

"Meaning?"

"I'm representing Angel Christian."

Tammy rolled her eyes. "No kidding? Well, ain't you just the lucky victim. I guess the question is, are *you* ready? His royal highness wants to deal with your client first thing. They brought her over from the jail about an hour ago. She's in the holding cell. There are already three television cameras in the courtroom and at least five newspaper photographers. Reporters all over the place. At least you'll get some free pub out of this."

I cringed at the thought of the media in the courtroom. Judge Green was always at his most belligerent in front of the television cameras. He'd often declared his belief that the voting public wanted judges who were tough on criminals, and when the media came to court, he made sure he didn't disappoint his constituency.

I walked through the clerk's office and into the hallway that ran parallel to the courtroom. When I reached the door, I stopped and stuck my head inside. Judge Green was not yet on the bench. Green and I had a long history of bickering that sometimes turned downright nasty. I thought he was pompous and effeminate. He thought I was a belligerent Neanderthal. Both of us were probably a little bit right.

The jury box was filled with television cameras, newspaper photographers, and reporters. I noticed they started huddling as soon as they saw me walk through the door and sit down at the defense table. Six uniformed Washington County sheriff's deputies flanked the courtroom. Six was a number reserved for the most dangerous defendants, and I certainly didn't think Angel qualified. The gallery on the civilian side of the bar was nearly full; there were close to a hundred people in the audience, most of them criminal defendants and their families. They would wait their turn without complaint, hoping to appear before the court in anonymity after the press had packed up and left.

District Attorney Deacon Baker was talking to a television reporter from Bristol near the jury box. Baker rarely made court appearances and hardly ever participated in trials, but he never missed an opportunity to preach the virtues of justice and law enforcement in front of the media. Baker's newest lead assistant, Frankie Martin, a bright but unseasoned youngster, sat at the prosecution table rummaging through a file.

At precisely 9:00 a.m., Wilkie Baines, one of the criminal court bailiffs, strode to the front of Judge Green's bench and faced the crowd. The door to Green's chambers opened, and the judge seemed to glide through the door, his perfectly groomed silver hair freshly cut, his black robe flowing behind him.

"All rise," Baines called in his best town-crier voice. "The criminal court for Washington County is now in session, the Honorable Leonard P. Green presiding. Please come to order."

Judge Green climbed the steps to the bench and took his seat in the high-backed black leather chair, directly beneath a massive portrait of himself.

"Thank you, Deputy Baines," he said. "Please be seated."

I, along with everyone else in the courtroom, dutifully sat down.

"Good morning," Judge Green said.

"Good morning." Nearly everyone in the courtroom responded, as though they feared the consequences of remaining silent.

"The first case we're going to address this morning is an arraignment in the State of Tennessee versus Angel Christian." He turned to the prosecution. "And I see that the district attorney himself has chosen to grace us with his presence today. To what do we owe this rare pleasure?"

Baker's face flushed the slightest bit. He stood up.

"This is a serious case, Your Honor. I'm merely here to ensure that all goes well."

"And to get yourself a little free publicity in an election year, I trust." Baker thought Judge Green was soft on sentencing sex offenders and wasn't shy about saying it to the local media. Baker had also openly and actively supported the judge's opponent in the last election. He was fond of telling people he wouldn't piss on Judge Green if the judge were on fire. Green, on the other hand, took obvious pleasure in harassing and humiliating Baker every chance he got. I'd seen them nearly come to blows on several occasions. They truly hated each other.

"I didn't invite the press," Baker said. "I believe their presence here has something to do with the first amendment."

"You may not have invited them, but you've certainly had plenty to say about this case over the past week. You've been on television more than *Law & Order* reruns."

Baker plunked back down into his chair, either unwilling or unable to spar with the judge, and Judge Green turned to me.

"What are you doing at the defense table, Mr. Dillard?"

"Representing the defendant, Judge." I knew he preferred "Your Honor."

"Has she hired you?"

It was a stupid question, but I resisted the urge to say something smart.

"She has."

Judge Green raised his eyebrows at me as if to say, "How much did she pay you?" He turned toward the deputy nearest the door that led to the holding cell and barked, "Bring in the defendant."

The deputy disappeared into the hallway. He returned in less than a minute with Angel beside him. The shackles on her ankles forced her to shuffle. Every camera was suddenly pointed in her direction. The courtroom went dead silent. Just behind the deputy and Angel were two more deputies and K.D. Downs, the sheriff of Washington County. Everybody was getting in on the show.

The bailiff gingerly escorted Angel to the podium in front of the jury box, directly to the judge's right. I noticed that he patted her on the shoulder before he stepped back. Angel looked tired, scared, confused, and gorgeous. I walked over and stood by her at the podium.

Green turned to Tammy Lewis. "Let me see the indictment."

She handed the document to the judge. He studied it for a few seconds, then offered it to Wilkie Baines.

"Give this to Mr. Dillard, and let the record show that the defendant's counsel has been provided a copy of the indictment. Mr. Dillard, your client has been charged with one count of first-degree murder and one count of abuse of a corpse. Do you waive the formal reading of the indictment?"

"We do, Judge."

"How does your client plead?"

"Not guilty."

"Very well." The judge looked at Deacon Baker. "I assume you've filed your death notice, Mr. Baker?"

"We have, Your Honor. We filed it this morning."

With the number of stab wounds, the case was probably second-degree murder at best. It certainly appeared to be a crime of passion. But Baker handed out death notices like grocery stores hand out coupons. It seemed that every murder defendant got one. He did it because it gave him an effective bargaining chip—Baker was notorious for offering to take the death penalty off the table in exchange for a guilty plea just before trial, no matter how heinous the murder.

"What about scheduling?" the judge said.

"We'd like a speedy trial," I said. "Miss Christian is incarcerated without bond. Since she's charged with a capital offense and since she's not from this community and really has no ties here, I'd be wasting my breath to ask you to set a bond. But she maintains her innocence and wants a trial as soon as possible. I think I can be ready to go in three months."

Baker stood up. "There is no way the state could be ready in less than nine months, Your Honor. This is a death—"

I cut him off. "I didn't want to get into this, Judge, but since Mr. Baker is going to resist a speedy trial, there are some things I think you should know. As you know,

I've been doing this for a long time, and I've never had a case quite like this one. The police and the district attorney have let everyone know that the victim in this case is a preacher. What they haven't told anyone is that he spent his last night on earth getting drunk at a strip club. Nobody knows where he went between the time he left the club and the time he was killed. This isn't one of those cases where the police have the killer dead to rights. My client swears she didn't see the victim after he left the club. She swears she didn't kill him, and she shouldn't have to wait almost a year before a jury hears this case."

"I object to this!" Baker yelled. "Mr. Dillard is taking this opportunity to sensationalize this case and poison the potential jury pool."

That's exactly what I was doing, but I wasn't about to admit it.

"All I'm doing," I said, "is asking you to set this case for trial as quickly as possible so an innocent young girl doesn't have to sit in jail any longer than necessary."

Judge Green ruminated for a few minutes, then looked down at Baker.

"God created heaven and earth in six days, Mr. Baker. Surely you can be ready for trial in ninety. If you weren't ready to prosecute her, you shouldn't have indicted her. How long is it going to take to try the case?"

"A week, maybe less," I said.

"I have an opening on July twenty-fourth. That's just under three months from now. Mr. Dillard, since you're the one who asked for a speedy trial, I won't expect to see you back in here asking me for a continuance. I'll send you a scheduling order that will deal with pretrial conferences, expert disclosures and deadlines, motion deadlines and plea deadlines. Anything else?"

"No, Judge, not from us," I said. It was the same week that we were planning to go to the Braves game, but I didn't say anything. It wouldn't have made any difference. It was also only ten days before the August 3rd election. It had to be Judge Green's not-so-subtle method of applying pressure to Deacon.

"Miss Christian," the judge said, "they'll bring you over from the jail on July twenty-fourth, and you'll get a fair trial. It will be your responsibility to see to it that you have civilian clothing, and I won't allow the jury to see that you're restrained in any fashion. I'll see you then unless there are motions or unless you decide to change your plea."

The bailiff took Angel by the arm and led her toward the door. I followed. Just before we reached the door, I noticed a man walking quickly toward the bar that separated the attorneys from the gallery. He was about six feet tall, wearing a blue polyester suit. I'd seen pictures of John Paul Tester in the newspaper. This guy looked like a younger version. The hair was shorter and darker, but he was working on the pot belly, and he had the same mutton-chop sideburns. He was pointing at Angel.

"*A fire* is kindled in mine anger, and shall burn unto the lowest hell!" he yelled. Everyone froze at the power of his deep voice. I stepped between him and Angel, more fascinated than frightened. "And shall consume the earth with her increase, and set on fire the foundations of the mountains! They shall be burnt with hunger, and devoured with burning heat, and with bitter destruction. I will send the teeth of beasts upon them, with the poison of serpents of the dust. You have taken my father's life, Jezebel, and upon you, I swear revenge."

I took a couple steps backwards as the bailiffs began to slowly converge. They were tentative, apparently frightened. Tester's eyes were as blue as robin's eggs and fiercely intense.

"And you, scribe!" he continued, turning his attention to me. His voice boomed off the walls, and I could see veins popping out of his neck. He stepped through the bar toward me and bumped me with his pot belly. He was so close I could smell his breath. "How dare you blaspheme my father! I swear you'll pay for it!"

I shoved him hard in the chest. He stumbled backwards as I heard Judge Green's voice cut through the chaos: "Bailiffs! Arrest that man!"

"She killed my father!" he screamed as he struggled against the bailiffs. "Jezebel killed my father!"

Angel, crying hysterically, was quickly ushered into a jury room just down the hall from the courtroom. I caught up with her and gently took hold of her shoulders.

"I didn't kill him!" Her shoulders were heaving. "Please tell that man I didn't kill his father."

"I'll tell him," I said, knowing I wouldn't be going anywhere near him. "Don't worry about this. It happens. People get upset. You just try to calm down. I'll come to the jail to see you in a couple of days."

The bailiffs took her away, and I walked back into the courtroom. The man was now in handcuffs, standing at the podium in front of Judge Green, looking down at his shoes. The judge had apparently just finished reading him the riot act.

"I understand the emotional turmoil you're going through," Green said, "but you, being a chaplain *and* a deputy sheriff, should know we cannot tolerate that kind of behavior in court. Now go, but sin no more in my courtroom. Court's in recess."

Tester's son a chaplain and a deputy? Any hopes I had of the district attorney's office acting reasonably were out the window.

As Green disappeared into his chambers, I scanned the courtroom. Erlene Barlowe was in the back row. I motioned for her to meet me in the hallway. She was wearing a black pantsuit and had toned down the makeup for court. If I didn't know better, I might have mistaken her for a lawyer.

"Now that we've done the arraignment, I can get some discovery," I said. "Why don't you come down to the office around four, and we'll take a look at what they've got."

"I'll be there, sugar."

As we stood together, I looked down the hall and saw Tester's son leaning against the wall, staring in my direction. There was no mistaking the look in his eyes. It was pure hatred.

APRIL 30
4:00 P.M.

E rlene Barlowe's granny trained her to be punctual way before everyone in Erlene's family disowned her because she ran off with Gus. Granny said tardiness was nothing but bad manners, and that people with bad manners lacked character. Erlene didn't want Mr. Dillard to think she lacked character, so she arrived at his office ten minutes early.

Joe Dillard was a big, strong, good-looking man, just like Erlene's Gus. If Erlene had been a younger woman and hadn't been so devoted to Gus, she might have thought seriously about trying to seduce Mr. Dillard. He dressed in dark suits and colored shirts, solid-colored ties, nice shoes. His hair was jet black and wavy, just flecked here and there with gray, and he had green eyes and the cutest dimples Erlene had ever seen. He was well-spoken, too, obviously an intelligent man. Erlene thought he was a little high on the fee he charged to represent Angel, but if he got her off, it'd be worth every dime. Besides, it wasn't like the fee was going to put Erlene in the poorhouse. If

Mr. Dillard had known what she was worth, he'd have asked for twice as much. Gus made a lot of money buying and selling different things on top of what they made at the strip clubs, and he had a fortune in life insurance. When he passed, the lawyer told Erlene she was worth as much as Jed Clampett.

Mr. Dillard showed her to a seat. He had papers spread out all over the table.

"Have you talked to Angel?" he said.

"She called me a little while ago. Poor baby is scared to death. That little outburst at the courthouse didn't help any."

"Tester Junior's a scary guy. Did you see him staring at me in the hallway? He looked like he wanted to cut my throat. That's why we took the back stairs."

He may have been scary to Mr. Dillard, but he didn't scare Erlene. She wasn't afraid of any man. If she'd learned anything in the adult entertainment business over the past thirty years, it was how to deal with men. She knew how to make them feel good, and she knew how to make them miserable.

Erlene knew how to deal with preachers, too. When she and Gus first came to northeast Tennessee, the preachers had all ganged up and wouldn't let them go into business. They put pressure on county commissioners, organized rallies, talked on the news. They did whatever they could to make Erlene and Gus look bad, but the couple had been through it before. They hired good lawyers. It cost them nearly thirty thousand dollars in legal fees plus another twenty in bribes and took over a year, but they finally got their business license and all their permits. Then danged if somebody didn't burn down their building as soon as they got it up. Erlene and Gus built another one, only to see it too go up in flames. The second time, though, Gus had hidden video surveillance cameras all around the building. Turned out the man who was burning the buildings was a preacher named Hastings. He went to jail. They left Erlene and Gus alone after that, but it didn't change her opinion of preachers. Bunch of danged hypocrites was all they were.

"Erlene," Mr. Dillard said, "I've spent the afternoon going through this discovery material. I know pretty much everything they have now, and there are a couple things I need to talk to you about. Do you own a red Corvette?"

Shitdammit. Why did he have to be so direct?

"I beg your pardon?"

"Do you own a red Corvette?"

"Why no, honey, I sure don't."

"Let me rephrase the question. On the day Tester was killed, did you own a red Corvette?"

Erlene had a feeling that before this was over, she and Mr. Dillard were going to get along like two peas in a pod, but right then she thought it best to keep a few things to herself.

"Why?" she said.

"Because the police have a witness who told them you owned a red Corvette and that it disappeared the day after Tester was murdered. That same witness also told them you and Angel left the club right after Tester left that night and neither of you came back. And they have another witness who saw a woman get out of a Corvette around midnight at Tester's motel."

"Well, I swan, honey pot. Who would say a thing like that?" She knew exactly who it had to be. Little Miss Julie.

"Is there any truth to it?"

"Is this conversation just between the two of us, sugar?"

"You're not my client, Erlene. The privilege doesn't apply, so be careful what you say." Erlene sat back and took a deep breath, like she was nervous. "Can you tell me who the witnesses are?" she said.

"One is a night clerk at the motel named Sheila Hunt. She says she saw a Corvette pull in behind Tester around midnight and saw a woman get out of the passenger side and go up the steps with him. It was raining pretty hard, and the woman was apparently wearing some kind of hooded poncho or cape, so she didn't get a good look at her. And she didn't see her leave. She didn't get a tag number and couldn't tell the cops anything about the driver."

"That doesn't sound like much to me."

"It isn't, unless the Corvette shows up somewhere down the road. Will it?"

"Who told them I owned a Corvette?" Erlene said.

"One of your employees. The night they raided your place. She said you'd been driving a red Corvette prior to Tester's murder and that it disappeared the day after he was killed."

"It was Julie Hayes, wasn't it?"

Mr. Dillard nodded.

"Did anybody else at the club tell the police anything like that?" Erlene said.

"No ma'am. She was the only one."

"What does that tell you, sugar?"

"It tells me that either she's lying or everyone else is lying."

"And what do you think?"

"I think I want to hear you tell me she's lying."

Erlene smiled. Mr. Dillard was so handsome, and she could just feel goodness oozing out of him.

"She's the one who's lying, baby doll."

Erlene told him about Julie and her drug problem and her crush on Gus. She told him how Julie came back on a bus from Texas with Angel after they'd met in the bus station down there. Julie noticed that Angel didn't have any luggage, not even a purse, so Julie knew right off that Angel was probably a runaway. Since Angel was so pretty, Julie asked her if she'd like to tag along and maybe work in the club. When Erlene picked Julie up at the station, Angel was with her.

"So you think Julie's setting you and Angel up for a murder because she's jealous?" Mr. Dillard said.

"I wouldn't put anything past her. She's a troubled girl. I've heard her talk about her arrest record. She bragged about it. She used to tell Gus she had a record as long as his terwilliger."

"As long as his what?"

"Terwilliger. It's what I call a man's thingy. You know... ." Erlene pointed between her legs, and Mr. Dillard's face turned red as her lipstick.

"What else do you know about Julie?"

"Just what she's told me. She said her mother's boy-friend tried to rape her when she was sixteen. When she told her mother about it, her mother accused her of lying and beat her up pretty bad. She took off and has been on the road ever since. I think her life has been pretty much nothing but drugs and prostitution. That's one of the reasons she likes to work here. The money's good enough that the girls don't have to sell themselves. But Julie just can't seem to stay away from the drugs. She has to know I'm about to fire her again."

"Okay," Mr. Dillard said. "That helps. It looks like we can impeach Julie if she testifies. But you still haven't answered my question."

"What question is that?"

"Is a red Corvette going to jump up and bite us on the backside sometime between now and the trial?"

"I just don't see how it could, sugar."

"Good. I'll put an investigator on Julie Hayes and gather all the background information we can on her. From what you've told me, we shouldn't have much trouble helping her make herself look bad in front of a jury."

Mr. Dillard didn't know it, and Erlene wasn't about to tell him, but Julie Hayes wouldn't be going in front of any jury.

"We have another problem," he said. "Two hairs they found on Tester's shirt match Angel's DNA."

"Is that bad, sugar?"

"It's a problem, but I don't think it's insurmountable. I'm going to suggest a couple of Angel's hairs could have passed to Tester while he was at the club."

"Why, he was all over her," Erlene said.

"That's not what you told the TBI."

Shitdammit again. "That TBI man scared me to death, honey. I didn't know what to say to him."

"From now on, Erlene, I'd suggest you just stick to the truth. In this case, it looks like the truth may set Angel free."

He was so cute and noble. Erlene just wanted to pinch his cheeks.

JUNE 6
5:45 A.M.

I liked to watch the sun rise on Sunday mornings. The Sunday after they arraigned Angel Christian, I got up around five-thirty, made a pot of coffee, and wandered up the driveway in the semidarkness in my bare feet and boxers to get the newspaper. As I got to the end of the driveway, I noticed a silver pickup truck, one of those macho Dodges with tinted windows, backed into the dirt road that led into the woods across the street from the mailbox. It was the same place where I'd counted Erlene's money. The lights weren't on, and I couldn't hear the engine running. The property where the truck was sitting belonged to me. It wasn't hunting season, and no one had asked me about camping, so I decided to check it out.

I got the paper out of the box and started walking toward the truck. Just as I got to within ten feet, the engine roared to life and the lights came on. I thought it was probably one of Jack's friends, so I started to wave and say hello, but the thing started coming right for me. I jumped out of the way before it hit me, but it couldn't have missed by more than a couple feet. When I landed, my foot caught on a small bush and I ended up flat on my back. The truck came off the dirt road and squealed off into the dawn. I didn't get a look at the driver over the headlights, and my clumsy leap kept me from seeing the license plate.

I cursed, picked myself up off the ground, and walked back down the driveway toward the house, wondering who in the hell could have been in the truck. I thought about the look Tester's son had given me and made a mental note to call Diane Frye, a retired state trooper who was now a private investigator. I'd already talked to her about working the Angel Christian case for me, but now I needed to know whether Tester's son had a silver Dodge truck registered in his name, and if he did, I needed to know anything and everything she could find out about him.

That's when I noticed Lilly's car was gone. We had room for only two cars in the garage, so Lilly's was always parked just outside, off to the side of the driveway. I knew it had been there the night before because Lilly had driven it to Knoxville and hadn't gotten home until midnight. I'd waited up for her.

I went back into the house and upstairs to Lilly's room. She wasn't the kind of kid to sneak out, but I was hoping against hope that she had. I found her sleeping the dead-zone sleep of a teenager.

As I walked toward Sarah's room, I was hoping the car had been stolen by some stranger, knowing it hadn't. Sarah's bed was unmade and empty.

She'd been doing relatively well under the circumstances. Caroline and Lilly had taken her to town to buy her some clothes a couple days after she showed up, and I'd brought her a catalogue from Northeast State Community College. She'd talked about enrolling in the fall and studying computer graphics. She spent a lot of time wandering through the woods down by the lake and watching television, and she'd been attending Narcotics Anonymous meetings four days a week.

But then I made a mistake. I took her up to see Ma on Saturday. Ma didn't recognize either one of us and was unusually belligerent. She told us to get out of her room and never come back. She made such a fuss that one of the nurses suggested we leave and come back another time. The visit obviously upset Sarah, who was hoping to make some kind of peace before Ma died. Sarah hadn't given any indication on Saturday night that she was about to do something stupid, but she was quieter than usual and went to bed early.

I walked back through the house to our bedroom and touched Caroline on the shoulder. She came out of sleep slowly.

"Mmm ... what? Is something wrong?"

"Sarah's gone," I said. "In Lilly's car."

She didn't seem to understand for a moment. Then she sat straight up. "Oh no," she said. "I dreamed last night that she ran away."

"We better take a look around and make sure nothing's missing."

"What do you think she took besides the car?"

"I don't know, but you better make sure she didn't steal anything out of your purse, and you should check your jewelry. Lilly's too. I'll check the electronics and the guns."

It was hard to think of my sister as a thief, but that's exactly what she'd been in the past. She'd stolen money from me, and Ma had been a favorite target. I wandered around the house for the next fifteen minutes, checking to make sure she hadn't hauled off a computer or a television or a stereo system. When I was finished, I walked back into the kitchen. Caroline was sitting at the table drinking a bottled water. She looked at me, and I knew the news was going to be bad.

"My diamond necklace is gone." I'd given Caroline the necklace for Christmas five years ago. She'd never owned anything expensive, and seeing the look on her face when she opened the box had given me great pleasure. She kept it in a jewelry box in a drawer in the bedroom. If it was gone, Sarah must have snuck in there and stolen it during the night.

"Goddammit," I said. "God*damm*it! How could she do this?"

"I guess we were expecting too much," Caroline said.

"I thought she might be ready to change. I thought I might be able to help her."

"When she's ready to change, if she's ever ready to change, she'll do it on her own. We can't force it on her. What do you think we should do?"

"She's taken a ten-thousand-dollar car and a five-thousand-dollar necklace. What do *you* think I should do?"

Caroline sighed. "I don't know, babe. Maybe you should go out and try to find her."

"I've been down that road before. You know she's high by now. I guarantee she's already sold the necklace for peanuts or traded it for coke. If I found her at some dealer's house, I'd end up defending myself in court after I killed the son of a bitch. I guess I'll just call Johnson City's finest and see if they can pick her up before she sells the car to some chop-shopper."

The phone rang. Maybe it was Sarah, ready to turn back before she crossed the line.

"Mr. Dillard?" a male voice said when I answered.

"Yes."

"Hi, this is Matthew Miller with the Johnson City Police Department. Haven't seen you in a while. You okay these days?"

I knew Matthew Miller. I knew most of the cops in Johnson City.

"I'm fine, Officer Miller. Tell me you found my daughter's car."

"A 2001 Chrysler Sebring, maroon in color, Washington County plate number QRS-433?"

"It was stolen last night."

"Well, sir, I'm afraid I have some more bad news. We found it wrecked this morning off Knob Creek Road. Went down an embankment and rolled across a creek. Ended up against a tree. I'd say it's totaled, and—"

"What about the driver?"

"No driver," Miller said. "No trace. Any idea who was behind the wheel?"

"It was probably my sister. She disappeared some-time last night."

"I thought she was locked up." Sarah was infamous. Everybody knew her.

"She got out a couple weeks ago. She was staying here."

"I guess no good deed goes unpunished," Miller said. "We're pretty much finished up here. I'm going to have the car towed down to Brown's Mill Chevron, and you can take it from there. The air bags inflated and there's no blood, so if it was your sister, she probably made it out okay."

"Thanks. Can you send somebody out here to take a report? She took some jewelry too."

"Probably be best if you just call 9-1-1," he said. "They'll send the right people."

I thanked Miller and hung up.

"She wrecked it," I said to Caroline. "She wrecked Lilly's car. I'm calling the cops. I'm through with her."

"I've heard that before."

"I'm serious. She committed two felonies under my roof. She stole and wrecked my daughter's car and stole your necklace. With her record, they'll ship her off to the penitentiary where she belongs. She won't see the light of day again for at least four years, maybe longer."

"Are you sure that's what you want to do?" Caroline said. "I don't want you beating yourself up about it later."

I picked up the phone and dialed 9-1-1.

JUNE 9
10 A.M.

Two days later I got a call from a drug enforcement agent I'd known for ten years. He said they'd picked Sarah up in a crack house on Wilson Avenue around midnight on Monday night. He thought I might like to know.

I drove straight to the jail. On the way, my cell phone rang. It was Diane Frye.

"The answer is yes," she said when I picked up the phone. "John Paul Tester Junior owns a silver 2005 Dodge Ram pickup." It was the same color, make, and model of the truck that had almost run over me.

"So what else did you find out about him?"

"Born December 1, 1972, to John Paul and Debra Jean Tester in Newport. His mother died of ovarian cancer when the boy was only two. Raised by his father, who was a journeyman welder when he wasn't preaching the gospel. When he was on the road, which was often, Junior stayed with an aunt. Talked to the aunt, nice lady named Wanda Smithers who has since moved to Ocala,

Florida. She said Junior idolized his daddy. She said the boy's favorite thing to do when he was a boy was to go to church and listen to his daddy preach. Said he'd sit in the front row and hang on every word.

"By the time Junior was ten years old, he was already studying the Bible and 'testifying' for his father. Started preaching when he was a teenager. When he wasn't preaching, he spent almost all his time in his room. Never had a girlfriend, didn't show any interest in any school activities or sports. The gospel was his whole life. The aunt says that after he got out of high school, Junior and his father started traveling together. They preached all over the Southeast. She says they're somewhat of a legend among the fundamentalists."

"Wow, Diane, you got all that in two days?"

"It's my charm and personality. That and the fact that the aunt talked my ear off."

"Anything else?"

"The aunt said she visited last year for a weekend. Said Junior stayed in his room and studied, just like when he was a boy. She also said Daddy Tester wasn't as committed to the faith as Junior. She said he tended to drink heavily every so often and that he liked the ladies."

"I wonder if the son knew about that," I said.

"Probably. Be kind of hard to hide for an entire lifetime. I also talked to a couple people down at the Cocke County sheriff's department. Daddy Tester apparently had some political clout and got Junior his job. He's been there for more than ten years as a chaplain. He counsels the officers, works with inmates at the jail, that sort of stuff. The people I talked to said everybody down there thinks Junior's a nut job. He apparently won't talk about anything but the gospel, and since his daddy was killed, he hardly talks at all."

"Anything violent?"

"No criminal record. The aunt said he's gentle. Doesn't remember him ever even getting into a fist-fight. But she said he's changed since his father's death. She came up for the funeral and said he acted awfully strange."

"Thanks. Send me a bill."

"It's already in the mail."

A half hour after I got off the phone with Diane, a guard brought Sarah into the interview room. She looked like she'd aged fifteen years. When she saw I was there, she didn't bother to sit at the table, she just put her hands over her face and slid down the wall onto the floor. The sight of her no longer made me sad. All I felt was anger.

"Have a good time?" I said.

"Screw you."

"Screw me? That's great. You did a nice job on Lilly's car. I really appreciate that."

"Yeah, well, tell her I'm sorry. I haven't driven in a while."

"Where's Caroline's necklace?"

"Gone."

"Gone where? Who'd you sell it to?"

"Like I'd tell you."

"Did you sell it or trade it?"

"What difference does it make?"

"I'd like to get it back."

"Not a chance."

"Are you really that far gone, Sarah? Do you really not give a damn about anything anymore? That necklace may mean nothing but a quick fix to you, but it meant a lot to Caroline, and I'd like to have it back."

She uncovered her face and glared at me.

"The only person that necklace meant anything to was you. It was just you showing everyone what a successful big shot you were, buying an expensive trinket. Do you really think it meant anything to her? You tried the same crap with me. Oh, come live with us, Sarah. Come stay with my perfect little family. We'll buy you stuff if you don't get high. We'll take care of you. What a crock. You can't buy people, Joey. You're so pathetic."

I'd gotten up and was leaning against the block wall, contemplating my fingernails. Sarah had long ago perfected the art of the addict's vitriolic tirade. The words floated past me like tiny ghosts. I didn't allow them to linger.

"I came up here for a couple reasons," I said. "The first is to tell you what you've done, in case you don't fully understand the situation. Stealing the car was a C felony, minimum three years, maximum six in your range. Stealing the necklace was another C felony, same sentence. With your priors and my connections at the district attorney's office, I think I can convince them to push for consecutive sentences at the top of the range. No more six months in the county jail and you're out to do it again, Sarah. You're going to the penitentiary for twelve years. You'll be at least fifty when you get out, if you live that long. I'm going to see to it personally."

I'd represented her five times in the past, each time telling myself I'd never do it again. I'd always managed to get her sentences reduced, to get them to go as easy on her as possible. But this time was different. I felt genuinely betrayed, and although I wasn't proud of it, I wanted a little retribution. The words I'd spoken seemed to sink slowly into her addled brain. She pulled her knees up to her chest and rocked against the wall. Then she began to whimper.

"You can't do that to me, Joey. You can't. I won't survive."

"Sure you will. You always have."

"I'm sick, Joey. You know I'm sick. Tell Lilly and Caroline I'm sorry. I'll get a job and pay you back."

"Too late. Last straw, Sarah. I'm through with you."

"You've said that before. You don't mean it. You're the one person who's never given up on me. You can't give up on me, Joey."

"My name is Joe," I said. "I stopped being Joey a long time ago, when I grew up. You should give it a try."

The crying turned into a mournful wailing. Tears were streaming down her face, and she was banging her head against the wall. The guard came to the doorway.

"Everything all right in here?"

"Yeah, I was just leaving. Mind letting me out?"

He unlocked the steel door and I stepped through. Sarah's sobs were almost unbearable. I quickened my pace as I walked down the hall to the stairwell and pushed the door open. Just before it closed, I heard her yell.

"Joey! You're supposed to protect me!"

JUNE 12
2:15 P.M.

News travels fast in the law enforcement community, both good and bad. The word was that Joe Dillard's sister had been popped again, only this time Dillard and his family were the victims.

Agent Landers regarded Dillard as a self-righteous prick who spent his life defending the scumbags Landers was trying to put away. As far as Landers was concerned, Dillard was as bad as the people he represented. When Landers heard Dillard had been hired to represent Angel Christian, he almost puked. He hated the thought of having to deal with Dillard through discovery and through a trial. But when Landers heard Dillard's sister had been arrested, it cheered him up. He immediately called the jail and found out she hadn't made bond. Then he called the jail administrator and asked her to move Dillard's sister into the same cell block as Angel Christian. The administrator said it would be no problem, so Landers waited a couple days and then went down to pay Miss Dillard a little visit.

He had the guards bring her to an interrogation room. Her shoulders were rounded and slumped, and her eyes were blank. Still, she was definitely good-looking enough to screw. And wouldn't that have been sweet, laying the wood to Dillard's sister?

She sat there like a stone, not looking at Landers. He thought he'd wait her out and let her talk first, but after a few minutes it was obvious she wasn't going to say a word.

"You're Joe Dillard's sister," Landers finally said.

"What about it?" she said without looking up.

"I hear he had you locked up."

She didn't respond. Landers watched her closely, trying to see whether she was silently agreeing with him.

"You haven't asked who I am, Miss Dillard."

"I don't care who you are."

"You should. I'm the man who could get you out of here."

She looked up for the first time. "And why would you do that?"

"I need some help. You need some help. You help me, I'll help you. Simple as that. I can offer you two things: a ticket out of jail and a chance to get back at your brother. Should I keep talking?"

Her eyes narrowed. "I don't trust lawyers."

"I'm not a lawyer. I'm an agent with the Tennessee Bureau of Investigation."

"I trust cops even less than I trust lawyers."

"Suit yourself. I'm sure I can find somebody else up there in the cell block who wants to get out of here. I just thought you might like a shot at your brother." Landers got up from the chair, walked to the door, and acted like he was about to push the button to call the guard.

"Wait," she said. "What do you want from me?"

"Like I said, I need a little help."

"What kind of help?"

Landers sat back down at the table. "Information. I need information. Your brother is defending a murderer named Angel Christian. She's in your cell block. Have you met her?"

"I keep to myself."

"Here's my problem. I don't know anything about her. I need to be able to check her out, you know what I mean? For starters, Angel Christian isn't her real name. I need to know what her name is. I need to know where she's from. I need to know where she went to school, whether she's ever had a driver's license in another name, whether she's ever been in trouble before, who her parents are, that kind of thing, and if she happens to bring up the murder, I wouldn't mind hearing about it. Do you think you might be willing to help me out with that?"

It was as though the Christian girl didn't exist. The only person who knew anything about her was Julie Hayes, and all Hayes knew was that she'd picked her up at the Greyhound bus terminal in Dallas back in February. Hayes said the girl wouldn't tell her what her name was, so she gave her the name Angel Christian on the bus. She thought it was funny. Landers desperately needed to come up with *something*. Hell, for all he knew, Angel might be a serial killer. But she wouldn't talk to him, the Barlowe woman wouldn't talk to him, and the people they'd interviewed at the strip club hadn't helped at all.

"So you want me to snitch for you?" Dillard's sister said.

"You can call it whatever you want. What I call it is providing substantial assistance to a law enforcement officer in a murder investigation."

"And what do I get in return?"

"People who provide substantial assistance in murder investigations often receive substantial reductions in their sentences. Like time served."

"What's your name?" she said. Landers didn't like the tone or the look on her face.

"My name is Landers. Special Agent Phillip Landers."

She started laughing.

"What's so funny?" Landers said.

"I heard my brother talking to his wife about you after he got hired on his big murder case. He said you're the biggest liar on the planet. He said you'll lie on the witness stand, plant evidence, frame people, and God knows what else. He said you're one of those cops who'll do anything to win a case."

"Your brother's a prick."

"My brother may be a prick, but he's an honest prick," she said. "I don't think I care to get involved with someone like you. Besides, I'm not a snitch."

Stupid little slut. Landers was offering her a way out, and she had to go all sanctimonious. He wanted to ask her if being a drug-addicted, thieving, little whore was better than being a snitch, but he didn't want to kill the possibility that she might be willing to help him later. He swallowed his pride and smiled.

"Fine," he said. "It was nice to meet you. If you change your mind, just give me a call."

Landers handed her a card and walked out the door. He'd wait and come back in a few weeks, maybe a month. If he was lucky, she'd be sentenced by then, looking at a trip to the women's penitentiary in Nashville. Landers had been down there a couple times. It was a miserable place. Maybe when the prospect of going to the penitentiary turned into a reality, Dillard's sister would change her mind.

JUNE 13
1:00 P.M.

Erlene Barlowe hated to do it to Virgil, he was such a sweetie. But Erlene had made an uncharacteristic mistake the night the preacher was killed—she'd let her emotions overcome her good sense, and she'd put her beloved Angel in an impossible position. Erlene's mistake had ultimately resulted in Angel's arrest, and now she was determined to do something that might begin to set things right.

Erlene had called Virgil and asked him to come out and meet her at the club at one o'clock in the afternoon. She could tell by his voice that he was a little apprehensive, but she assured him she just needed a teeny little favor.

He showed up right on time. Virgil Watterson was a homely sort of man, kind of short, and the hair in his gray wig stuck up in different directions. Erlene had never asked him why, but he always wore a bow tie and suspenders when he came to the club, at least until one of the girls took them off. Erlene had a collection of the bow ties Virgil had left behind.

Virgil was real well off—Gus told Erlene that Virgil owned six McDonald's restaurants and a whole bunch of real estate. He'd been coming to the club for years, but since he was married and a deacon in his church and a high-class businessman and all, Erlene and Gus had always made the VIP room available for him and let him come and go through the back door. Sometimes he brought a friend or business associate with him, but usually he just came by himself. He always wanted at least two girls to keep him company, and he always paid in cash. He was a good customer and a sweet little old man. Wouldn't hurt a flea, though he did have some sexual tendencies that ran a little to the strange side.

The VIP lounge was a fairly large room with its own bar and dance floor. Off to one side were three small rooms Erlene called bullpens. If a gentleman wanted even more privacy, he was welcome to take a lady, or two or three, off into one of the bullpens and conduct whatever business he needed to conduct.

Gus always called the video recording system he installed in the VIP bullpens his little insurance policy. He didn't tape everything that went on in there, but he taped enough to be able do a little trading if the need ever arose. He had tapes of judges and lawyers and doctors and police chiefs and preachers and businessmen and politicians. All the tapes were arranged in alphabetical order and kept in a fireproof safe in a mini-warehouse on the outskirts of the city. Virgil just happened to be one of the people Gus had taped several times, and Virgil was such a meek little man that Erlene thought he was perfect for what she needed done.

It was just the two of them in the club, and Erlene led Virgil down the hallway in the back to the girls' dressing room. There was a small lounge for the girls with a television back there, one of those televisions that had a video player built into it. The tape Erlene wanted to show Virgil was already in the machine. She pulled a chair up for him in front of the television.

"Now you just sit your cute little self down right here," Erlene said. "I've got something special I want to show you."

Virgil sat down and Erlene sat down next to him. She put one hand on his knee and pointed the remote at the television with the other.

The screen lit up and there was Virgil, naked, sucking his thumb and talking dirty to a couple of the girls. Erlene kept patting Virgil's knee as they watched him do some things he probably found a tad embarrassing. After a couple minutes, he asked her to turn it off. Then he turned to her with the most pitiful look on his face Erlene had ever seen.

"I can't believe you'd do this to me, Erlene," Virgil said. "After all these years and all the money I've put in your pocket, I just can't believe it."

"Do what, honey?" Erlene said. "I'm not doing a thing to you."

"Then what was the purpose of showing that to me?"

"I just need a little favor, sweetie. That's all. And if you'll do me just this one little favor, I swear on Gus's grave I'll give you every tape Gus ever made of you."

Erlene watched Virgil carefully as she laid out the proposal. He was reluctant at first, but the more Erlene talked, and the more she rubbed the inside of Virgil's thigh, the more he seemed to relax. Finally, he agreed to do what Erlene needed done.

He was such a sweetie.

JUNE 15
6:00 A.M.

O n the morning my daughter's last dance recital was scheduled, I was sitting at the breakfast table reading the paper when Caroline wandered into the kitchen rubbing her eyes.

"I need to tell you about something," she said. I put the paper down.

"Sounds bad."

"I'm not sure. I saw a silver truck yesterday afternoon, like the one you said almost ran over you. It drove by the house twice. Then when I went to the grocery store later, I came outside and it was parked right beside me, but I couldn't see the driver through the tint."

"Why didn't you tell me yesterday?"

"I was getting ready for the recital, remember? I was busy all day, and then last night when I came in, you were already asleep. I thought about waking you up, but I didn't think it would hurt to wait until this morning. I'm sorry."

"Tester's son—the one I was telling you about who made that scene at Angel's arraignment—owns a silver Dodge truck. It has to be him."

"But why, Joe? Why would he want to bother us? You're just a lawyer doing your job."

"You didn't hear him in court that day. Something very strange is going on in that man's head."

"What should we do?"

"There isn't much we can do. If you see him again, call the cops and tell them what's going on. Maybe they'll check him out. And make sure you tell Lilly to be watching for him. Show her a picture of a Dodge truck or something so she'll know what to look for."

After I finished the paper, I drove to the gym in Johnson City and worked out for an hour. Then I drove over to Unicoi County to represent Randall Finch, one of my two remaining appointed death-penalty cases. Randall was a twenty-five-year-old uneducated redneck who'd killed his girlfriend's thirteen-month-old son in a drug-induced haze. Randall and his girlfriend had been binging on crystal meth and hydrocodone for two days and had finally run out of drugs, so the girlfriend went out to find some more, leaving the child with Randall. While she was gone, the little boy apparently started to cry. Randall first dealt with him by using him for an ashtray, putting cigarettes out on the bottoms of his feet. Then, for some reason only Randall could understand, he laid the child on the metal protective rack of a hot kerosene heater, producing a sun-shaped burn that covered his back. Finally, when the baby still wouldn't stop crying, Randall shook him so violently his brain hemorrhaged.

Randall's girlfriend returned to find the carnage and called the police. They arrested her too.

Randall didn't deny killing the baby, he just said he didn't *remember* killing the baby. The only defense I could attempt was reduced mental capacity based on intoxication so severe that Randall didn't realize what he was doing, but I knew it wouldn't work. Once the jury saw the photographs of the cigarette burns and the burn on the tiny boy's back, Randall would be lucky to get out of the courtroom without being lynched. When I looked at the photos the first time, I wanted to lynch Randall myself. All I'd have needed was a rope and some privacy.

The preliminary hearing had been held two months earlier in a lower court in Erwin, and the evidence was gruesome. Since then, Deacon Baker had spent a great deal of time and energy proclaiming to the local media the fate he had in mind for Randall Finch. It was to be the death penalty, swift and certain.

Deacon, however, hadn't bothered to file his death notice, an absolute requirement in any death-penalty case, so I decided to try something sneaky. I told Randall that since the case against him was so strong and since Deacon hadn't filed the notice, Randall should plead guilty at arraignment, his first appearance in the higher criminal court. Nobody had ever tried to pull a stunt like that to my knowledge, and I had no idea what the judge would say. But I knew it would, at the very least, set up an extremely interesting appellate issue. Randall agreed.

The judge was Ivan Glass. I wasn't expecting any warm greetings. Glass had recently developed some kind of infection in his leg and was spending a lot of his time on the bench high on the same kind of painkillers Randall had been taking when he murdered the baby. If Glass was high during the Finch arraignment, I knew I'd probably be in for trouble.

The judge called our case around 10:00 a.m. The bailiffs brought Randall to the podium, and Glass glared down at him from the bench.

"So this is the man accused of killing the baby?" He wasn't slurring his words, and his eyes appeared to be clear.

"Yes, Your Honor," Deacon Baker said. He'd made yet another appearance for the cameras.

"Let the record show that I've appointed Mr. Dillard to represent him and that Mr. Dillard is present with his client today." I'd told Glass after he appointed me that I was planning on retiring and would appreciate it if he wouldn't appoint me to any more cases. He'd snorted and said he looked forward to not having me around. The feeling was mutual.

"I'm handing Mr. Dillard a copy of the indictment," Glass said. "Do you waive the formal reading?"

"We do, Judge," I said.

"How does your client plead?"

"He pleads guilty."

"Very well, as far as scheduling ... wait a minute. What did you say, Mr. Dillard?"

"I said Mr. Finch wants to enter a plea of guilty this morning. He doesn't want to contest the charges."

"I've never heard of such a thing," Judge Glass said. "A guilty plea at arraignment in a death-penalty case?"

"This isn't a death-penalty case, Judge," I said. "No notice has been filed."

I saw the light bulb come on as Judge Glass realized what I was trying to do. To my relief, he seemed amused rather than angry. He turned to the prosecution.

"What do you think about *that,* Mr. Baker?"

Baker stood, red-faced.

"This is unprecedented, Your Honor. He can't do it."

"There's nothing in the rules to prohibit it," I said. "The rules say a criminal defendant can enter a plea of guilty or not guilty at arraignment. We want to enter a plea of guilty. Mr. Baker hasn't filed his death notice. He's had plenty of time, and he's certainly let everyone in the media know his intentions."

"I was going to file it today," Deacon said, his voice even whinier than usual.

Glass snickered and looked at Randall. "Mr. Finch, do you understand what your attorney is attempting to do here today?"

"Yes."

"Have you and your attorney discussed this thoroughly?"

"Yes."

"Do you understand that if I decide to accept this plea, you'll be giving up your constitutional right to a trial by jury?"

"Yes."

Judge Glass sat back in his chair and ran his fingers through his snow-white hair. I could see the rusty wheels in his brain grinding. After a couple minutes, he leaned forward.

"Mr. Dillard, if I refuse to accept this plea, I assume you're going to file an appeal immediately?"

"That's right, Judge."

"And if I accept the plea, I assume you'll do the same, Mr. Baker?"

"Absolutely."

"Well, if I'm going to make a mistake, I prefer to err on the side of caution. I'm going to refuse to accept Mr. Finch's guilty plea. Go ahead and file your appeal, Mr. Dillard. We'll deal with scheduling after we find out what the wise men at the Supreme Court have to say about this."

"Thank you, Judge," I said. There wasn't any point in arguing with him. I didn't really expect Judge Glass to let a baby killer escape the possibility of a death sentence, but it was worth doing just to see the look on Deacon Baker's face. I told Randall I'd file the appeal immediately and watched the bailiffs lead him back toward his isolation cell. The other inmates in the jail had let the sheriff know that if Randall got into the general population, he wouldn't last an hour.

Since Lilly would be graduating soon and moving out, I knew her recital that night might be my last opportunity to watch her dance. Caroline told me she'd choreographed a solo for Lilly that was set to a song about sexual abuse. How ironic, I thought, given my situation with Sarah and some of the things Erlene had told me about Angel.

The dance was a lyrical, the song "I'm OK" by Christina Aguilera. Lilly had been dancing since she could walk. She was strong in acrobatics, tap, ballet, and jazz, but the lyrical dance was my favorite. I loved the smooth movements, the athletic jumps, the graceful turns.

My daughter was costumed in a long-sleeved, high-necked, solid white dress. There were puffs at each shoulder, and the chiffon skirt gave the illusion of a full circle when she turned. Rhinestones glued onto the costume sparkled under the blue and gold spotlights. Her long auburn hair had been pulled back from her face, and she floated back and forth across the stage as if she were riding on her very own cloud. I was amazed at the changes in both her body and her ability in the six months since I'd last experienced the pleasure of watching her dance. She was no longer a girl; she'd turned into a young woman, a beautiful and talented young woman.

I felt my heart soar as I watched Lilly turn her body into a powerful form of expression. Her long arms and slender hands caught the subtle accents of the music perfectly, and the flexibility and strength in her legs reflected the hard work and dedication required of a dancer. As the music built, a smile took over my face. She was so lovely, so pure. My day-to-day world was filled with cruelty and evil and ugliness. I experienced this kind of thing so rarely that at one point I realized I was lightheaded, apparently too moved to breathe. As I listened to the lyrics, I understood what Caroline had meant. The song was about a young woman who carried the guilt and shame of sexual abuse at the hands of her father.

When the dance was over, I quickly made my way around to the back of the stage and asked another dancer to retrieve Lilly from the dressing room. When she emerged, I kissed her on the cheek.

"Thanks, honey," I said, "that was incredibly beautiful."

"Are you all right, Daddy?"

"I'm great," I said. "I'm absolutely fine."

"Are you sure?"

She stood on her tiptoes, kissed me on the cheek, and pulled me toward her so that she could whisper in my ear.

"This is the first time I've ever seen you cry."

JUNE 16
6:00 P.M.

would've preferred concentrating on Angel's case, but I had to deal with Maynard Bush. Besides Angel and possibly Randall Finch, he was my last death-penalty client.

I'd been appointed to represent Maynard by the criminal court judge in Sullivan County, and the trial was quickly approaching. The judge had also appointed a young lawyer from Carter County named Timothy Walker II to help me, but Walker had quickly learned he didn't have the stomach for dealing with Maynard up close and personal. I couldn't blame him, but that left the jail visits to me.

Maynard was one of the most intimidating, dangerous men I'd ever had the displeasure of defending. He had a long, violent criminal history and had spent most of his adult life in prison. He was pure predator, always looking for a weakness, always trying to gain an advantage. Dealing with him was a constant game of cat and mouse. The problem was that both Maynard and

I wanted to be the cat. As a result, we weren't getting along.

During a change-of-venue hearing three weeks earlier, Maynard had suddenly told the judge I wasn't doing my job. He said he wanted a new lawyer. The judge knew better—Maynard was just trying to delay his trial—so he told Maynard he was stuck with me. The judge also granted our motion to change venue. The trial was to be held in Mountain City in June. I had only four weeks to finish preparing, and Maynard wasn't cooperating. I'd arranged for a forensic psychiatrist to evaluate him. Maynard wouldn't speak to the doctor. I'd hired an investigator to interview witnesses and check facts. When I sent him to the jail, Maynard told the investigator to go screw himself. He did the same thing with the mitigation expert.

I'd stayed away from Maynard for three weeks, in part because I was busy, in part to make him think the stunt he pulled in court had genuinely offended me, but primarily because being around him made my skin crawl. Three guards brought him into the interview room at the Sullivan County jail a little after eight in the evening. It had been a long day, but I didn't want to put off talking with Maynard any longer.

Maynard was about six feet tall, and years of methamphetamine and cocaine abuse had left him as thin as an anorexic. He had shoulder-length black hair he parted in the middle and a dark, smooth complexion. His eyes were almost as dark as his hair. I'd never asked him, but I assumed some Native American heritage, most likely Cherokee or Chickasaw. Both of his arms and his upper torso were covered with tattoos. Their intricate design announced to those who knew about such things that he was a member of the Aryan brotherhood. Most of the white inmates belonged to the brotherhood. It helped them stay alive. The tattoos on Maynard's chest and back were religious symbols. There was a large dove on his chest and an even larger cross on his back. I'd seen them when a guard brought him in shirtless one day.

Maynard was wearing a standard-issue jumpsuit that was much too large for him. He sat down and folded his long, thin fingers across his stomach. It looked as though he could easily slide his wrists through the handcuffs, which were attached to a chain around his waist. The guards had secured the shackles around his ankles to the legs of his chair, which was bolted into the concrete floor. He didn't look at me.

"Hello, Maynard," I said. "How have you been since you tried to ambush me in court?"

Silence.

"There are a couple things we need to discuss today if you're feeling up to it. Are you feeling up to it?"

Nothing.

"I'll take that as a yes. First of all, I need to know why you won't submit to a psychological evaluation. I'm not insinuating that you have mental problems, Maynard. I just need to have you evaluated to see whether the doctor can find something that might help us."

Maynard sat there like a stone. I wasn't even sure he was breathing.

"I'd also like to know why you won't talk to the investigator or the mitigation expert. They're trying to help you. Don't you get that?"

Silence.

"I've been through all the evidence, including your background, Maynard. How about you and I get real with each other? You've spent most of your life in prison. Killed your first wife and got the charge reduced, murdered some dude who was screwing around with your girlfriend and got convicted, served fifteen years. Killed at least two men in prison and got away with both of those murders. As soon as you got out, you started hauling cocaine and meth. While you were at it, you sold and smoked and snorted practically anything you could get your hands on. Now you've killed and cut up a couple teenagers. They can prove you tied the girl up and had sex with her before you shot her. They've got semen from her vagina—the DNA matches yours. They've got both victims' blood all over that little house you rented. Got your signature on the lease at the storage place where you stashed the bodies. That was bright. Didn't you think they'd start to smell after a few days? They've got the kids' blood and your fingerprints on the chainsaw you used to cut them up. And they've got a lot more."

"I don't care."

"Really? Why not?"

"'Cause I know I done wrong and I deserve to die."

I nearly fell out of the chair. I'd defended people who had decided to accept their fate and their punishment, but in a death-penalty case, it wasn't so easy to do. There was no way the prosecution was going to offer Maynard anything. He had raped, shot, and dismembered a young girl and shot and dismembered her boyfriend, and he was a career criminal. The only thing they'd accept would be Maynard's pleading guilty to two murders and agreeing to the death penalty, and there was simply no way I was going to let him do that. If the state was going to kill him, it was my duty to make sure they could prove their case. I couldn't just walk him into court and say, "Okay, we quit. Go ahead and kill my client." We were going to trial whether Maynard wanted to or not.

"I can appreciate that," I said, "but you have to understand that we're going to trial anyway. Jesus, Maynard, we just got a change of venue. At least you'll get a fair trial in Mountain City."

"I don't want you to put on no witnesses for me," Maynard said. "You put me up there, I'm gonna tell them I did it."

"So what the hell am I supposed to do?" I said. "Sit there like a deaf mute?"

"You just do the best you can. God will take care of the rest."

"Don't do that to me, Maynard. Don't tell me you've found God in here. I know he's here because everybody in here finds him, but if I'm going to try to defend you, you have to help me a little. Don't leave it in God's hands. God helps those who help themselves."

"There's only one thing I want you to do," Maynard said, "and it ain't got nothing to do with the trial."

"What's that?"

"I'd like a little privacy is all."

"What are you talking about?"

"I been writing to this woman on the outside. Her name's Bonnie Tate. Me and her have got real close, you know? She's the one that's made me realize I don't have to lie no more. God will forgive me and accept me into heaven. I think maybe I'm in love, Dillard. Can you believe it? Ol' badass Maynard, falling flat out in love with a woman I ain't never even met. I even tried to write her a little poetry. But that's the problem. It's these freaking guards. They look at my mail. They brought the poetry in and gave it to some of the other dudes in here. Them boys been giving me grief ever since."

It wasn't the first time I'd heard about guards trying to embarrass and humiliate inmates with the contents of their outgoing mail. He was probably telling the truth.

"What do you want me to do?" I said.

"You don't have to do much. They can't read letters if I put 'legal mail' on the envelope, can they?"

"They're not supposed to. Communication between client and lawyer is privileged, even if the client is an inmate."

"All I want to do is put Bonnie's letters in an envelope and address them to your office. So I'll write 'legal mail' on the envelope, and underneath that I'll write her initials. When you see it come into the office, all you have to do is either call her up and tell her to come get her letter or forward it on to her. I'll give you her phone number and address."

I thought about it for a minute. All he was asking was to be able to write love letters without being humiliated. But then I thought again about who I was dealing with.

"Sorry, Maynard, can't do it."

"Why not?"

"It's probably illegal, and I like life on the outside just fine. If the wrong people found out what I was doing, they'd lock me up."

"Well, can you at least fix it so she can visit me?"

I'd set up jail visits for plenty of clients. It seemed like a reasonable request.

"Now, that I *can* do. Put her on your visitor's list."

"You know something, Dillard?" he said. "I didn't like you much when I first met you. Thought you was like all them other mush-mouthed, pussy lawyers. But at least you try to do the right thing. You been coming up here to see me pretty regular, and you been straight with me. I ain't saying I want to marry you or nothing, but you're a pretty decent dude."

I didn't know what to say. A vicious, cruel, remorseless, murdering sociopath was doing his best to convince me he liked me, and I wondered why.

"Can I ask you a question?" he finally said.

"Sure."

"How come you do this kind of stuff, Dillard? Ain't no way you could like it much. How come you defend men like me?"

The question took me by surprise, and I leaned back in the chair for a second. I didn't want to get into talking about my motivations, and I didn't want to tell him I was getting out.

"Why do you care?" I said.

"C'mon, Dillard, humor old Maynard. How come you take these death-penalty cases?"

"Most of them are appointed. But if you have to know, Maynard, I guess I have this sort of simple philosophy about it. I just don't think it's right for a government to pass laws telling its citizens they can't kill each other and then turn around and kill its citizens. It just seems hypocritical to me."

Maynard grinned. "You're a do-gooder, Dillard. That's what you are."

"Maybe. Something like that."

"You'll take care of the visits, then?" he asked when I didn't say anything else.

"Yeah, Maynard. I'll set it up."

I thought it was the least I could do for a man who was soon to be condemned to die.

JUNE 16
9:15 P.M.

It was after nine o'clock when I finally finished with Maynard. Darkness was falling, but it was clear and warm, and I could see the stars shining above the lights in the jail parking lot. I was tired and wanted to get home quickly, so I took a shortcut along a back road that bordered Boone Lake. As I drove along with the windows rolled down, I started thinking about how Angel was getting along at the jail. She was locked up with murderers, child abusers, drug addicts, thieves, hookers, and cons. So was Sarah, but Sarah was tough as nails. It would have to be incredibly difficult for a young girl. I imagined what it would be like to be caged most of the day and herded like sheep the rest of the time, to be taunted and bullied by guards and inmates, to be subjected to all kinds of physical indignities, to have absolutely no privacy. And if she really was innocent? The thought made me cringe.

I was about halfway home when I noticed headlights in my rearview mirror. They were approaching fast. I thought about pulling over and letting whoever was in such a hurry pass, but I was on a narrow, curvy stretch of road with steep slopes on both sides. To my right were rocky cliffs, and to my left, thirty feet below, was the lake.

The vehicle behind me turned its headlights on bright when it got to within fifty feet or so. I had to turn the rearview mirror down to keep from being blinded. I slowed and looked in the side-view mirror. The vehicle was right on my tail.

I started tapping the brakes to try to get whoever it was to back off. They didn't. I sped up around a sharp curve but almost lost control in a patch of gravel. When I got the truck straightened back out, the vehicle bumped me.

"Why, you sorry sonofabitch. ..." I slammed on the brakes, and the truck skidded to a halt in the middle of a short straightaway. I kept an old aluminum baseball bat under the seat, and I fully intended to use it on the person behind me. I reached down and felt for the bat, hoping whoever it was didn't have a gun.

With a sudden loud crash, my truck jerked forward. I twisted around and looked out the rear windshield over the bed. I could tell that the vehicle silhouetted behind me was a pickup, bigger than mine, but between the surrounding darkness and the glare of the headlights, I couldn't make out the color. It was pushing me along the road.

I turned back and grabbed the wheel, trying to hold the truck straight and pushing on the brakes with all my strength. The tires screamed, but the truck began slowly to turn toward the lake. I tried to turn hard to the right, but the truck behind me had gotten its bumper into my left-rear fender and was turning me. I was moving faster by the second, and I had absolutely no control.

A moment later, I felt the right front tire drop off the embankment. I'd been turned almost a hundred and eighty degrees. I looked and at last caught a flash of the truck that was pushing me. It was a silver Dodge. Then the right rear dropped, and my truck was rolling. My head slammed into the steering wheel, and I saw a flash of bright light. I felt a brief sense of dizziness as images flashed. I thought I heard a splash, then an explosion, then I thought I was being smothered.

And then it was silent and still. I felt fingers gently rubbing across my forehead.

"Joe," a voice said. "Joe, honey, it's time to wake up. C'mon, baby, you have to wake up." It was Caroline's voice.

I awoke to the sound of a rushing waterfall. It was dark, and my wife was nowhere to be found. I looked around. I was leaning hard to my right and being restrained by something. I reached down and realized it was a seat belt. Something was pushing against my face. An air bag. My eyes adjusted to the darkness, and I remembered that the Dodge had pushed me over the embankment. I was in the lake, and the sound I heard wasn't a waterfall, it was the lake rushing in through the open passenger window. As I struggled with the seat belt, the truck began to level off, and more water started pouring in through the driver's side.

"I am *not* going to drown!" I said out loud. "I am *not* going to drown in this freaking lake!"

I got the belt off, scooted out from beneath the air bag, and crouched in the middle of the seat. Water was pouring in so fast on either side of me that there was no way I could get out. I knew I'd have to wait until the truck was submerged. I looked around frantically. The headlights were still on. I could see bubbles rising as the truck sank in the water. I pulled my shoes off. The water continued to pour and roar.

And then it was black. The water began to cover me. It was so cold I could barely breathe. My face was nearly against the roof as the cab finally filled. I took a deep breath and pushed myself through the passenger side window. The truck had started to roll in the water, and for a second, I had no idea which direction to swim.

I thought about the bubbles in the headlights. Bubbles rise, Joe. Follow the bubbles. I let out some air and felt the bubbles rise across my face. I kicked for my life, and a few seconds later, I broke the surface. It was eerily quiet, but the moon gave off enough light that I could make out the features of the landscape around me. I was only about twenty feet from the steep, rocky bank where I'd gone over. I looked up to see whether whoever tried to kill me—and I knew it had to be Tester Junior—was still there. I couldn't see or hear anyone.

Boone is a mountain lake, and the water was bone-chilling. My teeth started chattering, and my hands and feet were already beginning to tingle. I knew I had to get out fast. I swam for the bank, got hold of some over-hanging brush, and pulled myself up onto the rocks. I sat there for a couple minutes, caught my breath, and tried to compose myself.

I took inventory of my body first. I didn't seem to be hurt too badly. My ribs and chest were sore, but I didn't think I had any broken bones. All my joints seemed to be in working order, and I didn't have any trouble making a fist with either hand. I noticed something warm running down my face and touched it. I was bleeding from a cut above my left eye. It was tender and beginning to swell, but I didn't think it was too serious. I looked up the bank and realized how far the truck had fallen. I was lucky to be alive.

It took me at least ten minutes to crawl up the rocky slope to the road. I crouched in some brush for several minutes. A couple cars went by, but I was afraid to stand up and wave for fear that Junior might come back. I finally mustered the courage to get up and start walking down the asphalt road. I knew there were houses about a mile away. After about a quarter mile, I found myself wishing I hadn't shed my shoes.

As I walked down the road with my socks squishing and the warm blood running down the side of my face, I wondered if Junior thought he'd succeeded in killing me. What about Caroline and Lilly? Would he be crazy enough to go after one of them? I felt my heart quicken, and I began to jog.

A short time later, I made my way to a farmhouse set about a hundred yards off the road. Nearly every light in the house was on. As I climbed the steps, I looked down and noticed the front of my shirt was soaked with blood. I wondered what kind of reception I'd get when whoever answered the door saw a blood-soaked stranger wearing a tie and no shoes standing on the porch.

I knocked. A small dog immediately started yapping, and a woman who looked to be around seventy soon appeared at the door. She pulled the curtain aside and peered up at me through oval-shaped glasses. Her gray hair was pulled into a tight bun. A look of horror immediately came over her face—I must have looked even worse than I felt.

"What do ye want?" she yelled through the door.

"I've been in an accident," I said. "I need to use your phone."

"Air ye drunk?"

"No ma'am."

She looked me up and down. "Soaking wet and ye ain't got no shoes. Where's yer shoes?"

"In the lake," I said. "My car went into the lake. I had to swim out."

"Ye drove yer car into the lake? What'd ye do a dang fool thing like that fer?"

"I didn't mean to, ma'am. It was an accident. Please, if you could just hand the phone out the door, I'd really appreciate it."

"Yer bleeding like a stuck hog."

"I know. I hit my head."

"Got a name?"

"Dillard. My name is Joe Dillard."

"Dillard? Any kin to Hobie and Rena Dillard out Sulphur Springs?"

"I don't think so. Please, ma'am, do you have a phone I can use?"

"Well, I reckon," she said after a thoughtful moment. "You don't look like a hoodlum."

She opened the door and I stumbled in. It must have been the tie.

JUNE 16
11:00 P.M.

'd called Caroline from the mountain woman's house, and she and Lilly had come to pick me up. Lilly started crying when she saw me. After I got into the car and things settled down a little, I told Caroline what happened and who I thought had pushed me into the lake.

"What are you going to do?" she said.

"I'm not sure. Guess I'll start by calling the police."

I used Caroline's cell phone to call 9-1-1 from the car. Mine was at the bottom of Boone Lake in the console of my truck. I told the dispatcher what had happened and that I was headed to the emergency room. She said they'd send someone up.

Since the attack had occurred in the county, jurisdiction for my attempted murder fell to the Washington County Sheriff's Department. An investigator showed up and stood beside the gurney while a doctor stitched up my eye.

The damage amounted to a bruised sternum, a few bruised ribs, and a two-inch gash above the orbital bone that surrounded my left eye. The doctor covered the eye while he stitched, so I could see the investigator who'd been dispatched to talk to me only out of my right eye. His name was Sam Wiseman. Sam was almost seven feet tall and had to weigh in the neighborhood of four hundred pounds. He was a surly man, and he had no compunction about letting me know that he didn't like me. His feelings stemmed from a case I'd defended a couple years earlier. A group of teenagers had vandalized a Baptist church in the county. They broke every pane of glass in the place and threw paint and mustard and anything else they could find all over the sanctuary. By the time they were finished, they'd done more than fifty thousand dollars' worth of damage. Sam caught the case, and unfortunately for my client, a fifteen-year-old girl named Delores McKinney, the church they vandalized happened to be the church that Sam attended every Sunday with his mother.

Sam insisted that every one of the juveniles go off to detention for at least a year, a demand I considered unreasonable since my client was a good student, had no record whatsoever, admitted what she'd done after she sobered up, and her parents were more than willing to reimburse the church for her share of the damages. She pleaded guilty to vandalism, and I hired a psychologist for the sentencing hearing. When the juvenile court judge heard how much the kids had to drink, heard that they stole the booze and the pills they took from their own parents, and heard the shrink testify about peer pressure and gang mentality, she put them all on probation. Sam blamed it on me.

As I lay on the gurney, I ran back through the night's events for Sam and told him about Tester's son and what had happened in the courtroom at Angel's arraignment. The problem was that I hadn't actually *seen* the person driving the truck either time. I didn't even have a tag number.

"I can't get a warrant based on what you've told me," Sam said.

"I know."

"I can find out where he lives and see if the sheriff will let me go down and talk to him tomorrow."

"I doubt he'll admit to anything."

"There might be some damage on his truck, but you have to understand it'll be hard to prove anything. If you're going to accuse a sheriff's deputy of doing something this crazy, you're going to need more than suspicion."

"I understand."

Sam finished taking his notes and gruffly told me he'd make sure my insurance company got a copy of his report. The doctor finished stitching me up, and Caroline, Lilly, and I walked out the door. We started home in silence.

"What are you going to do?" Caroline asked again about ten minutes later.

"I'm not sure, but you and Lilly have to be extra careful now, do you understand? Maybe you should go away for a couple weeks."

"I'm not about to let some lunatic run me out of my home," Caroline said.

"He's a dangerous lunatic, Caroline. Aren't you just a little afraid?"

"A little, but if he comes anywhere near the house Rio will tear his leg off, and if he gets past Rio, I have a big strong Ranger to take care of me."

"He almost got the best of your big strong Ranger tonight."

"But he didn't, did he? My Ranger lives to fight another day."

It was past midnight when we got home, and I was sore and tired. Lilly was still upset, so I told her to sleep in our bed. After we were sure she was asleep, I double-checked to make sure all the doors and windows were locked. Caroline had taken a seat on the couch in the den, and I went in and lay down with my head in her lap.

"You saved my life tonight," I said as she stroked my forehead.

"Really? How?"

"When I went over the bank, I hit my head on the steering wheel. It knocked me out, but this voice kept telling me to wake up. It was your voice. You woke me up before I drowned."

She leaned over and kissed me softly.

"I'll always be there when you need me, babe," she said. "Always."

I closed my eyes with the taste of her mouth lingering, and somehow managed to drift off to sleep.

JUNE 17
MIDNIGHT

I was so sore the next morning I could barely get off the couch, so I spent the day at home, looking out the window, worrying and wondering. I got hold of Jack a little before noon, but I didn't tell him anything about Junior Tester. He'd been invited to play baseball for Martinsville in the Coastal Plains League over the summer and was having the time of his life. He said he was still hitting the ball great and had talked to several big-league scouts. I promised him I'd make it up there to see him play sometime soon.

Sam Wiseman called at two thirty in the afternoon and told me he'd called the Cocke County Sheriff's Department and learned that Tester had taken a week's vacation.

"I called his house, but nobody answered," Sam said.

"Are you planning to go down there?"

"I ran it by my supervisor. He said since you didn't see the driver and don't have a tag number, it'd be a waste of time."

"What if the front end of his truck is banged up like you said at the hospital? What if it has paint on it the same color as my truck?"

"You know how it is around here. We've only got five investigators to cover three shifts. There's been a string of burglaries we're working, and the boss wants me to keep concentrating on that. He said he can't let me go chasing around Cocke County on a case I don't have much chance of making."

"This is bull, Sam. What about my family?"

"What about them?"

"Can't you spare anyone to look out for them? At least for a few days?"

"We barely have enough road deputies to cover patrols. Besides, you haven't exactly. ..." His voice trailed off without finishing the sentence, but the tone alarmed me.

"I haven't exactly what, Sam?"

"You haven't exactly made a bunch of friends around here over the years, you know. Not many people here are willing to go out of their way to help you."

"So you're telling me that the sheriff's department won't help me because I'm a defense lawyer?"

"I'm telling you we only have five investigators to cover three shifts, we don't have enough patrol deputies to provide security for one family, we have a lot of other cases, and you're accusing a law enforcement officer of a serious crime with no real evidence to back it up. I'm afraid there isn't much I can do."

"So what the hell am I supposed to do? Wait for him to come back?"

"Maybe you ought to buy a gun."

"I already have guns. I was hoping you guys would do something so I wouldn't have to use them."

"Sorry. Like I said, we're not going to be able to do anything right now."

"Thanks, Sam. Thanks for nothing."

I hung up the phone, walked into the den, and sat down at the computer, as angry as I'd ever been in my life. It didn't take me long to find Junior's address and phone number on the Internet. MapQuest gave me directions to his house. I printed the directions and memorized the phone number, something that had always come easy for me. Once the numbers were in my brain, they stayed there for years. I spent the rest of the day trying to think of the various situations I might run into if I actually did what I was thinking of doing.

At 11:30 p.m., after the evening routines were all finished and Lilly had gone to bed—in our room again—I asked Caroline to sit down at the kitchen table. I told her about my conversation with Sam Wiseman and that the police weren't going to help. Finally, I took a deep breath.

"I'm going down there," I said.

"Where?" Caroline said.

"To Newport. To find Junior."

"When?"

"Tonight. Now."

"No you're not."

"Yes. I am."

"No you're not. No way."

"I'm going, Caroline. You can't stop me."

"And just what do you propose to do when you find him?" Her voice took on some intensity, and she stood up. Neither was a good sign.

"I'm not sure, but I can't just sit around here. The police aren't going to do anything, so I have to take care of this myself. Sit back down and talk to me. Try to be rational."

"Rational? Did I just hear you say rational? You're talking about going out in the middle of the night to an insane man's house to do God knows what, and you're telling *me* to be rational? You're as crazy as he is!"

I stood up and started toward the bedroom with Caroline right on my heels.

"He's a police officer, Joe," she said. "He's going to have a gun, you know." The words were staccato, and her voice was a tone I'd only heard a couple times during all the years we'd been together.

"Keep your voice down. Lilly's sleeping."

"Don't tell me to keep my voice down. Wake up, Lilly! Your dad's about to do something insane! You better kiss him goodbye because *you might never see him again*!"

Lilly stirred and groaned, but she could sleep through a hurricane.

"Leave her out of this," I said. I walked into my closet and grabbed up a pair of black jeans, a navy blue hooded sweatshirt, a pair of old combat boots, and a black stocking cap. Then I hurried back out to the kitchen and started to change clothes. Caroline was hovering like an attack helicopter.

"I have to *do something* to this guy," I said as I pulled off my shirt. "If I don't, we're all going to spend our lives looking over our shoulders. I mean, for God's sake, Caroline, think about what he did. He staked us out. He stalked you. He followed me and ran my truck into the lake. He tried to *kill* me. What do you want me to do? Sit back and give him another chance, because I guarantee you he'll try again as soon as he finds out I'm still breathing. Or maybe he'll try to kill you next time. Or Lilly. Hell, maybe he'll wait until he gets a shot at all of us at the same time. Three for the price of one."

"I don't care, Joe. I—"

"Yes, you do. You care. You care about me and you care about Lilly and you care about living. And as much as you want to think we should be civilized right now, as much as you want to deal with this *rationally*, there comes a time, Caroline. There comes a time when meeting violence with violence is the best way, the only way."

"So you're going to hurt him?"

"I'm not planning to kill him, but I'm not going to give him a hug, either. I have to let him know if he comes after any of us, there'll be consequences. I have to show him that I'm willing to cross the same line he crossed."

"I'm going with you."

"No. You have to stay here with Lilly. We can't leave her here alone. I promise I'll stay in touch. I'll—"

"No, Joe. This is too weird."

I looked her in the eye. "You know I love you, and you know I respect you, but—"

"Don't patronize me."

"I'm not patronizing you, but I'm telling you I'm going. You can yell and scream all you want. You can call the cops for all I care. I've made up my mind, Caroline. I'm going."

She took a long, slow breath. "Have you thought this through?"

"Of course I've thought it through." I sat down in one of the chairs at the table and started lacing my boots. "I've thought about it all day, and to be honest, I have no clue what's going to happen when I get down there. Maybe nothing will happen."

"I'm too young to be a widow."

"And I'm too young to make you one."

I got up and grabbed a lighter out of a drawer in the kitchen and a bottle of water from the refrigerator. I opened the bottle, poured the water into the sink, screwed the cap back on, and headed for the garage. Leaning against the wall was an old hickory walking stick I'd bought during a trip to Grandfather Mountain, North Carolina, a few years ago. It was four feet long and hard as steel. I picked it up and looked at it. Caroline was standing in the doorway, eyeing me.

"I need your cell phone," I said.

"Why?"

"Because mine's at the bottom of Boone Lake. Just get it. Please?"

She disappeared for a second, came back to the doorway and tossed me her phone.

"You're taking a walking stick to a gunfight?" she said.

"If things go right, he won't get a chance to shoot at me."

"Sometimes things don't go the way you plan them. And speaking of plans, do you have one?"

"Sort of."

"What is it?"

"You don't want to know."

"Yes I do."

"Trust me, you don't."

I walked over to the five-gallon container that held gasoline for the lawn mowers and filled the water bottle with gas.

"Are you going to throw a Molotov cocktail at him?" Caroline said.

"Not exactly."

"Then what's the bottle of gas for?"

"Diversion, if I need it. Or maybe bait."

The last thing I picked up was a small flashlight off the shelf in the garage. Rio was following me every step of the way, whimpering. He knew I was going somewhere and didn't want to miss out on the fun. I tossed the stick, the plastic bottle of gas, and the flashlight into the passenger side of Caroline's Honda and shut the door.

"Keep Rio close while I'm gone," I said. Caroline was still standing in the doorway with her arms folded. "The shotgun's locked and loaded behind the door in the bedroom. You know how to use it."

She started chewing on her fist. I could see tears welling in her eyes. "I want to go," she said. "I can't stand the thought of sitting here waiting. By the time you get back, *I'll* be insane."

"I'll be fine," I said. "Try not to worry."

"Yeah, sure."

"I have to do this."

"No, you don't."

"I can handle myself, Caroline." I walked up to the door and took her in my arms. "I'll call you on the house phone when it's done. Don't call me, please. I don't want to worry about the cell phone ringing."

"You be back here by four," she said, "and you better be in one piece."

"You sound like my mother." I kissed her and got in the car.

Junior's place was almost seventy miles away. As I drove down Interstate 81 toward Newport, I ran through the possibilities. The more I thought about it, the more I realized that Caroline was right. I was doing something crazy and dangerous. I had a vague plan in mind, but I wasn't sure how I was going to get close to him, *if* he was home. It was after midnight, so I couldn't just waltz up to the front door and knock. Junior would have to be paranoid after what he'd done to me. If I went to the door after midnight, he'd be sure to answer it with a gun in his hand. And to make matters worse, I didn't know anything about his house, his neighborhood, whether he had a dog. ... I didn't know a thing. When I was a Ranger, I went on several recon missions. During the missions, my job was to make accurate assessments of enemy strengths and positions so that the commanders would know what they were up against. It would have been nice to have had the same luxury before I went to Junior's, but I was going in blind.

The miles passed quickly, but not quietly. A debate was raging inside my head, as though a tiny Caroline was perched on one shoulder and a tiny Joe was perched on the other.

Turn around and go home. You might get yourself killed.

He tried to kill you. He tried to kill you. He was stalking your wife. Your kids might be next. The police won't do a thing.

I kept driving.

I made it to Newport in just over an hour. It's a small town, so it took me only a few minutes to find Junior's place, which was about a half mile outside the city limits. I was relieved to see that it was relatively isolated, the nearest neighbor more than a hundred yards away. I drove by slowly the first time. There was a black mailbox on a post at the end of the driveway with "Tester" stenciled on it in slightly crooked, white letters. The house was a small brick ranch that sat on a rectangular lot bordered by scruffy pines. There were no security lights, and I didn't see any lights on in the house. One of two small outbuildings looked like a garage. After I made the first pass, I drove about a mile down the road, turned around, and made another pass. I thought about Junior driving by my house and stalking Caroline. Now it was my turn.

I found an apartment complex about a half mile from the house, parked the car in a corner of the lot, grabbed the hickory stick, the bottle of gas, and the flashlight, and started walking. The streets were deserted. It was around fifty degrees, and the moon was low in the west. Some cloud cover would have been nice, but the Rangers had trained me to use the shadows. They'd trained me to make myself invisible in all kinds of terrain and conditions. They'd also taught me the value of surprise in an ambush, and they'd taught me plenty about hand-to-hand combat. If I could surprise him and get my hands on him, I knew I could handle Junior Tester.

When I got back to his place, I cut in and moved along the pine trees to the back of the lot. I crept around the entire lot, staying in the shadows of the pines, looking for a light in the house or signs of movement. Nothing. From what Diane Frye had told me, I knew Junior didn't have a wife or kids, but I wasn't sure about a dog. I was relieved when nothing moved or barked. Once I was sure nobody was stirring, I walked out of the trees and up to the garage. It was big enough for only one vehicle, and it was empty. The other outbuilding was just a storage shed that contained a few tools and a pile of junk, but there was plenty of fuel for a small fire. I crept to the back of the house and stood there listening for several minutes. It was silent.

I moved slowly around the entire house, trying unsuccessfully to see something inside through the windows. No television, no radio, no bathroom light or night light, nothing. When I'd circled the house and was again near the back door, I moved quietly up the concrete steps and turned the doorknob. It was unlocked. I stood there for a second, debating whether I should step inside and add breaking and entering to what could soon be a long list of crimes I'd committed. I decided against it. If he was there, I needed to get him outside. It was time to put my "plan" into action.

I jogged back out to the shed and stepped inside. I turned on the flashlight, grabbed up some rags and several pieces of wood, turned the flashlight off, and walked back outside. I piled the wood and rags up about ten feet from the shed, where Junior could see it if he looked out the back door. Then I took Caroline's cell phone out of my pocket, turned it on, set the block function, and dialed the number I'd memorized earlier in the day. In less than ten seconds, I heard a phone ringing in the house. Once. Twice. Three times. Four.

A light came on at the back corner of the house. I quickly doused the pile of rags and wood with the gasoline from the bottle, trailed some gasoline to a safe distance, and lit it with the lighter. The pile ignited with a *whoosh*. Eight rings. Nine.

I ran back toward the house and crouched down by the back stoop. *Answer the phone! Answer the phone!* Ten rings.

The cell phone clicked in my ear.

"Hello?"

"Junior," I said. "It looks like your shed's on fire."

"What? Who is this?"

"It looks like your shed's on fire. I'm calling the fire department."

I hung up, stuffed the phone back into my pocket, and waited. I could hear quick, heavy steps coming toward the back door. I stood and flattened my back against the side of the house.

Come outside. Please, come outside.

I heard the doorknob turn, and the door opened. A form appeared on the stoop within three feet of me. It was him.

"What the ...?" I heard him say.

He started down the steps. Just as he got to the bottom, I gripped the walking stick with both hands and came off the wall. I dropped to one knee and swung the stick with everything I had. There was a loud crack as the stick caught him across the shin. He howled and fell to his knees.

I dropped the stick and threw myself at him. I managed to get my forearm beneath his chin and climbed onto his back. I got him into a strong chokehold and squeezed as hard as I could. I felt him kicking as I wrapped my legs around his torso and pulled him backwards on top of me.

He tried to reach back to claw my face, but the more he struggled, the tighter I squeezed. After fifteen seconds or so, his strength began to wane.

"Good thing I can swim," I said quietly into his ear.

At the sound of my voice, he stiffened.

"You see how easy this was?" I said, letting up just a little. "If you ever come near me or anyone in my family again, I swear to God I'll kill you. They'll never find your body."

I tightened my grip on him again, and he passed out in less than thirty seconds. As soon as I felt him go limp, I let go and started patting him down. The front of his pajamas was soaked, and I smelled urine. To my relief and surprise, my little ruse had worked better than I'd hoped. He didn't even have a gun. I moved over to where I'd dropped my stick, picked it up, then crawled back on top of him.

He opened his eyes about a minute later to find me straddling him. I'd pinned his shoulders to the ground with my knees and had the hickory stick pressed firmly against his throat. He stared at me with the same intense hatred I'd seen at the courthouse.

"Consider me your living, breathing restraining order," I said. "Don't ever come near me or my family again. Do you understand?"

He began to breathe heavily and his blue eyes looked as if they were about to pop out of his head. He was like a volcano, about to explode with fury.

"You took my daddy from me!" he yelled.

What? Took your daddy? The strange comment surprised me.

"Bull," I said. "I didn't do a thing to your daddy."

"You told people he went to that terrible place! You told people he was drowning in sin! I heard you in the courtroom."

"I told people the truth. Your father took money from a revival and spent it at a strip club."

"Liar! Blasphemer!" He tried to raise up, but I shoved down hard on the stick, cutting off his breath. He froze again, and a sudden realization came to me. The look on his face, the outlandish comment, the pain in his voice, told me I'd shattered a powerful image, the image of a father held by a son. What was it Diane had said? *"He idolized his daddy."* The words I'd spoken in court had apparently opened a gaping wound in his soul, and the wound was festering.

I kept the pressure on with the stick and leaned closer to him.

"Your daddy wasn't the man you thought he was," I said. "That's not my fault. I didn't take him away from you—he did that all by himself. You remember what I said. If you come anywhere near me again, you'll be joining your daddy. I'll shoot you on sight."

His eyes narrowed and bored into me. "Yea though I walk through the valley of the shadow of death," he said, "I shall fear no evil—"

"Shut your mouth!" The words came out of me with such force that I sprayed him with spit. I grabbed his chin with my left hand, rolled his head to the side, and pressed the stick down hard on his carotid artery. Fifteen seconds later, he was unconscious again. For a moment, I envisioned myself smashing his head to a pulp with the stick. *If you kill him, you won't have to worry about him anymore.* But I couldn't do it. I stood up, turned around, and took off running.

A half hour later, driving along in the dark silence, the anger and bravado I'd felt earlier started to subside. In my mind, I envisioned Junior's head exploding as I beat him with the stick and relived the fleeting feeling of satisfaction the fantasy had given me. I smelled the urine and felt his labored breath on my face. I began to shake, and before long I was trembling so badly I had to pull to the side of the road.

What the hell had I just done? I'd gone to a man's home in the middle of the night, attacked him, threatened him, and even fantasized about killing him.

But he tried to kill you.

That doesn't matter and you know it. You're not a vigilante. How many people have you defended who did something stupid and violent because they thought it was right? You're rationalizing.

I thought about the look in his eyes while I was straddling him. My intention had been to scare him so badly that he'd leave me and my family alone, but that look—that angry, pained, insane look—told me I'd failed. He wasn't afraid of me. He either hated me too much to be afraid, or he was just too crazy to care. As I tried to control the trembling, I looked at myself in the rearview mirror.

"Caroline was right," I said aloud. "You're as crazy as he is."

JUNE 23
9:20 A.M.

gent Landers's head was pounding, his back and shoulders aching. The little college cheerleader he'd laid hold of last night must have been more athletic than he thought. Not that he remembered much about her. He drank almost a fifth of Jim Beam.

Landers was sitting at his desk going through a box of physical evidence from the Angel Christian case. He had to meet with Joe Dillard later. Dillard had a right to inspect the physical evidence. Landers wouldn't go to Dillard's office and Dillard wouldn't come to his, so they were going to meet in a conference room at the courthouse in the afternoon.

Landers was worried about the case. Deacon Baker had indicted the Christian girl without much evidence hoping she'd either confess or roll on Erlene Barlowe. She hadn't done either one, and now Dillard was representing her. Dillard was a prick, but he knew how to try a case. Landers knew there was a good possibility they might lose, and to make things even worse, Judge

Green had scheduled the trial a couple weeks before the August election. If Deacon lost this case, he could very well find himself on the outside looking in the day after the election.

Landers didn't give a damn about Deacon, but he'd been around long enough to know that the crap flows downhill. If the case was lost, Deacon would immediately start looking around for someone to blame. Since Landers was the case agent, Deacon would look in his direction first. Deacon would tell anyone who'd listen that it was Landers's fault, that Landers had been sloppy, or that Landers had talked Deacon into indicting Angel without enough evidence for a conviction. If that happened, Landers knew he could kiss his chances at a promotion goodbye when his boss finally retired.

Landers had just picked up the photograph of Angel with the bruise on her face when the secretary buzzed.

"There's a man on the phone says he has information about the Tester murder," she said.

Landers punched the flashing button.

"Who is this?"

"My name is Virgil Watterson. I have some information you may be able to use."

"What information is that?"

"My understanding is that a body part was found out near Picken's Bridge?"

A crank call. Some pervert wanting to talk about the dead preacher's dick.

"That's right. What about it?"

"I crossed the bridge the night of the murder, around one in the morning. When I got onto the bridge, I noticed there was a car stopped right in the middle. As I got closer, I saw a woman standing outside the car near the railing. She could have thrown something in the water."

What the hell? A witness? Where had this guy been?

"Did you get a look at her?"

"Sure did. Her car was facing me in the other lane, and she was walking back toward it. Caught her full in my headlights. Middle-aged woman, wearing some kind of animal print jacket and the tightest pants I ever saw. Bright red hair."

Erlene Barlowe. It had to be her. Landers started scratching notes on a pad. "Would you recognize her if you saw her again?"

"Probably."

"What about the car? You get a look at it?"

"Yes, sir. The bridge is narrow, so I had to slow way down to get past her. It was a Corvette. A nice one."

"Get a plate number?"

"No. Sorry."

"What about the color?"

"It was dark out there, but I'm pretty sure it was red."

"Was anyone else with her on the bridge?"

"I didn't see a soul."

"Anyone else in the car?"

"Not that I saw."

"Why'd you wait so long to call and tell us about this, Mr. ... did you say your name is Watterson?"

"Yes. Virgil Watterson. I'm afraid it's a little embarrassing."

"Embarrassing?"

"I wouldn't want this to get out."

"Wouldn't want what to get out?"

The man's voice got quieter, as though he was trying to keep someone nearby from hearing what he was saying.

"It's my wife, you see. I'm a married man."

"So?"

"I'd been on a business trip and came back a little early. I was on my way to someone's house."

"Whose house?"

"I'd rather not say."

The light came on in Landers's mind.

"So you came back early from your trip and were going to visit someone besides your wife?"

"That's possible."

"And you didn't go home until the next day?"

"That's right."

"And then you heard about the murder and put two and two together?"

"Exactly."

"I understand," Landers said. "So why have you suddenly changed your mind? Why are you coming forward now?"

"I can't stop thinking about it. I dream about that woman on the bridge every night. I'm afraid you may have arrested the wrong person. My conscience just can't bear it."

Landers sat back and rubbed his forehead with the back of his hand. A steady pressure was beginning to build just beneath his temples.

"Is there anything else you want to tell me, Mr. Watterson?"

"Not that I can think of."

"Would you be willing to give me a written statement if I need one?"

"I guess I could if I have to."

"Would you be willing to testify in court?"

"I'd rather not."

Landers wrote down Watterson's address and phone number and told him he'd be back in touch. If Watterson was telling the truth, Erlene Barlowe could well have tossed Reverend Tester's dick into the lake. Maybe even the murder weapon. Landers wrote himself a note to have the sheriff's department drag the lake under the bridge again. They'd already done it once, after the cat found the reverend's dick, but they hadn't come up with anything.

Since Watterson said the woman on the bridge was alone, Angel Christian was either still at the club or Erlene had taken her home. Either way, it probably took Angel out of the picture so far as the murder was concerned. Deacon Baker—that moron. Landers told him he was pulling the trigger too early. He told him the case was thin. Now it looked like Watterson might be right— they arrested the wrong person.

Landers sat there trying to decide what to do. He could go out and take a written statement from Watterson and add it to the district attorney's file, but if he did that, Dillard would be entitled to a copy of the statement and Deacon would accuse Landers of sabotaging the case. Payback would be hell. Landers figured the better option would be to tell Deacon about Watterson's call and force *him* to decide what to do. Landers had a pretty good idea what Deacon would say. He wasn't one to openly admit a mistake.

Landers called Deacon's office, and for once, he was in. Landers told him about Watterson and the woman on the bridge.

"Doesn't sound like a very reliable witness to me," Deacon said. Landers knew it. He *knew* Deacon would say something like that.

"You know what this means, don't you?" Landers said. "If Erlene Barlowe was standing in the middle of the bridge that night and she was alone, we probably arrested the wrong person."

"I don't recall any of the Barlowe woman's DNA being found on the victim," Deacon said, "and it had to be dark out there. No way this guy could make a positive ID."

"You didn't hear his description. It was her."

"So? What do you want me to do, Phil? You want me to publicly announce that we charged the wrong person with first-degree murder? What do I say? Oops? Gee, we're sorry? Six weeks before an election? You're out of your freaking mind."

"So you're asking me to ignore a material witness in a murder investigation."

"I'm asking you to ignore an unreliable and irrelevant witness who will do nothing but muddy the water and give Dillard more ammunition when we go to trial. As far as I'm concerned, we've got the right person. Her DNA was found on the body, she had contact with the victim earlier that evening, we have a witness who says she left the club at the same time as the victim, and she's refused to talk to us. And what if we did dismiss on the girl and arrest Barlowe? What evidence do we have that *she* committed the murder?"

"She lied to me from the start, and I can't quit thinking about that car. Watterson said he saw a red Corvette on the bridge."

"Then find the thing! But until you do, I'd appreciate it if you'd *stop trying to help the other side!*"

With that, Deacon hung up. Landers wadded up his notes and tossed them into the trash.

JUNE 23
3:30 P.M.

O n Monday, I called Phil Landers's office to set up a time when I could take a look at the physical evidence they intended to present at Angel Christian's trial. It was my right as a defense attorney, and I was always diligent about doing it, but the meeting loomed like a dentist's appointment for a root canal.

The bad blood between us went back more than ten years, to when I first began practicing criminal defense law in Washington County. Landers had been sleeping with a woman who'd just gone through an acrimonious divorce. The woman told Landers her ex-husband was a small-time pot dealer and asked Landers to arrest the guy as a favor to her. She gave Landers the make and model of her ex's car and told him which bar her ex was likely to be hanging out in. She said if Landers would just wait in the parking lot outside the bar for her ex-husband to leave, he'd be sure to get a DUI arrest and probably find more than a little marijuana.

So Landers did what she asked. He waited in the parking lot until the ex left and then, when the guy didn't give him a legitimate reason to stop his vehicle, Landers made one up. He arrested the man for DUI, searched the car, and found an ounce of marijuana.

The ex-husband, a man named Shane Boyd, hired me to represent him. He had no idea he'd been set up until his ex-wife grounded their teenage daughter for staying out too late on a Saturday night two weeks after he was arrested. The girl was pissed off, so she called Shane and told him that both she and her boyfriend had heard her mother and Landers talk about the setup. The teenagers came into my office and signed sworn affidavits. I filed a motion to suppress all the evidence based on Landers having had no legitimate reason to stop the vehicle.

When it came time for the hearing, Landers got on the witness stand and lied. He denied he even knew Shane Boyd's ex-wife. He said he stopped my client's vehicle "because he failed to activate his turn signal before making a left turn." I knew TBI agents didn't routinely make traffic stops, and so did the judge. I called the daughter and boyfriend to the stand and subpoenaed Shane's ex-wife. She was afraid of getting charged with perjury, so she admitted the affair with Landers, admitted she'd asked him to arrest her ex, but swore she never dreamed he'd do it.

The judge was so outraged that Landers had committed perjury in his courtroom that he dismissed the case and wrote a letter to Landers's supervisor at the TBI, but nothing happened. It was my first reality check when it came to cops committing perjury. Since then, I'd questioned everything Landers did in every case I had that involved him. I didn't trust him, and I didn't have any problem letting him know it.

We set our evidence meeting for 3:15, but knowing Landers would enjoy making me wait, I didn't show up until 3:30. He wasn't there, so I sat down at the table and fumed for a little while. I was about to leave when he finally walked through the door in his expensive gray suit, carrying a cardboard box under his arm. Landers is around my age, a couple inches shorter than me, in pretty good shape, and has blue eyes and short brown hair. I suppose he's handsome—he certainly thinks he is—but there were dark circles under his eyes, and I could smell booze on him. It was the kind of smell you can't shower off, the kind that comes from your pores.

"You're a half hour late," I said as I stood up.

"Yeah," he said with a smirk.

He started taking things out of his cardboard box, the last item being a photograph of Angel. She was sitting at a table looking up at the camera, and she had what appeared to be a nasty bruise on her left cheek. The photograph was dated two days after Tester's murder. Angel hadn't mentioned anything to me about the police taking her picture, and the photograph wasn't in the initial packet of discovery material I'd picked up from the D.A.'s office. As soon as I saw the photo, I knew I'd need to file a motion to keep them from being able to use it at trial. Unless they had some concrete proof of how Angel got the bruise, the photo could unfairly prejudice a jury.

"So I hear Bill Wright's about to retire," I said, trying to keep things civil. "Who's next in line?"

"No such thing as next in line," Landers said. "The job will go to whoever the suits think is best."

"Who do you think it will be?"

"What do you care?" He looked at me as if I were a fly on his wrist, nothing more than a nuisance.

"Just trying to make a little friendly small talk. No point in us being at each other's throats all the time."

He raised his nose in the air like he was sniffing me. It wrinkled, as though he found the scent repugnant.

"Hate to disappoint you," he said, "but I don't think me and you will ever be friends. I don't like lawyers, especially defense lawyers who do everything they can to get criminals off on technicalities."

"You misunderstand my role," I said. "I just try to make sure you guys follow your own rules. If you were in the same boat as my clients, you'd want everybody to play fair, wouldn't you?"

"If I were in the same boat as your clients, I'd sink the thing and swim away. Now, are you going to look at this stuff, or did you get me down here to chit-chat? Because to be honest with you, I'm not in a real chatty mood today."

I slid the items across the table and looked them over.

"Why'd you take this picture?" I said, holding up the photo of Angel. "And what's it doing in your evidence file?"

"Why do you think I took it? Look at her. Somebody cracked her in the face. We're gonna show it to the jury."

"Any proof of how she got the bruise? What if she slipped on a banana peel?"

"She can explain it on the witness stand."

"*If* the judge lets it in." I tossed the photo back onto the table. "I'm going to file a motion to keep it out."

"You see?" Landers said. "That's exactly what I'm talking about. This photograph was taken two days after the murder. Her hair was found on the dead guy, and she just happens to have a nasty bruise on her face. The logical conclusion is that she got the bruise during a struggle with the victim. But then some dickhead like you comes along and wants to keep the jury from finding out about it."

"Is this all you've got?" I said. "I see some photos of Tester, a photo of what looks like a shriveled penis, a photo of Angel, a couple hairs, a couple lab reports, and some bank records showing that Tester withdrew money from the strip club's ATM. Is that it?"

"It'll be enough to convict that little slut of murder."

"It's not enough to convict her of simple assault."

"That's what I like to hear," Landers said. "You just keep thinking that way."

"The evidence in this case is as weak as any I've ever seen."

"Since when is DNA evidence weak?"

"Her hair probably got on him while he was groping her at the club," I said.

"Maybe. You can go ahead and try to sell that to the jury, but the *fact* is that her hair was found on his corpse in his room."

"It's not enough."

"Our witness says your girl and Barlowe followed the victim out of the club that night. They were the last people to see him alive."

"Your witness is a lying prostitute with a drug problem."

"And your *client* is a mystery woman who was working in a strip club. A stranger. Not from around here. Jury won't exactly love her, especially when they see that bruise on her face."

"You don't have a murder weapon or a motive."

"Don't need either one. We've got enough circumstantial evidence to get a conviction. And you know what? I think something else will come up before this is over."

"Something else already has come up. You've heard of Virgil Watterson, haven't you? I think you talked to him this morning."

There was a long, tense silence.

"How the hell would you know that?"

"He called me first. He described what he saw on the bridge that night. He said he thinks you guys arrested the wrong person. Just trying to do the right thing, you know? I told him he should call you and tell you what he saw and maybe you'd try to make it right. He called me back after he talked to you. Said you didn't sound all that interested in his information. I should've known better."

"He's not reliable. He waited two months before he even bothered to call."

"He's worried about his marriage."

"It was dark out there, after midnight. No way he could have made an identification."

"He saw Erlene. She was alone. He saw the Corvette. It's consistent with what Julie Hayes is saying. What the hell's the matter with you? You guys should be taking a closer look at Erlene Barlowe."

"And you should mind your own shop. I don't need your advice."

"So you're going to ignore him."

"Ignore who? Far as I'm concerned, he never called."

Someone banged on the door, and it opened. A police officer named Harold "Bull" Deakins walked in. He and Landers were drinking buddies, legendary carousers. Deakins's nickname was well deserved. His shoulders barely fit through the door.

"They told me I'd find you down here," he said to Landers. Landers's eyes didn't move, and neither did mine. Deakins stopped short. "Everything all right with you boys? Are we playing nice?" His voice did nothing to break the tension.

"Your buddy and I were just talking about arresting innocent people," I said, still locked onto Landers. He stared back, saying nothing.

"Watterson saw Erlene Barlowe on the bridge that night," I said. "She was alone. My client wasn't around. You know what that means, don't you?"

"It doesn't mean jack. For all I know, you put the guy up to it. For all I know, you paid him to say he saw the Corvette."

"Sorry," I said, "that's more along the lines of something you'd do."

"You know something, Dillard? You're wasting your breath talking to me. My job was to investigate this case and make an arrest, and that's what I did. Now my job is to go to trial, testify, and make sure your client gets what she deserves—a needle in her arm."

He started packing up his little box as Deakins loomed over my shoulder. I turned to leave. As I was walking out the door, I stopped and faced Landers. He finished putting items in the box, picked it up off the table, and looked at me.

"She's innocent," I said. "She didn't kill anybody."

His shoulders lifted the slightest bit. What was that? A shrug?

"Are you listening to me? *She didn't kill anybody.*"

He knew it. He knew. He looked back down at the table, and I walked out the door.

JUNE 25
1:00 P.M.

'd been going down to the jail to see Angel once a week, but the conversations I'd had with her were more personal than professional. I'd already heard her version of what happened the night Tester was killed, so I spent the time trying to get some background information out of her. She was reluctant, but during the second visit she decided she trusted me enough to tell me her real name and where she was from.

I gave the information to Diane Frye. She'd been working for weeks, and I'd also sent Tom Short, a forensic psychiatrist, down to the jail to interview Angel three times. I set up meetings with both of them on the same afternoon.

Diane had traveled to Oklahoma and Ohio, running down witnesses and documents. I was anxious to hear what she had to say. When I walked in, the conference room table was covered in papers.

"Your chickie is a ghost," Diane said in her Tennessee drawl. She was nearly sixty, but she styled her light brown hair short and spiked. She was wearing her perpetual smile and her favorite casual outfit, a bright orange Tennessee Volunteer T-shirt—she's a rabid fan—khaki shorts that exposed knobby knees and varicose veins, and orange high-top Converse basketball shoes.

"No Social Security number, no driver's license, no school records, no credit history, no nothing. She doesn't exist, at least not on paper. But I've talked to everybody I could find, and I think I've got everything pretty well organized. At least you'll know a little more about what you're dealing with."

Diane said Angel was born in Columbus, Ohio, on March 15, 1989, to a young woman named Grace Rodriguez. Her biological mother gave her up for adoption the same day to the Columbus Freewill Baptist Home for Children. Angel was adopted five months later by Airman First Class Thomas Rhodes and his wife, Betty. They named her Mary Ann Rhodes.

Diane had flown out to Oklahoma City to talk to Angel's adopted parents. They told Diane that when they adopted Mary, they thought they were unable to have children of their own, but Ms. Rhodes became pregnant a year later. She subsequently had three more children.

"They said they treated her like a princess," Diane said. "The mother called her a thieving, ungrateful little wench. She said her husband kept a stash of cash in a box in the ceiling, and Angel apparently cleaned it out before she left. But I always leave a card and tell people if they have any other information to give me a call. A couple hours after I left, I got a call on my cell phone. It was one of their daughters, a seventeen-year-old named

Rebecca. She was scared to death and I didn't get to talk to her for long, but she said her parents didn't tell me the whole story."

Diane paused and stared up at the ceiling. She loved drama.

"What?" I said. "C'mon. Out with it."

"She said her daddy did bad things to Angel."

"What kind of bad things?"

"Sexual abuse. She said it went on for years, and she thinks Angel finally just had enough. She also said her mother used to beat Angel pretty badly."

"I wonder why Angel never told anyone."

"The mother is a religious freak. Their living room looked like a sanctuary. She said she homeschooled the kids and was particular about what they were allowed to watch and read. I got the impression she didn't even allow them to have friends. Angel probably didn't have much of an opportunity to tell. Either that or she was just scared. Her sister told me Angel tried to run away a couple times and the police had to bring her back, so I went down to the Oklahoma City police department and got copies of the reports. In 2001 she only made it ten blocks. She locked herself in the bathroom of a convenience store. The police came and took her straight home. She took off again in 2003. They found her walking along the highway about seven miles from her house. The police took her home again. If she told them about the abuse, they didn't believe her."

Diane then turned her attention to Erlene Barlowe. I'd asked her to quietly check into a few things, and I'd paid her out of my own pocket.

"No criminal record. Her husband was the sheriff of McNairy County from 1970 to 1973. He resigned under some pretty suspicious circumstances and went into the strip-club business. She was with him every step of the way until he died of a heart attack last year. She doesn't seem to have any enemies, at least none I could find. I talked to a couple of her employees. They're flat-out loyal."

"Corvette?"

"No Corvette. Or I guess I should say no record of a Corvette."

"And what about Julie Hayes?"

"Very naughty girl. Three drug possessions, two misdemeanor thefts, three prostitution convictions. Most of the arrests are in the Dallas-Fort Worth area. Nobody had anything good to say about her. She's a mess."

"You talk to her?"

"I tried. The first time I went out to her place she was so stoned she could barely speak. The second time she told me to buzz off, so I buzzed off."

An hour later, I drove over to meet with the forensic psychiatrist I'd hired to examine Angel. Tom Short was head of the psychiatry department at East Tennessee State University, a short, wiry academic who seemed to spend a lot of time in a world no one else understood. I'd met him at a death-penalty seminar in Nashville five years earlier where he taught a class on the role of psychiatric evaluation in mitigation. I'd used him in seven cases since then, and we'd become friends. I'd never placed a lot of faith in psychiatry before I met Tom, but his uncanny ability to diagnose personality disorders and psychotic illnesses made a believer of me. I trusted him completely.

"PTSD," he said as soon as I walked into his office. He was sitting behind his desk, chewing on the end of the pipe he kept in his mouth like a pacifier. I'd never seen him without the pipe, and I'd never seen it lit.

"Post Traumatic Stress Disorder?"

"Chronic and severe. But she's being evasive about the stressor. I suspect she was raped by her adopted father."

"Why?"

"Because if the stressor was a car accident or something she witnessed, she'd tell me about it. She became agitated and evasive when I asked her about her father."

"Is she a candidate for murder?"

"Everybody's a candidate under the right circumstances. Unfortunately, I don't have a crystal ball."

"I don't see how she could possibly have killed Tester," I said. "For one thing, he was a 260-pound man. What does she weigh? 110? I just don't see her being able to overpower a guy like that."

"His blood alcohol level was .27, and he was drugged. A ten-year-old could have killed him."

"I know, but she just doesn't *feel* like a murderer when I talk to her," I said.

"I look at her clinically," Short said. "You look at her emotionally. Her beauty and vulnerability cloud your perspective."

"So you think she killed him?"

"I didn't say that. I'm just saying it's possible. Some PTSD victims go into a dissociative state if the stressor is severe enough, and if it's repeated. Let's say her adopted father sexually abused her for years, which I suspect he did. She runs away. Then she finds herself being sexually abused by this Tester man. It's possible she could have had sort of an out-of-body experience and killed him. It would also explain the extraordinary number of stab wounds and the mutilation."

"Would she remember it?"

"It'd be like a dream, but she'd remember it."

"Would she be responsible for her conduct, legally, if that's what happened?"

"Probably not. I think I'd be able to testify that under those circumstances she would *not* be responsible for her conduct. At that point, she wouldn't have been able to discern the difference between right and wrong."

"The problem is that in order for us to assert that defense, she'd have to admit she killed him."

"That's right."

"She says she didn't kill him."

"I know."

"So where does that leave us?"

"She didn't tell me she did it, so as far as I'm concerned, she didn't do it. Everything I've told you is purely theoretical."

"Have you made notes on all of this?"

"Of course."

"Shred them."

Since I had Tom's attention, which was sometimes hard to get, I decided to ask him about Junior Tester. I described to him in detail everything that had happened between us, including the look of torment and hatred on Junior's face the night I went to his house.

"Was it a mistake?" I said.

"Actually," Tom said, "going down there wasn't as bad an idea as you might think. You may have showed him there could be serious consequences to his actions. Maybe you shocked him back into reality, at least for a little while. Have you seen him since?"

"No."

"You must have frightened him."

"He didn't look scared. Do you think I'll see him again?"

"Can't say for sure."

"Is it likely?"

"I'd say it depends."

"On what?"

"On how you portray his father in the courtroom if you go to trial. You might want to give that some serious consideration."

JUNE 25
4:00 P.M.

After the meetings with Diane and Tom, I was both confused and concerned. I decided it was time to go have a serious conversation with my client. I wanted to discuss some of the more incriminating evidence with her, but more important, I needed to see how well Angel would hold up under cross-examination. If I could catch her in a lie, so could the district attorney.

She wasn't shackled or handcuffed when the guards escorted her into the interview room—apparently she was no longer considered a security risk. I'd asked her what she wanted me to call her after I found out her real name. She said she wanted to be called Angel. Mary Ann, she said, was gone.

"How are you holding up?" I said.

"I'm okay. The guards are nice to me."

Each time I went to visit, I was struck by something different: the smoothness of her skin, the contours of her face, the fullness of her lips. She was an extraordinarily beautiful girl, a fact that made what I was about to do even more difficult.

"There are a couple things I need to ask you about, some things that are bothering me. I want you to tell me the truth."

A puzzled look came over her face, but she nodded.

"First off, I need to know about your relationship with Julie Hayes."

"What about it?"

"Do you have any idea why she would tell the police that you and Erlene left the club right after Reverend Tester the night he was killed?"

"What? Julie said that?"

I reached into my briefcase, pulled out a copy of Julie's statement, and set it down in front of Angel.

"This is a copy of the statement she gave to the TBI. Read it for yourself."

Angel looked down at the statement for a few minutes, then back at me.

"Why would she say something like that?" she said.

"Good question. Why would she?"

"I don't know."

"Did you and Erlene leave the club right after Reverend Tester?"

"No."

"Are you sure?"

"Yes."

"Well, Julie says you did, and since she signed this statement, I'm sure she'll testify at the trial. Is she mad at you about something?"

"I don't think so."

"Is she mad at Erlene about something?"

"I don't know."

"Was she jealous of the relationship between you and Erlene?"

"She never said anything to me about it."

"Did you ever see Julie and Erlene argue or fight about anything?"

"No."

"Did Erlene take you home that night?"

"Yes."

"What kind of car was she driving?"

She hesitated. "What?"

"What kind of car was Erlene driving that night?"

"I don't know anything about cars."

"Do you know what a Corvette looks like?"

"No."

"Come on, Angel. It's a sports car. Shiny and fast. It would have been red."

"I really don't know anything about cars."

"Was Erlene driving the same car the next day?"

She hesitated again and asked me to repeat the question.

"Erlene took you home with her the night Reverend Tester was killed, right?"

"Yes."

"She gave you a ride home in her car, right?"

"Yes."

"Did she have the same car the next day or a different car?"

"I don't know. The same car, I guess." She looked upward when she answered. I thought she might be lying, so I stayed with the subject of the car.

"Julie told the police Erlene was driving a red Corvette the night Tester was killed. She said Erlene got rid of it and was driving a different car the next day. Is that true?"

"I don't think so."

I sighed. I wanted to believe her, but the vagueness of her answers wasn't helping. I decided to press harder, so I raised my voice a notch and slammed my palm down on the table.

"Is that what you're going to tell the prosecutor when he asks you the same question on the witness stand? Are you going to say 'I don't think so'? If that's what you're going to say, he'll tear you apart. Now give me a straight answer! Was Erlene driving a different car the next day or not?"

The sound of my hand on the table had startled her, and I could tell the tone of my voice was beginning to unnerve her.

"No. I think she was driving the same car."

"You think? You *think* she was driving the same car? That's not good enough, Angel. That's an evasive answer. Juries don't like evasive answers."

"What should I say?"

"How about the *truth*? This is just between you and me. If you tell me Erlene was driving a different car the next day, I'm not going to run out and tell the police, and I'm not going to tell Erlene that you told me."

She folded her arms across her chest and crossed her legs—the classic defensive position—and started rocking back and forth in her seat. She was obviously struggling with herself, trying to make some kind of decision.

"Miss Erlene didn't kill anybody," she said finally.

"I didn't say she did."

"That's what you're thinking. I can tell." She was right. I was beginning to believe that Angel was protecting Erlene. If she was, it was a mistake that could cost her her life.

"Julie says Erlene switched cars the day after Tester was murdered. Julie says you and Erlene left the club right after Tester left. Now either Julie's lying, or you and Erlene are lying. If Julie's lying, I need to know why. If you're lying, I need to know why. Now, who's lying?"

"Julie's lying."

"Why?"

"I don't know."

"Then tell me about Erlene's car. Did she switch cars the day after Tester was killed or not?"

"No."

I was back to square one. Julie was lying, and the only explanation I could offer a jury was that she was a drug addict, perhaps bitter, or perhaps jealous of the relationship between Erlene and Angel. I didn't know whether a jury would buy it.

"You can uncross your arms now."

"What?"

"People cross their arms when they feel like they're being threatened or attacked, Angel. It's a sign of defensiveness, and I don't want you to do it if you ever get up on a witness stand. Now tell me about the bruise on your face. The one the police took a picture of."

She hesitated again and unconsciously raised her fingers to her cheek. Her eyes began to blink quickly.

"I got hit by a door," she said.

"When?"

"The day after, I think."

"Where?"

"At the club. I was about to walk through the door and someone opened it from the other side. It hit me in the face."

"Erlene told me you didn't go back to the club after Tester was killed."

"Oh, right, well, it must have been the day before then."

"The same day Tester was killed?"

She nodded.

"You're sure?"

"Uh-huh."

"Who was on the other side of the door?"

"I'm not sure."

"You don't remember who hit you with a door so hard it put a bruise on your face?"

"It was Heather. I remember now."

Small beads of perspiration were forming on her forehead, and I decided to ease off. I wondered whether Heather would confirm that Angel had run into a door, and I made a note to have Diane Frye speak with her. Angel had self-consciously unfolded her arms and placed her hands on the table. I noticed they were discolored—not severely, but they were both slightly pale to about an inch above her wrist. I remembered Erlene telling me to ask Angel about her hands. Very gently, I touched one of them.

"Did something happen here?" I said.

"I burned them when I was little." The words were flat, monotone, and the expression on her face went completely blank.

"How?"

"I was making oatmeal for my brothers and sisters." She paused for a long moment. "And I ... I dropped the spoon into the pot ... by accident." She paused again.

"And?" I said.

"Mother Betty. She pushed my hands down into the oatmeal and made me get the spoon out."

"Jesus, Angel. And your hands look like that from the burns?"

She nodded.

"How old were you?"

"I'm not sure. Maybe five. Or six."

I shuddered. She'd described the event as if she were describing a walk down an empty hall in a burned-out building. She'd become distant, disconnected, as though she'd suddenly been unplugged.

"What about your adopted father? Did he do bad things to you too?"

Another nod.

"Do you want to tell me about it?"

Tears were forming in her eyes. She didn't answer the question. She didn't have to.

"Did it happen a lot?"

She nodded again as a tear slid down her cheek.

"Angel, is there something you're not telling me?"

She started to speak but stopped herself. I suddenly realized I was in a tug-of-war, and Angel was the rope. Someone else was pulling on the other end, and I suspected it was Erlene. She broke into tears and stood up, leaning against the table. Her shoulders began to shudder, and her lips were quivering. The intensity of the sobs increased with each passing second, and before I knew it, she was hysterical.

"Please," I said when she paused for breath after a high-pitched wail, "you need to stay calm, Angel. All I want is the truth."

She gave me a look that told me I'd gone too far and gathered her breath.

"*Why won't you believe me?*" she shrieked. "I told you I didn't kill him! Why are you asking me all these questions? I thought you were on my side! I thought you were my friend!"

She turned and started to pound on the door with her fist.

"Wait, please. Please calm down, Angel. I *am* on your side." I got up from the table and reached out to touch her arm.

"*Don't touch me! Stay away from me!*"

The door opened, and she nearly fell into one of the two guards' arms. I started out the door toward her, but the second guard stuck his finger in my chest.

"Step back," he said. He meant it, he was armed, and I had a feeling he would do anything to protect this particular prisoner.

I raised my hands and stepped backwards into the interview room as he slammed the door in my face.

JUNE 28
1:30 P.M.

Ronnie came into the back office on Saturday afternoon while Erlene was catching up on her paperwork. She could see right away that something was bothering him. Ronnie had this cute little cleft in his chin, and when he was upset, he set his mouth a certain way and the sides of the cleft swelled up like little knots on a birch branch. The cleft reminded Erlene of Gus, which was only natural since Ronnie was Gus's nephew. He wasn't as handsome as Gus, but he was still a looker, tall and well built, with dark blond hair and blue eyes. Erlene just wished he didn't have those icky tattoos all over him. They came out of his shirt up his neck and ran clear down his arms to his hands. They made him look like a thug.

"What's the matter, sugar?" Erlene said. "You look like somebody just shot your dog."

"They shorted us again."

Shitdammit. Erlene hated that he was bringing up such unpleasantness, especially after the visit she'd had with sweet little Angel down at the jail. Angel was as tore up as Erlene had ever seen her, poor thing. She said Mr. Dillard had come down and asked her all sorts of embarrassing questions. She even asked Erlene if she thought they needed a different lawyer, but Erlene set her straight real quick on that. Mr. Dillard was exactly what they needed. Erlene talked to Angel for as long as they let her stay, and by the time she left, she could tell Angel was feeling a whole lot better. Erlene even managed to make her smile a couple times. But she still felt so bad for Angel. She'd already been through so much. It hurt Erlene's heart to see her suffer more.

"How much did they short us?" Erlene said to Ronnie.

"A little over two ounces."

Erlene didn't much like fooling with the candy trade, but Gus had made so much money doing it over the years, she'd have been a fool not to pick up right where he left off. It was an all-cash business, and since Ronnie handled the pickups and the deliveries and the inside sales, it wasn't too much of a bother for Erlene. The problem she was having was that some of the people she bought the candy from were greedy and mean. They were always trying to pull one over on her, as if they thought she wouldn't notice or wouldn't do anything about it even if she did. She reckoned because Gus was gone, they thought they could get away with most anything. Shitdammit. Why couldn't they just play fair?

"Do we have other folks we can use?" Erlene said.

"Four besides these guys. One in Atlanta—"

"Don't tell me, baby doll. I don't want to know where they are. I don't want to know much of anything about them."

"Sorry," Ronnie said. He was such a considerate boy.

"I tell you what let's do, then," Erlene said. "First off, you go ahead and deal with your people in Atlanta or wherever you said. Can they give us the same price?"

"The price will be the same and the quality will be better," Ronnie said. "The only reason I was dealing with these fools was because they were so much closer and they were willing to meet me halfway. Saved me a lot of road time."

"I think it's worth the inconvenience, don't you?" Erlene looked up toward the ceiling and pursed her lips. "Now," she said, "what to do about those others?"

Erlene knew Ronnie had a mean streak in him as wide as the Tennessee River, but underneath all that meanness, he was really a good boy. He'd just hit a few bumps in the road was all, although Erlene had to admit that Ronnie hit the bumps a little harder than most boys. He'd spent several years down at the state penitentiary in Morgan County after he got into some trouble with the law. When he got out, he didn't have a place to go and couldn't get a job, so he called his uncle Gus. Gus had always felt close to the boy and invited him to come up to work in the club. When Ronnie got there, Gus sat him down and told him that if he'd pay attention and be honest, Gus would see to it that his brother's oldest son made a good living.

Erlene had to give Ronnie credit—he took right to it. The first thing Gus told him was that people who sell candy have to stay out of the candy. One of Ronnie's biggest problems when he was younger was that he snorted and smoked so much candy he couldn't think straight, so Gus told him if he got so much as an inkling that Ronnie was using, he'd be gone. The second thing Gus told him was that he who steals pays the price. Ronnie had gone to prison for stealing, among other things, and Gus told him he wouldn't tolerate his stealing a single dime.

Ronnie went to work in the club, tending bar and selling candy. Gus kept a close eye on him the first year, and he did a wonderful job. Before long, he was pretty much running Gus's whole candy business. Gus got to where he trusted Ronnie so much that if something went wrong, Gus just stepped back and let Ronnie take care of it. And from what Gus told Erlene, Ronnie was excellent at taking care of problems, especially if it involved Ronnie getting to hurt somebody.

The best part, though, was that Ronnie never stole the first penny. Erlene was proud as punch of that boy, although she suspected his honesty was at least partly due to the fact that he was afraid his uncle Gus would kill him if he took anything. Gus wasn't a man to trifle with, especially when it came to money.

After Gus died, Ronnie asked her whether he could keep doing what he'd been doing. Erlene thought about all the money Gus had made and said, "Sure, sugar. I'd be a fool to make you stop." Ronnie paid Erlene every night, cash, like clockwork. Ronnie had turned out to be a real good boy, and Erlene kind of felt like she was at least partly responsible.

"Tell you what," Erlene said. "How about you just go ahead and do whatever you think Gus would have told you to do. I don't even have to know about it."

"Sounds good to me."

"That's wonderful," Erlene said, "and speaking of dealing with bad people, I have another little problem I'm going to need you to help me with."

There was a certain girl needed tending to, and Ronnie was the right man for the job.

JULY 1
10:10 A.M.

T he Tate woman wrote to Maynard Bush out of the blue. Maynard figured killers must get her hot. He didn't have nothing better to do, so Maynard wrote back. He wasn't real good at writing, but what the hell? He knew enough to get by. She wrote again and he wrote again and before Maynard knew it, they're writing to each other every few days.

Maynard laid it on thick as jelly on a biscuit. Played her like a banjo. At first he was just screwing off, but then he got a bright idea. He didn't know if it would work, but it was sure as hell worth the try.

First thing Maynard did was talk his dumbass lawyer, Joe Dillard, into fixing it so the Tate woman could visit him. Then he started working on her. He shoveled so much crap on her she damned near turned brown. He told her he was lonesome and that he needed a friend. It was a lie. Maynard didn't have friends and didn't want none. They always just ended up pissing him off, and then they ended up dead. To Maynard, killing a human being wasn't any different than killing a dog or a rabbit.

When he told Bonnie Tate he needed a friend, Maynard could see it damned near broke her heart, so he just kept pouring it on. He told Bonnie how when he was a boy his mama was a drug addict and his daddy got hauled off to prison. It was about the only thing Maynard told Bonnie that was true. He told her he went to bed hungry every night, which was bull. He told her he didn't have no shoes that fit. Another lie, good enough to make her cry. When she cried, it made Maynard think of how he used to make his baby cousin cry. When the girl's mother turned her back, Maynard would pinch her up under her arm as hard as he could and she'd wail like an ambulance passing in the night. Maynard never did get caught. He was too smart and quick.

Four days before Maynard's trial was supposed to start, he made sure Bonnie came to visit. It was time to take his shot.

"You're my only visitor, you know," Maynard said as he gazed across the table at the plump, homely brunette. "You're the only person I trust." He watched her close. She was eating it up.

"I want to thank you for everything you've done for me, Bonnie," Maynard said. "You gave me hope when there wasn't none left." Maynard had to concentrate as hard as he could to keep from gagging. He'd told a couple of his buddies at the jail that Bonnie Tate was ugly enough to make a freight train take a dirt road.

"I think about you all the time, Bonnie. I dream about you every night. I think maybe I love you."

She looked at him and he could see tears forming in her eyes. It was working.

"Do you think maybe you love me too, Bonnie?"

She nodded. "I think maybe I do, Maynard."

"If I was to ever get out of this place, would you stay with me, Bonnie? Please say you'd stay with me. It'd mean so much to me."

"I reckon I'd stay with you."

"Bonnie, I need to ask you something. It's real important, and you can't breathe a word of it. Can I trust you?"

"You know you can trust me, Maynard."

"If I was to tell you I know a way out of here, would you help me? Would you, Bonnie? It's the only chance I've got. They'll kill me if you don't help me."

It didn't take her long to say yes.

"Okay then," Maynard said. "You listen real close now. You gotta do exactly what I say."

JULY 2
9:05 A.M.

I walked into Judge Glass's courtroom a little after nine
and took a seat in the back behind a column where the
judge couldn't see me. Sarah and her appointed attorney had worked out an agreement with the assistant district attorney, and she was about to enter a plea. To my
relief, there were no reporters in the jury box.

I'd lost a lot of sleep thinking—and worrying—
about Sarah. As time passed, I'd gotten over the anger.
I still thought Sarah needed to pay for what she'd done,
but I knew prison time wouldn't do her any good. I'd
never seen prison time do anyone any good.

She'd agreed to plead guilty to two counts of felony
theft, to accept the minimum sentence of three years on
each count, and to forego a probation hearing. The two
three-year sentences were to run concurrently. Under
Tennessee law, she'd be eligible for parole after serving
ten months, and I had every intention of speaking on her
behalf at her first parole hearing. Because of the over-
crowding in the state penitentiary system, inmates who

were sentenced to fewer than three years served their time in the county jails. That meant Sarah wouldn't be shipped off to the woman's prison in Nashville but would stay in the Washington County Detention Center. I'd be able to visit and try again to patch things up. I should have already gone down to see her, but I was afraid we'd just end up in the same old place.

Judge Glass was his usual cantankerous self, barking at defense attorneys and sniping at defendants. A woman in the audience had forgotten to turn her cell phone off, and when it rang, Glass ordered her to the front and castigated her so fiercely that she was reduced to tears.

He called Sarah's case twenty minutes after I sat down, and a bailiff brought her in. She looked small and frail in the baggy jumpsuit, and I thought the handcuffs and shackles were totally unnecessary. She shuffled to the podium and stood looking at the floor.

"State of Tennessee versus Sarah Dillard," Judge Glass said. He looked at Lisa Mays, the assistant district attorney. "Is this Mr. Dillard's sister?"

"She is, Your Honor."

I hoped Glass wouldn't use his dislike for me as a reason to reject the plea agreement and give Sarah a harsher sentence. I scooted down in my seat.

"What did she do this time?" Glass said.

"She stole Mr. Dillard's daughter's car and a necklace that belonged to Mr. Dillard's wife," Mays said. "She traded the necklace for cocaine and wrecked the car."

"So she's an indiscriminate thief," Glass said. "She steals from everybody in the family. How'd she get the keys to the car? She break in?"

"No, Your Honor. As I understand it, she had recently been released from jail, and Mr. Dillard had taken her in. He was trying to help her. This is how she repaid him."

I was hoping Glass would just go through the motions and not ask any questions. It was a run-of-the-mill plea. He took hundreds of them every year.

"This judgment form says she was charged with two Class C felonies," Glass said. "I read her presentence report last night. She's been stealing and drugging for almost twenty years. Why are you agreeing to concurrent sentences?"

"We agreed at the victim's request, Your Honor. We do it all the time."

"You mean to tell me Mr. Dillard requested that she only serve three years for this? After everything else she's done?"

"Yes, sir."

"Where is he?"

"He's probably in court somewhere."

"Well, get him down here. I want to talk to him."

I stood, my face hot, and walked toward the front.

"I'm here, Judge."

"Well, well, Mr. Dillard, glad you could join us, especially since you've been so successful at manipulating the system."

"I haven't manipulated anything," I said. Lisa Mays seemed surprised to see me. Sarah looked at me hopefully. I stopped just to the right of the defense table. "I'm just not asking for blood, Judge. This is her first felony."

"It's her first felony *conviction*," Judge Glass said. "She's been charged with felonies three times in the past, but they've all been reduced to misdemeanors. I suppose you didn't have anything to do with that either—did you, Mr. Dillard?"

"Are you accusing me of something?"

"You're darn right I am. I'm accusing you of manipulating the legal system to gain favorable treatment for a member of your family."

"And you wouldn't do the same?"

"Watch your mouth, sir. I'm not in any mood to put up with any disrespect from you."

"This district attorney, the public defender, and my sister have apparently come to an agreement they think is fair," I said. "I didn't have anything to do with it. The only thing I told Miss Mays was that I wasn't going to insist on the maximum punishment. She'll serve almost a year as it is."

"Let me ask you a question, Mr. Dillard," Judge Glass said. "If this young lady was a complete stranger to you and she'd stolen your daughter's car and an expensive piece of jewelry that belonged to your wife, would you be in here asking me to accept a minimum sentence? Especially with her list of priors? Tell the truth for a change."

"She's not a complete stranger, so the question is meaningless," I said. "And I always tell the truth in this courtroom. You just don't like to hear it sometimes."

"Watch your tone, Mr. Dillard. You're on the verge of a contempt citation." His voice was beginning to tremble, a sure sign that his anger was about to overcome his reason.

"My tone is no different than yours, Judge," I said. "Is this hearing about accepting a plea from my sister?

Or is it about something else? Because if it's about some personal animosity you hold toward me, perhaps you should consider recusing yourself from this case and let her enter her plea in front of an impartial judge."

Glass was a bully, and like all bullies, he became angry and confused when people stood up to him. He certainly had the power to put me in jail, but I knew I hadn't done anything to deserve it. If he ordered them to arrest me, I'd just embarrass him in front of the court of appeals.

"Don't flatter yourself," he said. "I save my personal animosity for important people. You're certainly not in that category."

"Good. Then let's get on with it," I said.

"I'm not accepting this plea as is," Glass said. "She can plead to two consecutive three-year sentences, or she can plead to concurrent six-year sentences, or she can go to trial. She's not walking out of my courtroom with less than six years."

"Why?" I said. That simple, three-letter word was the one I knew judges hated the most. Most of them didn't feel like they had to explain themselves. They were judges, after all. They wore a robe, and the robe gave them the power to do pretty much whatever they pleased.

"Why, Mr. Dillard? Why? Because I say so. Because your sister is the scum of the earth. She won't work, she doesn't pay taxes, she sucks up drugs like a vacuum cleaner, and she's a thief. She's a drain on society, and she belongs in jail. If you didn't want her to go to jail, you shouldn't have reported her crimes to the police. You did call the police, didn't you?"

As much as I hated to admit it, he was right. When I picked up the phone, I knew I was putting Sarah at risk of a long jail term. Hell, I'd wanted her to go to jail. But my anger had subsided, and I'd convinced myself that what she'd agreed to was more than enough.

"What's the matter, Mr. Dillard?" Glass said. "Cat got your tongue?"

"This is between you and the district attorney and her lawyer," I said. "I'm leaving."

"Have a nice day," Glass said.

I turned and walked out the door, angry and embarrassed. I called Lisa Mays an hour later. She said the public defender had taken Sarah into the back and explained that if she went to trial and was convicted, Judge Glass could, and probably would, sentence her to twelve years in prison.

"She agreed to the six," Mays said. "But the judge went into his routine again about you calling the police. She's angry at him, but she's *really* pissed off at you."

JULY 5
8:20 A.M.

I was sitting with Thomas Walker II, an assistant district attorney named Fred Julian, and a couple of bailiffs in the judge's office in Mountain City, getting ready to go to trial with Maynard Bush. The bailiffs were Darren and David Bowers, a pair of cheerful, inseparable identical twins in their late fifties. Every time I saw them, they were laughing. After graduating from high school in Mountain City in the late sixties and thinking they'd be drafted, Darren and David enlisted in the army so that they could stay together. Darren, in his brown deputy's uniform, was telling a war story. David, also in uniform, was sitting across the room red-faced.

"We're in this little bitty brothel in Saigon," Darren was saying. His accent made Jeff Foxworthy sound like a city slicker. "Been out in the bush damned near a month. Hornier than three-peckered billy goats, both of us. Davie's drunker'n Cooter Brown, and he staggers up to this ol' Vietnamese madam and puts his hands on his hips like John Wayne and says, 'How much fer a suckie thar, Miss Slanty Eyes?'

"Now, I reckon that ol' girl, she knew a little more English than Davie figgered she did, 'cause she give him a look that'd peel chrome off a bumper. Then she smiles at him all nice and says, 'You *beaucoup* big boy?' Davie didn't know what she's a-talkin' about at first, but then she points down at his pecker and she says, 'Show me. You big boy?'"

Darren was giggling. He started to talk and then stopped and giggled some more. The memory was almost too much for him to take.

"So Davie, he goes, 'Ahh, so you want to take a gander at old G.I. Johnson, huh? You reckon it might be too big for your girls?' So Davie, he ... he. ..." Darren broke down again. He was laughing so hard tears were streaming down his cheeks.

"Davie, he just drops his fly and pulls his pecker out right there for everybody to see. And that madam, she looks down at it and then she looks back up at Davie's face all serious, and I swear on my mama's grave, this is what she says to him. She says, 'Normal price for suckie ten dollah. But for little guy like you, I take five.'"

Darren slapped his leg and roared. Laughter was bouncing off the walls as Judge Rollins walked in. Rollins was a no-nonsense guy who traveled the Second Judicial Circuit. He didn't bother to ask what all the commotion was about.

"Go get him," he said to the Bowers twins. "Let's get started."

Darren and David got up to go fetch Maynard Bush. He was being held in the old Johnson County Jail, which was about a hundred feet behind the courthouse, across a small lawn.

The judge sat down behind his desk, and we started talking about some of the issues that would come up in the trial. After about ten minutes, I heard what had to be gunshots.

Pop! Pop!

There was a short pause.

Pop!

The second-floor window behind the judge's desk looked out over the lawn behind the building toward the jail. I got to the window just in time to see Maynard Bush climbing into the passenger side of a green Toyota sedan. A woman was helping him get into the car. She slammed the door, ran around to the driver's side, jumped in, and the car drove away.

Darren and David Bowers were sprawled in the courtyard. Darren was facedown. David was lying on his back. The first thought that hit me when I realized what had happened was that they both had grandchildren.

It took me less than a minute to run down the steps, out the back door, and across the courtyard. David was gasping for breath, blood gurgling from a hole in his throat. Darren wasn't moving. I pressed my finger against his carotid. No pulse. Two officers from the jail were only seconds behind me. One of them took a look at the two fallen men and raced back inside.

I rolled up my jacket and placed it underneath David's feet. I took off my tie, folded it, and laid it across the wound in his throat. I put my left hand behind his head and held the tie over the wound with my right, trying to keep pressure on it to reduce the bleeding.

"Stay with me, David," I said. "You're going to be okay. Just stay with me until the ambulance gets here." He didn't respond. "David! Please, hang in there. You want to see those grandbabies again, don't you?" His eyes flickered slightly at the mention of his grandchildren, but blood was pouring from the wound and his breath was labored. I didn't think he was going to make it.

Beside me, a young Johnson County deputy rolled Darren onto his back and started CPR. The deputy who'd gone back inside returned with a first-aid kit and three more officers. They helped me replace my tie with a bandage.

"What happened?" one of them said.

"I don't know," I said. "I heard the shots, looked out the window, and they were down."

I held the bandage for what seemed like forever when suddenly, finally, I became aware of sirens; the air seemed to explode with noise and activity. Two ambulances and a crash truck arrived from the EMS station, which was only three blocks away. All of them jumped the curb and pulled to within a few feet of me. Uniformed men and women began to surround me, and I stood and backed off a ways. There was nothing more I could do.

They patched David up as best they could, strapped him onto a gurney, and loaded him into the ambulance. They did the same for Darren, but everybody knew he was already dead.

As they drove away, I stood there in a daze. A thought began to form in my mind, and I instantly felt nauseous.

Had Maynard used me to plan his escape? It was routine for attorneys to help their clients set up jail visits, but I was certain the woman I'd seen helping Maynard get into the car had to be Bonnie Tate. I hadn't actually seen her before, but it had to be her.

I thought about what Maynard said to me that day: *"I ain't saying I want to marry you or nothing, but you're a pretty decent dude."*

Decent dude. I dropped my head and began to trudge back toward the courthouse. My legs felt as heavy as tree trunks. I noticed my hands and shirt were covered with blood, David Bowers's blood. *Decent dude.* As I walked slowly through the courtyard in the bright sunshine on a beautiful July morning in the Tennessee mountains, I felt anything but decent. I felt dirty, and I just wanted it all to end.

JULY 7
11:45 P.M.

Being a single man with a rather large supply of discretionary income, and having had the opportunity to provide certain legal services to Mr. and Mrs. Gus Barlowe in the past, Charles B. Dunwoody III, Esq. saw no harm in occasionally availing himself of the pleasures of the Mouse's Tail Gentlemen's Club. To his closest associates, he privately referred to his adventures at the club as slumming with the naked hillbilly girls. He wasn't always particularly proud of the things he did there, but as he told his country club buddies, "Pardon the pun, but sometimes a gentleman just has to let it all hang out."

Gus Barlowe had sought Dunwoody's advice on a wide range of topics—most of which Dunwoody was not at liberty to discuss. Dunwoody had quickly learned that Mr. Barlowe was an enterprising gentleman who generated large streams of revenue and who required an attorney with a creative mind and a deft touch in order to dissuade curious institutional minds from examining his affairs too closely. Since Dunwoody's academic and legal backgrounds were steeped in corporate law and international banking and finance, he'd been able to satisfactorily accommodate Gus Barlowe's needs. The fact that Barlowe paid handsomely, and paid in cash, only made the relationship more palatable for Dunwoody.

Mrs. Barlowe, who had very capably taken over her husband's affairs since his untimely death, had made the VIP lounge available to him on a Thursday evening in July, and he'd spent two delightful hours with three of the finest-looking floozies he'd ever laid eyes on. Dunwoody had to hand it to Mrs. Barlowe—she had excellent taste when it came to hiring whores. It was getting rather late, and Dunwoody was beginning to wind down. He'd ingested a little more cognac than usual and had made three separate trips to the bullpen. God bless Viagra.

Dunwoody was sitting at the bar in the private room, conversing with a topless bartender named Tina, when Mrs. Barlowe suddenly appeared at his shoulder. They exchanged the usual pleasantries, and she asked him whether they could talk privately for a few moments. Anything for her, Dunwoody said, and they retired to a small booth in the corner. Mrs. Barlowe shooed the girls away, and lawyer and strip-club owner were left alone in the room.

Because Dunwoody had done so much work for her husband, he knew he was sitting across the table from a very wealthy woman, especially if one measured by local standards. He'd never been so crass as to directly ask her late husband how he managed to accumulate such large amounts of cash, but it didn't take a Rhodes scholar to deduce that Barlowe must have been doing something at least marginally illegal. Dunwoody suspected Barlowe was most likely selling narcotics, but so long as he paid Dunwoody's hefty fees and maintained a certain amount of decorum in Dunwoody's presence, the lawyer had no qualms about camouflaging the cash.

"What can I do for you, madam?" Dunwoody said. He thought Mrs. Barlowe a handsome woman. She dressed like a tart and spoke like a farm girl, but she had a sort of crude charm about her, not to mention a delicious body, especially for a woman her age.

"I need some legal advice, sugar."

"Charles B. Dunwoody the third, at your service."

"I'm going to pick up your tab tonight, sweetie pie, so I can retain you for the next little while. I wouldn't want you to think I was trying to take advantage of your good nature."

"You can take advantage of me anytime you like," Dunwoody said. The generous offer came as a pleasant surprise, since he was certain his tab would be in the neighborhood of two thousand dollars. Privacy does have its price sometimes.

Dunwoody must have taken too much Viagra because in spite of the fact that he'd performed brilliantly earlier in the evening during the bullpen sessions, he suddenly found himself strongly attracted to Mrs. Barlowe. She was wearing a low-cut, zebra-striped top that revealed a significant portion of her magnificent breasts. Dunwoody had to force himself not to stare, and he suddenly felt himself getting a chubby. He hoped he wouldn't have to rise quickly from the table.

"I know you don't do criminal work," she said, "but I have a difficult situation on my hands, and I need a sugar plum like you to help me figure out how to handle it."

Sweetie pie and sugar plum. No one had ever referred to Charles Dunwoody in such a manner, and he was not a young man. Mrs. Barlowe was correct in her assertion that Dunwoody did not indulge in the vulgar practice of criminal defense. He believed the arena of criminal defense was reserved for con artists and grandstanders. Nonetheless, any attorney worth his salt who paid attention in law school was well versed in the basics of constitutional law, and as any fool knows, constitutional law is the cornerstone of criminal defense.

"Tell me your predicament," Dunwoody said, "and let's see what we can come up with."

She leaned forward and lowered her voice. Her breasts were resting on the tabletop, which made it a bit difficult for Dunwoody to concentrate.

"I need to know the best way to lead a horse to water and then not let him drink," she said.

Dunwoody began to question her, and before long he was able to ascertain that Mrs. Barlowe was involved in something dicey and was attempting to manipulate a situation that could very well blow up in her face. Nonetheless, the odd couple spent a very pleasant hour together, and by the time Dunwoody left, he was convinced that he'd provided Mrs. Barlowe with some sound legal advice and had given her at least an idea of what she would have to do in order to accomplish her ends.

It wasn't until later that Dunwoody learned Mrs. Barlowe had followed his advice to the letter. He told his closest friends at the country club that he was proud to have been a part of it.

JULY 9
10:50 A.M.

F our sleepless days after Maynard's escape, I attended the funeral of the Bowers twins in Mountain City. I sat outside the church in my truck—the used one I'd bought to replace the truck that had been pushed into the lake—gargling mouthwash and waiting for everyone to get inside. Once they were all in, I slipped in the back. There were at least a hundred police officers there, and I felt like they were all looking at me. As soon as it was over, I left without speaking to anyone.

An hour later, I went through the complicated process of visiting a maximum-security inmate at Northeast Correctional Center just outside Mountain City. Northeast is a bone tossed by the Tennessee legislature fifteen years ago to a rural county that found itself on the brink of economic ruin. The planners of Johnson County had missed an important prerequisite to modern economic survival. They failed to recognize that in order for people to trade in your county or your towns, they need to be able to drive there in less than half a day.

The roads leading to Mountain City were narrow and slow. You couldn't get there from anywhere. As a result, nobody went there. As a result of that, Johnson County couldn't generate any tax revenue and therefore couldn't hire enough police or fund their schools.

But in 1991, the great state of Tennessee was about to embark on a vast expansion of its prison system, and it was looking for victims. They lobbied economically depressed counties, and economically depressed counties lobbied them. With the political stars in perfect alignment, Johnson County, in the heart of the Appalachian Mountains and one of the most scenic places in the whole country, was rewarded with its very own 2,000-bed medium-security concrete prison. Their plans, they said, were to put the inmates to work in a public/private enterprise, a slick mixture of capitalism and communism.

As I passed through the front door of Northeast Correctional Facility, a grand total of eighty of the two thousand inmates were participating in the prison's employment programs. I walked into the reception area and waited for a guard. He asked for my identification, frisked me, and took my photograph. I signed the log book, and he led me across a yard fenced in by twelve-foot chain link topped with concertina. The sky was a vivid blue, and the beauty of the surrounding mountains provided an ironic contrast to the razor wire and concrete.

Once in the communication center, a robotic guard in a black uniform spoke to me through bulletproof glass and demanded my identification. I slipped it into a stainless steel tray. It disappeared, and the guard ordered me to move on. I followed my guide back into the sun-light and down yet another fence-framed sidewalk to the maximum-security unit, which primarily housed inmates who had attacked guards or other inmates.

Many of the hundred men inside the maximum security ward had killed after being imprisoned. They were treated the way you'd treat a dangerous animal—with *extreme* caution. They were kept locked alone in their cells 24/7 except when they were escorted to the shower twice a week. If for any reason they went out, they were cuffed and shackled and trussed. The only way they could communicate was to yell through the slots in the cell door that allowed food to be passed through.

And yell they did.

When I walked through the fourth security check-point and into the cell block, the cacophony began. A man in a suit could mean only a few things to a max-imum-security inmate. Cop, lawyer, or prison admin-istrator. They hated them all. By the time I made the thirty-foot walk into the office where I was to conduct my interview, I'd heard every mama, sister, wife, and daughter insult known to man.

The cell block was two-story, open, and oval-shaped. The guard who sat at the desk had a view of all twenty cells on the block, and they all had a view of him through the tiny windows in the cell doors. The guard, a sturdy young man who looked to be about twenty-five, led me into the office.

"I'll go get him," he said. "Won't take but a minute."

He started to leave, then hesitated and turned back toward me.

"I feel sorry for you," he said.

"Thanks," I said. "So do I."

Maynard Bush had been recaptured four hours after his daring daylight escape from the Johnson County jail. Bonnie Tate's body was found in her car in the parking lot at the Roane Valley golf club. Maynard had apparently gotten what he wanted from her and then shot her to death as soon as she stopped the car and unlocked his cuffs.

After he killed Bonnie, Maynard headed straight for his mother, who'd kicked him out of her home when Maynard was fourteen years old. Mama Bush saw Maynard approaching the house, called the cops, and the cops came running, guns drawn. When they got there, they heard a series of gunshots inside. Maynard wouldn't respond to them. The Tennessee Highway Patrol's SWAT team lobbed tear gas and rushed in an hour later. They found Maynard sitting at the kitchen table, clutching his burned eyes, a half-eaten sandwich sitting on a plate in front of him. His mother's bullet-riddled body was lying less than five feet away. When they asked Maynard why he didn't fight, he said he used up all his bullets on his mama.

I'd spoken to Bernice Bush—Maynard's mother—while preparing for Maynard's trial back in May. She'd been left to raise Maynard alone after his father was carted off to prison for shooting his neighbor during a property-border dispute. The strange thing about it was that Maynard's father was a tenant—he didn't even own the property.

Bernice was a slight, feeble woman of fifty-five who lived in a four-room shack about two miles off Highway 67 in Carter County, not far from the Johnson County line. Her place was as run down as she was. It smelled of dog crap and cigarette smoke. There were plastic bags filled with Keystone beer cans all over the house and the tiny front yard.

Bernice existed on Social Security disability benefits, food stamps, and the prescription drugs provided to her by TennCare, the state's noble but misguided effort at providing health care to indigents. She told me that by the age of fourteen, Maynard had become a drug addict. He kept stealing her nerve pills, she said, and had started experimenting with a street drug called ice. He stopped going to school and was running with what she described as a very rough crowd. Sitting there looking at her, I couldn't imagine a rougher crowd than the one she belonged to.

Bernice said she had an old mutt she called Giggles because of its peculiar bark. When she mentioned the dog, ten years dropped off her face, and her harsh voice softened. One evening fourteen-year-old Maynard came home late and high and sat down on the couch. She went into the room to try to talk to him, but he was rambling and agitated, so she started to go back to bed. Giggles, she said, jumped onto the couch and licked Maynard on the face. Maynard picked the dog up by the scruff of the neck. He carried it, squealing, into the yard at the side of the house, pulled a pistol from his belt, and shot it in the head.

The next morning, after Maynard had sobered up, she gave him a choice: leave or go to jail. He'd been in trouble before and was on probation. They both knew that if she called the law, he'd be shipped off to a juvenile home somewhere. Maynard chose the road. She was glad, she said, because she was afraid if they locked him up she might lose some of her Social Security benefits. He packed up a few things in an old duffel bag and got into a car with some of his friends around three that afternoon. She hadn't seen him since. She hated him, she said. He killed her dog.

About six hours after Maynard was arrested and hauled back in, Judge Glass called my office.

"I want to go ahead and reschedule the first trial as soon as possible," he said, "and you might as well represent him on the new charges. He's got an escape, four counts of first-degree murder, two counts of conspiracy to commit first-degree murder, and four counts of felony murder. You don't mind, do you?"

Did I mind? It may have been the dumbest question ever uttered. Angel's trial was bearing down on me, I was constantly on the lookout for Junior Tester, my mother was dying, my sister was in jail, and I felt at least partially responsible for David and Darren's deaths. And to top things off, I knew if I represented Maynard after he'd killed two well-liked deputy sheriffs, I'd make a bunch of brand-new enemies in Johnson County and probably wind up practicing law for another two years. Did I mind?

"Judge, I told you I don't want any more appointed cases. I'm getting out of this business."

"We've all got problems, Mr. Dillard," he said. "And right now my biggest problem is dealing with this POS.

You're already appointed on the first two, a few more won't hurt you. Make a package deal. Get it over with."

"You're not hearing me, Judge."

"The case law says I can appoint you to a case if I so choose. If you refuse, I can hold you in contempt. Now, you'll either deal with this like a professional, or I'll cite you for contempt and throw you in jail."

"Where are they holding him?" I said. He had me by the balls, and he knew it.

"My understanding is they've moved him up to Northeast, to the max block. We need to get him arraigned as soon as possible, unless you can get him to waive the rule. Do you think you can do that?"

"I have no idea. I'll have to ask him."

"Get up there by Friday."

"I'll go after the funerals," I said.

The sturdy young guard, along with two of his sturdy young buddies, returned with Maynard Bush in tow. He was smirking. There were bruises on his face and arms—I assumed from the police. The guards sat him in a chair across the room from me. There was no way to secure him to the floor, so the guards ran chains through his shackles and around the legs of the chair. That way, if he decided to make a run at me, he'd have to drag the chair with him.

"Do you want us to stay in the room?" one of the guards said.

"No thanks. I've talked to Mr. Bush many times before."

"If you have any problems at all, just holler," he said. "We'll be right outside the door."

I looked over at Maynard sitting there in his striped jumpsuit with MAXIMUM SECURITY emblazoned on the front and the back. He was staring at nothing in particular with that disgusting smirk on his face.

"You've been a busy boy," I said.

"Appreciate the help," he said.

"You son of a bitch. You used me."

"You're right about both things, counselor. My mama was a bitch, and I played you. Don't worry about it though. I played everybody. Why do you think I wanted that change of venue so bad? I knew them crackers in Mountain City wouldn't have good security."

"Why, Maynard?" I said. "Why did you have to go and do something so stupid?"

"Been wanting to plug that worthless old hag for twenty years. I shoulda done it when I was a kid. The only thing I regret is that I didn't have more time with her. I was looking forward to seeing her suffer."

"Is that the only reason you broke out? So you could kill your mother?"

He smiled.

"And the Tate woman? Why?"

He shrugged his shoulders. "She got the drop on them deputies, handed me the gun, and then drove me out of there, just like I told her. She was as responsible as me for them getting killed. I didn't figure she'd like it in jail, so I did her a favor. Besides, I didn't need her no more."

"So now you've got four more counts of murder," I said. "The two deputies, Bonnie Tate, and your mother."

"I know how many was killed. I can count."

"The judge wants to try you for the teenagers first, then the police officers, then Bonnie, and then your mother, but they have a little problem. The law says they have to arraign you on these charges as soon as possible. Normally they do it within seventy-two hours of your arrest, but with your security situation, they have some leeway. I have a waiver here I need you to sign. It gives them up to thirty days to arraign you on the new charges, but they'll probably do it in the next week or two. You don't have to sign it, but you might as well. You're eventually going to end up on death row anyway."

I pulled the document from my briefcase and stood to approach him. He was trussed up like a chicken, but I'd be lying if I said I wasn't apprehensive. I set my briefcase on his thighs and put the pen in his right hand. He scrawled his signature on the line.

"They can't kill me but once, you know," he said.

"Are you finished now, Maynard? You've killed your mother. Is that enough? Or are you going to kill anybody you can kill between now and the time they stick a needle in your arm?"

"You ain't gonna have to worry about me much longer."

"Why? You contemplating suicide?"

"Nah, I like myself too much for that. But they'll get me in here, Dillard. You mark my words."

"Who?"

"I killed two cops in this county. You think they're about to let me live?"

"You're in a max block, in case you haven't noticed. Nobody can get to you in here."

"The guards can. I won't make it another week. But that's all right. I've lived my life, and now I got my revenge."

I walked to the door and opened it, and the three sturdy young guards stepped in. They took Maynard back, and I ran the gauntlet of catcalls again on my way out. Once I was clear of the max unit, I thought about what Maynard had said. The chances that Darren and David Bowers had friends and relatives working at the prison were good. For a moment, I thought I should do something, maybe file a motion and have Maynard transferred out of Johnson County for his own protection. Then I thought about the argument I'd have to assert—that it was likely the guards at Northeast would conspire to murder him. I imagined myself making that argument in front of Judge Glass. He'd throw me under the jail.

Maynard, I decided, was on his own.

JULY 10
9:45 A.M.

Agent Landers looked down at his ringing cell phone, then over at the naked blonde lying next to him. His head was throbbing again. The woman wasn't nearly as young as she looked last night. Must have been the bad lighting in the bar. Or the whiskey.

He was supposed to have the rest of the week off. He and Bull Deakins were planning to drive down to Hotlanta for a couple days. They were going to catch a Braves game and visit the Golden Pony, maybe round up a couple fillies and ride them for a night or two.

The phone number on the caller ID was the district attorney's. Damn. He pulled a sheet up over the woman's head so that he didn't have to look at her and answered the call.

"Landers."

"Phil, it's Frankie Martin. We have a serious problem. Our only witness against Angel Christian is dead."

Deacon Baker had assigned the Angel Christian case to Martin, who was only four years out of law school and had never tried a murder case. Martin didn't know it, but Deacon was setting him up to be a scapegoat. If the case went south, Martin might as well pack the suntan lotion because he'd end up going south with it.

"Julie Hayes?" Landers said. "How?"

"They found her at her place yesterday afternoon. She didn't show up for work, so Erlene Barlowe sent one of her gofers over to check on her. She was dead on the kitchen floor. The Washington County investigator who worked the scene said it looked like she might have been poisoned, so I asked the medical examiner to rush the preliminary autopsy. M.E. says she was full of cocaine and strychnine."

Landers had heard of lacing cocaine with strychnine at a DEA seminar. It was a relatively simple process that produced an agonizing death.

"Any ideas on who might have done it?" Landers said.

"I certainly have a candidate in mind."

"You think it was Erlene Barlowe?"

"Hell yeah I do. Who else would kill her?"

"You think she killed her to keep her from testifying against Angel? I think you're reaching, Frankie. Why would she risk murdering somebody to help Angel out? The kid had only been around a couple months when we arrested her. Barlowe barely knows her."

"At this point, I think Barlowe probably murdered the preacher too."

"Then why would she kill a witness who was about to help us convict someone else? Doesn't make any sense. And in case you haven't looked close, we have less on

Barlowe than we do on Angel." Landers hated working with kid lawyers. They were too dumb to live.

"Deacon told me this morning about the witness who saw Barlowe on the bridge," Martin said.

"Do you know what Deacon told *me* about that witness? He said the guy was unreliable. He said there was no way he could have made an ID like that in the dark. He said for me to ignore him."

"What are we going to do, Phil? This case was weak enough with Hayes. Without her, I might as well dismiss it."

"I wasn't hot to take it to the grand jury in the first place. You can thank your boss for that. He said he wanted to shake the tree."

"Him and his damned tree. Dillard's going to kick my butt. I'm going to be a laughingstock. Every newspaper and television station within fifty miles is covering this case, and everybody around is going to be watching while I go down. There's an election coming up, and in case you guys over there at the TBI don't pay attention to stuff like that, losing a high-profile murder case a week before an election is not good politics. Baker will fire me over this."

"It's not going to help my career either, Frankie."

"Why didn't we have her tucked away as a material witness?"

"Because she never gave me any indication she was going anywhere."

"Did you know she was a coke head?"

"I had my suspicions." Landers felt a hand running up his leg and pushed it away. It returned, and he pushed it away again. He was thinking about how much he hated lawyers, prosecutors included. Every time something went wrong with a case, they blamed it on the police. He also hated aging bleached blondes like the one next to him. He wished she'd just get up and leave.

"We need to try to make the best of this," Frankie said. "I talked to Deacon a little while ago, and we've come up with a plan. We're going to make Dillard an offer he can't refuse on the Christian case, but if it doesn't work, we're going to need your help."

"I have the rest of the week off, Frankie. Call me on Monday."

Landers hung up and turned to the woman, who was peeking out over the sheet. Her left eyelash was twice as long as her right one, which must have come off during the sexcapades last night. No doubt he'd find it in the bed later. Ugh. The roots of her blond hair were dark and so was the mole just above her left nostril. Landers had absolutely no clue what her name might be.

"Get up," he said. "Time to go."

"Don't you want to play some more?"

"Get up and get out."

The woman began to collect her clothing, which was spread out across the floor between the bed and the door. She was naked, and as Landers watched her, he wished she'd cover herself. The backs of her thighs were layered with cellulite, and her butt sagged and jiggled. When she straightened to look at Landers, he decided she had to be well into her forties. Landers liked younger women, much younger women. Jesus, how much did he drink? He pulled the sheet over his head and leaned back.

"You can dress downstairs, on your way out," Landers said. He was beginning to feel sick.

He heard her walking toward the bedroom door and pulled the sheet back down so he could take one last look at her and remind himself why he shouldn't drink so much. As she opened the door, she turned to face him.

"You're a lousy lay," she said, and then she was gone.

Lousy lay, my ass. Landers needed to take a shower. He threw back the sheet, and there it was. The false eyelash, about an inch from his thigh. It looked like a freaking centipede. Landers felt his stomach heave. He made it to the bathroom just in time.

JULY 11
7:00 A.M.

We'd brought furniture up from Ma's house when we moved her into the nursing home: a dresser, a couple small tables, a lamp and a chair, thinking it might help ease the transition and make her more comfortable. I spent an entire afternoon hanging and arranging photographs. One of my dad in his high school football uniform was hanging just to the right of the television. She'd asked me to place it there so that she could look at it from the bed. Now she didn't even know who he was.

I arrived at 7:00 a.m. to find her lying on her back staring at nothing. She hadn't spoken in weeks, and she'd wet herself and was drooling. The saliva had run out the corner of her mouth and soaked her pillow case. I dug a fresh one out of the closet, then went and found a nurse's aide. I waited in the hallway while she changed Ma's diaper. I couldn't bear to do it myself.

When she was finished, I walked back into the room and sat down. Ever since the day I told her about

Raymond, I'd gotten into the habit of talking to her, even though she was oblivious to everything I said. I'd turned my visits into mini-therapy sessions without the shrink. Mostly, I talked about my cases and the constant state of conflict in which I found myself.

"Just my luck, huh Ma?" I said. "I get a case with a client who's innocent, and the victim's son turns out to be a psychopath. Everybody in the family's scared to death. We check to make sure the doors and windows are locked every night. I've got guns spread out all over the house. We all spend half our time looking in rear-view mirrors and over our shoulders. It's crazy.

"But you know what? The whole system is crazy. For over ten years, I've been traveling every day to this bizarre world of lies and deceit. There's no honor in it anywhere. It's all just a sick game, and the people who win the most are the ones who lie the best. They call it the criminal *justice* system. What a crock. Defendants lie and cheat, police officers lie and cheat, prosecutors lie and cheat, defense lawyers lie and cheat, and judges—Jesus, don't get me started. The American legal system would do itself a great service if it could somehow execute half the sitting judges in this country and start all over again—"

My cell phone rang. It was Caroline.

"Deacon Baker just called. They found Julie Hayes dead at her house yesterday. He wants you to come down there. He wants to talk about a deal."

I leaned over and kissed my mother on the forehead, something I never did when she was conscious.

"Love you, Ma. I have to go, but I'm glad we had this little talk. Next time I'll tell you about Maynard Bush."

JULY 11
9:00 A.M.

Deacon Baker and Frankie Martin were waiting for me in the conference room. There were a couple plastic plants sitting on small tables in two of the corners, and the walls were lined with bookshelves stuffed with outdated law books and police magazines. The ceilings were low, and I noticed that mildew had formed in the corners. The lighting was almost as bad as the lighting at the jail.

"Mr. Dillard," Baker said as I walked in, "I trust you know my assistant, Frankie Martin?"

"I do." I shook hands with each of them and took a seat at the long table with my back to the wall. Baker and Martin sat across from me. Baker looked like an oompa-loompa from *Willie Wonka and the Chocolate Factory*. He was short, plump, and bald, and he always wore suspenders. He was also smoking a fat cigar, despite the fact that smoking wasn't allowed in the building. The smell and the smoke were sickening.

"Ready for trial?" I said. "Sorry about your witness." I couldn't resist.

"Of course we are," Baker said. "We have plenty of evidence without her."

"I understand you gentlemen would like to talk about a plea bargain."

"That's right," Baker said. "Let's try to be honest with each other. Perhaps we can put the posturing aside."

Plea bargaining was entirely about posturing. There was no way anyone was going to "put it aside."

"We have a strong case," Baker said, "but I've given this a great deal of thought and I don't think the case is appropriate for the death penalty. We might be willing to take it off the table in exchange for a plea."

So much for honesty. Their case was anything but strong, especially now that Julie Hayes was dead.

"What do you have in mind?" I said.

"Twenty years, second-degree murder."

"Not a chance. Not on the evidence I've seen. Surely you didn't bring me all the way down here for that."

"Make a counteroffer," Baker said.

"I've given it some thought too," I said. "The way I see it, you had a weak circumstantial case before your most important witness died, and you've got an unappealing victim. You're going to have to spend a great deal of time at trial proving that your preacher went to a strip club. Then I assume you're going to try to prove he solicited a prostitute, since you're going to introduce evidence about the money he withdrew from his bank account right before he left. I don't think the jury will have much sympathy for him, and I'll do everything I can to make sure they don't."

"Let's assume he was, as you say, there to solicit a prostitute," Martin said. "That doesn't mean he deserved to be brutally murdered and mutilated. The jury is going to want to see someone pay for that."

"I'm sure they will," I said. "But not Angel. I don't think she did it, and you can't prove she did. Barlowe could have killed him, any of the other girls at the club could have killed him, he could have gone somewhere else and picked up someone else, or someone could have been waiting for him when he got back to the room. Hell, it could have been anybody, and you know it."

"Nobody else's hair was found in that room," Baker said. "Only your client's."

"If they'd found the hair in the bathroom or on the headboard or even on the floor it would be different. But they found it on his clothing. It's entirely possible that her hair passed to him when she was serving him booze at the club and he was rubbing up against her. And the only way you could possibly make the jury even *suspect* Angel was at the motel was through Julie Hayes, and she's gone."

"We have plenty of other evidence," Baker said.

"I know what other evidence you have, Deacon. And I know what I have. I was planning to surprise you with this, but since we're not posturing, I have a witness who says he saw a woman fitting Erlene Barlowe's description on Picken's Bridge around midnight the night of the murder. His name is Virgil Watterson. I believe you've heard of him."

Baker flushed. It apparently hadn't entered his feeble mind that Watterson might take his testimony to the defense attorney, and Landers obviously hadn't said anything about our conversation at the courthouse.

"That testimony has no credibility," he said. "All the witness saw was a woman on a bridge in the middle of the night. He can't make a positive ID and he wasn't even sure about the color of the vehicle."

"Bull," I said. "You know as well as I do that if anyone from that club killed Tester, it was most likely Erlene Barlowe." I felt a twinge of guilt as I said it. After all, Erlene had paid me a handsome sum of cash, but my job was to represent Angel. I couldn't concern myself with Erlene.

"I can't prove that," Baker said.

"You can't prove Angel killed him either."

"So where does that leave us?" Baker looked like he was ready to say "uncle."

"We're willing to roll the dice."

"What would it take to resolve this case without a trial? Make some kind of reasonable counteroffer."

This was the tricky part. If Angel was innocent, I wanted her to walk away without any strings, but the only way to do that was to win in front of a jury, and winning murder cases in front of juries was easier said than done. I also knew Deacon. Like most prosecutors, he wasn't going to admit that he'd made a mistake and dismiss the case outright. I knew I'd have to give him *something* in order to make a deal and remove the risk that Angel might be found guilty and sentenced to life in prison or death.

"She might be willing to enter a no contest plea to some offense so long as you agree to probation," I said. "She's already served more jail time than she should have."

"You don't really think she's innocent, do you?" Frankie said.

"As a matter of fact, I do. She has no history of criminal behavior, no drug or alcohol use, no history of psychological problems"—a white lie—"and she seems very gentle. I don't think she did it. And I'll tell you something else. She's going to be a helluva good witness. You know how pretty she is, and she comes across as sincere."

"Probation is impossible," Baker said. "I can't reduce a death-penalty case to a probatable offense. I'd look like a fool."

"You can sell it, Deacon," I said. "Think about it. You announce to the court that an important witness has passed away and that the investigation has revealed some things you can't divulge, but those things convince you that the plea agreement best serves the interests of justice. You tell the press your job as district attorney is to see that justice is done, not just to try to win at all costs. Then you build a case on Erlene Barlowe and get it right. You could come out of it looking like a hero, and believe me, you won't hear a bit of criticism out of me. I'll tell the press the district attorney has done the right thing and that you acted in good faith throughout the entire course of this tragic situation. I'll publicly sing your praises a couple weeks before the election."

Baker sat back and removed the cigar from his lips. He looked at Martin, then at me. A crooked smile began to form on his lips.

"You're devious," he said.

"I'm just trying to grease the wheel," I said. "Win-win. My girl goes home, and you look like a good guy.

We'll take three years of probation on aggravated assault. You'll have her under your thumb for three years. If she screws up, she serves the sentence."

"I have to think about it," Baker said.

"What are you going to do about Tester's son?" I said.

"Screw him. From what I hear, he got fired from his job at the sheriff's department. Besides, he's not a registered voter in this county. I'm not even going to tell him about this."

I stood to leave. "I don't want to sound arrogant, Deacon, but if you take this to trial, you're going to lose. She didn't kill him."

Baker was silent, apparently lost in thought.

"We'll see about that," Martin said.

"Call me and let me know what you decide," I said. "I'll be getting ready for trial."

The call came two hours later.

"She can plead to aggravated assault as Range I and take the minimum, three years," Frankie Martin said.

"It will have to be a no contest plea, and you'll have to agree to probation," I said.

"Fine."

"Deacon is going to sell it?"

"He's already working the phones," Martin said. "He'll hold a press conference after the plea and explain why we agreed to this."

I hung up the phone and went down to talk to my client.

JULY 14
9:00 A.M.

A s Judge Green made his entrance and sat down beneath his portrait, I glanced around the courtroom. The jury box was once again filled with members of the media who'd been called by Deacon Baker. I was edgy and tired. I'd spent most of Sunday night troubled by Angel's willingness to take this deal. I told myself that the plea took nearly all the risk off the table, guaranteed her release from custody, and spared her the ordeal of a trial. But I also knew that if I'd been accused of a crime I hadn't committed, nothing would persuade me to stand up and accept a three-year sentence, probation or no probation. Angel hadn't needed much persuasion.

"I understand we have a plea in case number 35666, State of Tennessee versus Angel Christian," Judge Green said. "Bring the defendant in."

Angel appeared through the doorway to my right, and I smiled at her as I walked to the podium. She looked away. I thought she'd forgiven me for being so hard on her the day I questioned her about Erlene, but maybe not.

"Let me see the forms," Judge Green said.

I'd taken plea-agreement forms along with me when I explained the deal to Angel, and she'd signed them. I now handed them to the bailiff, who in turn handed them to Judge Green. The judge didn't allow lawyers to approach the bench to hand him forms or other evidence. He insisted that everything be passed forward through the bailiff, as though he was repulsed by the idea of having to deal directly with a lowly lawyer.

Judge Green studied the documents for a few minutes. His brow furrowed. When he was finished, he looked over at Frankie Martin and Deacon Baker, both of whom were staring straight ahead.

"Would you care to explain this to me, Mr. Baker?"

"Explain what, Your Honor?"

"The state is reducing a first-degree murder charge to an aggravated assault. You're agreeing to probation. Did your victim somehow miraculously come back to life?"

"No, Your Honor. He's still dead." The reporters laughed. I thought about Junior Tester, and for a moment, I actually felt sorry for him.

"Then why are you allowing this woman to plead as though the victim were still alive?" Green said.

"I think it's clear we have some problems with the case, Your Honor. This is a compromise plea agreement. An important witness has passed away. There are also some things that have come up in the investigation, things I'm not at liberty to discuss at this time, that convince me that this plea agreement is in everyone's best interests."

"Why don't you just dismiss the case?" Judge Green said. "You can always refile it if another witness pops up or if your other problems are resolved. There's no statute of limitations on murder."

"We think this is a better way to resolve it. Mr. Dillard's client is willing to enter a no contest plea to aggravated assault."

"No, I'm not." The soft voice came directly from my right.

Judge Green turned his attention toward me.

"Did your client say something, Mr. Dillard?"

"I think so." I looked at Angel. "What did you say?"

"I don't want to do this. I changed my mind."

Baker stood. "But we had a deal—"

"Be quiet," Judge Green said. "Mr. Dillard, what's going on?"

"I'd be happy to explain it if I knew," I said. "When I spoke to Ms. Christian on Friday afternoon, she seemed pleased. She's apparently changed her mind."

"You're wasting my time," the judge said. "I don't like it when people waste my time."

"This is a complete surprise," I said. "If you'll give me a few minutes to talk to her, maybe we can straighten this out."

"Don't bother," Judge Green said.

"Your Honor," Baker said, "Mr. Dillard and I reached a compromise agreement that brings what I believe to be a fair and satisfactory end to this very difficult case."

"It sounds like Mr. Dillard's client has other ideas."

"But she signed the forms," Deacon said. "She—"

"It's not a *contract*, Mr. Baker. She can change her mind if she wants to. Her plea has to be willing and voluntary, and she obviously is no longer willing. I might have rejected it anyway, but it appears she's saved me the trouble. Looks like we're going to trial after all, gentlemen. Court's in recess."

Green was almost jaunty as he stepped off the bench. He had to know that Deacon wouldn't have made such a lousy deal if his case was strong, and if Deacon's case wasn't strong, that meant he might lose just before the election. If he lost the case, he'd probably lose the election, and Judge Green would be rid of him.

I went back to the jury room and asked the bailiff to give Angel and me some privacy. She sat down at the table and wouldn't look at me.

"What's going on?" I said. "I thought you were happy with this."

"I changed my mind," she said.

"Have you talked to Erlene?" She didn't answer. "I'll take that as a yes. So Erlene told you not to take this plea?"

"She thinks you're going to win."

"I appreciate the confidence, but you're taking a big risk."

"You will win, won't you? I'm innocent. Promise me you'll win."

I didn't say anything. I wished I could promise, but I'd been through enough trials to know that I could never predict the outcome.

"We go to trial two weeks from today," I said. "I'll be ready. I'll come to the jail and we'll go over everything again. Are you sure about this?"

"Not really," she said.

I had to admire her courage, even though I thought it might be a bit on the reckless side. But what was more important was that I'd heard the magic words again: *I'm innocent.* Once again, I believed her.

JULY 14
11:45 A.M.

Landers quickly found out what Frankie Martin had meant when he said he and Deacon would need Landers's help if Dillard didn't accept the "offer he can't refuse." Less than an hour after the plea bargain fell apart, Deacon had called Landers and asked him to come down to the D.A.'s office. When Landers walked into Deacon's office and sat down, they told him they'd decided to go to Plan B, which was to try to get Dillard's sister to help them by snitching on Angel.

"I thought of that a month ago," Landers said. "I already took a run at her. She turned me down, but I was planning to go back. Her attitude might be different now that Judge Glass threw the book at her."

"Great minds think alike," Baker said. He'd thought of approaching Dillard's sister as soon as he heard about the six-year sentence. "Have they shipped her off to the penitentiary yet?"

"Nah. It's so crowded they don't have a bed for her yet. She's on a waiting list. The jail administrator told me she'd probably be around another month or so."

"I don't like using jailhouse snitches, but in this case, it looks like we don't have much choice," Baker said. "All the polls my people have taken say the election is going to be close. I can't afford to lose this trial."

"What if she won't go for it?"

"She'll go for it. We'll offer to let her out as soon as the trial's over."

"What about Judge Green? He'll never agree."

"Screw him. I'll get Judge Glass to sign the agreement. He's the one who put her in jail, and he hates Dillard. He'd love the idea of Dillard's sister getting on the stand and frying one of Dillard's clients. He'll probably come to court and watch."

Landers smiled. "Not bad," he said.

"I didn't get elected to this position by being stupid."

Landers thought of a couple wiseass responses to the comment, but chose to keep his mouth shut. He rose to leave.

"Wait just a second, Phil," Baker said. "There's one more thing we need to discuss."

Baker didn't come right out and say it, but over the next few minutes, he made it clear to Landers that he didn't care whether Dillard's sister told the truth in court or not. He said he needed "direct testimony that Angel Christian confessed to Sarah Dillard that Angel killed John Paul Tester." Landers was authorized to offer Sarah a get-out-of-jail-free card in return for her "truthful" testimony.

The more Landers thought about the idea of Dillard's sister as the star witness against Dillard's client, the more he liked it. He couldn't wait to see the look on Dillard's face when his sister stepped up on the witness stand and helped the state convict Angel Christian of murder. And Dillard would have to go after sis hard on cross-examination. What a great show *that* would be.

Since Baker gave Landers the impression he wasn't going to be too particular about the truth, Landers figured he'd make the process a little easier. Before they brought Dillard's sister into the interview room at the jail, he sat down and wrote out a statement, wording it in the way Landers thought would help the most. If Sarah Dillard signed the statement, Landers would leave her a copy and she could use her time in the cell to memorize it. Then, when she took the witness stand at the trial, all she'd have to do was repeat what she'd memorized. It would be perfect.

Landers looked up and smiled when the guard brought Sarah in. She nodded in return, a good sign. She looked pretty hot.

"I thought it might be you," she said.

"I hear you're about to be shipped off to the pen. Bet you're looking forward to that."

"About as much as I'm looking forward to my next enema."

"I heard what your brother did to you. It's a cryin' shame. I don't see how anybody could send their own flesh and blood to a place like the women's prison in Nashville. Doesn't he know how bad it is down there?"

"He doesn't seem to care."

"And how does that make you feel?"

"Pissed off."

"Pissed off enough to help us?"

"What's in it for me?"

"In exchange for your testimony, your sentence will be reduced to time served, plus you get to make your brother look bad."

She sat back and thought about it, but it didn't take her long. She took a deep breath and looked Landers in the eye.

"Tell me what you want me to do," she said.

Landers slid the statement across the table, and she started to read.

JULY 16
9:20 A.M.

Maynard Bush's arraignment on the new charges of killing Bonnie Tate and the Bowers twins in Mountain City had taken only fifteen minutes, but it was fifteen of the most intense minutes of my life. The courtroom was packed with relatives and friends of Darren and David Bowers. Judge Glass was at his most belligerent, Maynard at his most flippant. He wouldn't stop smiling. I wanted to crawl under the defense table and hide until it was over.

The people of Johnson County didn't understand that I'd been appointed to represent Maynard Bush by a heartless judge who dumped terrible cases on me for his private amusement. What they understood was that I was dressed in a suit, standing beside and speaking on behalf of a sociopath who'd killed two of their own. If they'd known that Maynard had manipulated me into helping him, they'd have strung me up right then and there.

I'd parked my truck a block from the courthouse in an alley. As soon as the arraignment was over, I grabbed my briefcase and headed straight for the back stairs. Once I got to the bottom, I jogged across the spot where David Bowers was shot, got to my truck as quickly as I could, and drove the hell out of Johnson County.

Judge Glass's plan was to arraign Maynard in Mountain City in the morning and in Elizabethton—for the murder of his mother in Carter County—in the afternoon. The two towns were forty-five minutes apart. Under normal circumstances, I would've enjoyed the drive. The road wound through the Cherokee National Forest and along Watauga Lake, which acted as a gigantic mirror for the surrounding mountains. The views were breathtaking. There were times in the past when I might have stopped along the way to take in the scenery, but I didn't even notice.

I drove all the way back home and went through the mail. There was an opinion from the Supreme Court on Randall Finch's case. The opinion said Randall had a right to plead guilty at arraignment, and if the state hadn't bothered to file their death notice in a timely manner, too bad. I couldn't believe it. I'd won. For once, they put the sophistry aside and used a little common sense. I was pleased until I thought about what I'd really done—helped a baby killer escape the death penalty.

I returned a few phone calls and drove over to Elizabethton. I tried to eat lunch at a coffee shop on Main Street, but I only picked at the food. Ever since Maynard had killed the Bowers twins, I'd lost my appetite. Food made me nauseous. And I was having trouble making myself work out. Exercise had always been an important part of my daily life. Exercise produced endorphins, and endorphins made me feel good. But I didn't seem to care about feeling good. I was having more trouble sleeping than ever, and when I looked at myself in the mirror in the mornings, I noticed circles under my eyes that seemed to be getting darker with each passing day.

After I paid the check at the coffee shop, I headed for the Carter County Courthouse, a truly unique structure. I don't know who the architect was, but the taxpayers should have taken him out and shot him the day he decided it would be a good idea to build the jail directly above the courthouse. It may have seemed like a grand idea at the time, but the reality soon set in. The inmates quickly realized that they could flood the jail by stuffing rolls of toilet paper into the commodes. They also realized that the raw sewage overflowing and spilling onto the floors soon seeped into the courtrooms and clerks' offices below. I could imagine some inmate having just been sentenced to ten years heading back to his cell and dropping a little dump of his own onto the judge below. It happened often enough that the place smelled like an outhouse.

When I pulled into the parking lot, I saw an ambulance with its lights flashing near the sally port at the jail. There were also several patrol cars, all with their lights flashing. Somehow, I knew what had happened. Instead of heading inside to the smelly courtroom, I parked and walked directly toward the ambulance.

They were bringing someone out on a gurney just as I turned up the sidewalk toward the sally port. Several police officers were milling around the door that led to the jail. A short, burly female paramedic with bright orange spiked hair was pushing the gurney. It was obvious that whoever was on the gurney was dead. A blood-soaked sheet had been pulled over the head.

"Step back, sir," the paramedic said as I approached.

"Is that Maynard Bush?"

"You need to step away and mind your own—"

I reached down and snatched the sheet back from the head. Maynard's eyes were wide open, frozen in what must have been a last moment of terror. His tongue was black and swollen and sticking out of his mouth at a macabre angle. There was a dark bruise across his throat. I'd seen enough ligature marks to know what it meant. Maynard had hung himself, or, more likely, someone had hung him.

The orange-headed paramedic was glaring at me. I flipped the sheet back up over Maynard's head and glared back.

"He was right," was all I could think of to say. "He was right."

I walked into the courthouse to tell Judge Glass I was leaving. He didn't bother to thank me for representing Maynard or say anything about Maynard's death. He just nodded his head and grunted. When I got back out to the parking lot, I noticed Caroline's car backed in next to my truck. The door opened and she stepped out. Her eyes were red and puffy.

"I'm so sorry to have to tell you this, baby" she said. "The nursing home called right after you left. Your mother died a little while ago."

JULY 17
10:20 A.M.

We went up to the nursing home to clear out Ma's room the day after she died. Jack had flown in on a red-eye the night before, and he helped me carry the furniture out to the truck. Then Caroline and I went to the funeral home while Jack and Lilly took the furniture back over to Ma's house. A tall, slim, bespectacled man who spoke in a quiet voice with a slight lisp showed us into the room where the caskets were kept.

About twenty caskets were spread around the room, mahogany and teak and oak and stainless steel. The man led us first to a round table in the corner.

"Please, have a seat," he said. "Can I offer you something to drink? Some cookies, perhaps?"

Cookies. I didn't want any cookies. I gave him a look that would have silenced most people, but he just smiled. He set a pad of paper down on the table and produced a pen.

"I've read a lot about you, Mr. Dillard," he said, "but I didn't know your mother. Tell me about her."

"Why?" I knew he didn't care about her or me. He just wanted to get as much money out of me as he could.

"We take the responsibility of contacting the newspaper on your behalf for the obituary," the man said. "I just need some basic information. Try to think of all the good things you remember about your mother."

"She was a tough woman. She raised my sister and me all by herself after my father was killed in Vietnam. She worked as a bookkeeper for a roofing company and did other people's laundry for extra money. She wouldn't accept help from anyone. She didn't say much and thought the world was a terrible place. How's that?"

"Where did she go to church?"

"She didn't believe in God. She thought the Christian religion was a global scam set up to control people and extract money from them by making them feel guilty. Do you think they'll print that?"

"Did she have brothers and sisters?"

"One brother. A jerk who drowned in the Nolichucky River when he was seventeen."

"And her parents?"

"Both dead."

"Would you excuse us for a minute?" Caroline said. She reached over and took my hand and led me out the door into the lobby.

"Why don't you let me handle this?" she said.

"I hate these jerks. Preying on other people's misery."

"You look tired. Why don't you go out to the car and nap while I finish up here?"

"I can't sleep in a bed. What makes you think I'll be able to sleep in the car?"

"Please? Just try to relax. You'll feel better. I'll be out as soon as I can."

I was beginning to think I was going insane. I'd been half-jokingly telling myself I was nuts for years, but with everything that had happened over the late spring and summer, beginning with Sarah's release from jail and subsequent return, I'd found myself falling deeper and deeper into a mental abyss. No sleep. No appetite. No exercise. Nothing seemed to give me pleasure anymore, not even music. My attitude was becoming more and more fatalistic and hopeless. I had no enthusiasm, and no particular interest in anything, including sex. It was as though I'd become a passionless robot, simply existing from day to day without feeling.

I went back out to the car and sat in the passenger seat for a while. I closed my eyes a few times, but I couldn't doze. I finally wrote Caroline a note, got out of the car, and started walking toward home. It was at least seven miles and my legs felt like lead, but I thought the exercise might help and it would give me some time to try to sort things out. At first, I tried to force myself to think pleasant thoughts. I envisioned Jack hitting home runs, Lilly dancing across the stage, Caroline's jubilation when I brought her a quarter of a million dollars in a gym bag. ...

But after only a few minutes of walking, my mind began to flash images that were much more sinister, the same images I was seeing when I tried to go to sleep night after night. Johnny Wayne Neal being gagged and dragged out of the courtroom. The bubbles rising in the headlights of my truck the night Junior Tester pushed me into the lake. The look in Tester's eyes when he said I'd taken his daddy from him. The fantasy of clubbing him to death. The bruise on Angel Christian's face in the photograph. David Bowers's blood on my shirt. Maynard's smirk, and the terrible image of his tongue sticking out of his mouth. My mother, wearing a diaper and lying helpless in a hospital bed with spittle running down her chin. And finally, Sarah. Always Sarah, when she was young and innocent. *"Get him off of me, Joey. He's hurting me."*

By the time Caroline rolled up next to me and pushed the passenger door open about two miles from home, I'd reached an entirely new level of self-loathing. I hated myself for putting Sarah in jail and for not being able to break through with Ma. I hated myself for helping monsters like Maynard Bush and Randall Finch and Billy Dockery and a long list of others. I was a whore, a pathetic excuse for a human being.

"I love you, Joe," Caroline said as soon as I got into the car. Caroline is intuitive, especially when it comes to dealing with me. I knew what she was trying to do, but the words bounced off me like a rubber ball off concrete. I didn't feel a thing.

"Did you hear me? I said I love you."

"I know."

"Do you know how much your children love you? Jack worships the ground you walk on. Lilly thinks you're the greatest man who ever lived."

"Please, Caroline, don't. Not right now. I'm in no mood to be patronized."

"What are you thinking? What's wrong with you?"

"You don't want to know what I'm thinking."

"Your mother just died, baby. You're grieving."

"My mother and I weren't even close. All those years, all that time together. I grew up in her house. She *raised* me, Caroline, and I can't remember a single meaningful conversation between us. Do you know what I was thinking a little while ago? In four years of high school, I played in over forty football games, over a hundred basketball games and over a hundred baseball games, and she never came to a single one. She never saw me play. Not once."

"You've been through a lot in the past few months," she said. "We've all been through a lot."

We rode the rest of the way home in silence. Jack distracted me for a couple hours by taking me out to his old high school baseball field. I didn't hear her say anything, but I felt sure it was at Caroline's suggestion. I'd bought a pitching machine a couple years earlier, and I fed balls into the machine while Jack pounded them over the fence. Watching him hit a baseball was a truly beautiful thing to me. He was so quick, so powerful, so fluid. He was so much better than I ever was, and watching him gave me more pleasure than I'd had in months. The sun and the exercise felt good, and by the time we got back to the house, I was feeling a little better.

But then the night came, and with it, another bout of sleepless self-flagellation. We drove to the cemetery at eleven the next morning. I felt like a dead man walking when we climbed the hill to the gravesite. It was overcast and drizzling rain. There was a crowd of people there. I sensed their presence, but I couldn't really see them.

It was as though they were all standing in a bank of thick fog.

And then I caught a glimpse of Sarah. Caroline had called the sheriff's department and made arrangements for them to bring her to the funeral. She arrived in the back of a cruiser, wearing an orange jail jumpsuit and handcuffs and shackles. The deputy who brought her up wouldn't let her under the tent with Caroline, Lilly, Jack, and me, so she ended up having to stand outside with the others in the rain.

Caroline had contacted Ma's best friend, a woman named Katie Lowe, to give the eulogy. I sat there, not really listening, until she began to talk about Elizabeth's children. I heard some things about my mother that I hadn't known before, things that Ma had told Katie about Sarah and me. One of them was that Ma had been so proud of me when I graduated from law school that she cried. I'd never seen my mother cry, and I'd never heard her say a word about being proud of me.

When the service was over, the deputy took Sarah by the arm and led her straight back down the hill. I watched as she climbed awkwardly into the backseat of the cruiser. I felt tears forming in my eyes as the cruiser pulled away, and I turned to Ma's casket. I put my palms on it and stood there, not knowing what to say or do, embarrassed to be showing weakness in front of my children. I stood there until the crowd had dispersed, and then, for some reason I didn't understand, I felt the impulse to bend down and kiss her casket. I'd kissed her at the nursing home, but not until she was too far gone to feel it. When I kissed her casket, I realized that I hadn't ever given her a meaningful kiss. The thought made it almost impossible to keep from breaking down.

I leaned against the casket with my shoulders shaking and tried to compose myself. *She's gone and you're still here*, I said to myself. *She's gone and you're still here. You're alive. You have people who love you. Stop feeling sorry for yourself. ...*

Stop feeling sorry for yourself. It was a phrase I'd heard many times, straight from my mother's mouth, and as I stood there leaning against her casket, I knew I had to try. The same people who loved me also depended on me for strength and support. I couldn't let them down.

"Goodbye, Ma," I whispered. "I'm sorry."

I took a deep breath, straightened up, wiped the tears from my face with the back of my hand, and lifted my chin. I put one arm around Caroline and the other around Lilly, and nodded to Jack.

Together, the four of us walked back down the hill toward the car in the drizzling rain, and went back to our lives.

PART III

JULY 24
6:15 A.M.

Agent Landers woke up in a foul mood, knowing he had to spend the next few days in a courtroom on a case he might lose, even with Dillard's sister's testimony. Just as he was starting to get in the shower, his cell phone rang. Who in the hell calls at six fifteen in the morning? The caller ID said the number was blocked. What was the point in a caller ID if the person on the other end could block it? Cell phone company morons.

"Landers."

"I have some information for you." It was a female. Landers could barely hear her.

"Who is this?"

"I used to work for Erlene Barlowe."

"How'd you get my cell phone number?"

"Julie Hayes gave it to me. I was going to call you sooner, but when she got killed, it scared me."

"So why aren't you scared now?"

"Because I'm gone."

"Tell me your name."

"Can't do it. You're making a mistake. Angel didn't kill anybody."

"How do you know that?"

"Because I was there that night. I know what happened."

"Are you saying Erlene killed him?"

"I don't think you even have to ask me that question."

"If you know something, we can protect you. You need to come back and sign a statement and testify."

"You didn't protect Julie."

"You're not helping me if you won't come in."

"I can help you find something you've been looking for."

"I'm listening."

"I'll give you a hint. It's red and has four wheels."

"The Corvette?"

"I knew you were smart."

"Where is it?"

"In a barn."

"Stop playing games with me. Where's the car?"

"Do you have a pen and a piece of paper? You're going to need to write this down."

Landers called Frankie Martin and told him he wouldn't be around for jury selection in the morning, but he didn't tell him why. Landers could tell from the tone of Martin's voice that he was pissed off, but Landers wasn't about to tell Frankie or anyone else where he was going. He'd been jerked around enough on the Angel Christian case. If the girl on the phone was sending him on a wild-goose chase, he was going to be the only one who knew about it.

Landers made the drive down I-181 from Johnson City to Unicoi County in thirty minutes. It was already 78 degrees, and there was a thick mist hanging over everything. It was going to be hotter than hell and humid. He took the Temple Hill exit and turned onto Spivey Mountain Road.

Two miles up the mountain, Landers came to an unmarked gravel road, right where his source said it would be. He turned right and followed the gravel road through a gulley and along a tree-covered ridge. After a mile, he came to a cattle gate that was secured by a padlock. He climbed the gate and followed the trail on foot through a stand of white pine for another quarter mile. As he broke into a clearing, Landers spotted the barn a hundred yards to his right. So far, it looked like she was telling the truth.

Landers pulled his gun and walked slowly up to the barn. He saw something move in the woods to his left and froze. Must have been a deer. He peeked through the wooden slats until his eyes adjusted to the semidarkness inside. Sure enough, there it was. A vehicle covered by a tarp. The barn door was padlocked, so Landers crawled in through an open window, walked over to the car, and lifted the tarp. A Corvette. A beautiful, red Corvette. And he could make out dark stains on the passenger seat. The *mother lode*. Finally.

Landers pulled a notepad from his pocket and wrote down the vehicle identification number, climbed back through the window, and jogged all the way back to his car. Sweat was pouring off him. As soon as he got to a spot where he had a cell phone signal, he called Bill

Wright and told him what he'd found. Wright said he'd arrange for two agents to secure the property. No one would go in or out until Landers did what needed to be done. Wright also said he'd call the forensics team. They'd be on the way soon.

Landers drove back down the mountain and straight to the tax assessor's office at the Unicoi County courthouse. They'd just opened and there was no one there besides Landers. The woman who worked there helped him find the property he'd just left on one of the tax maps. From that, he learned that the taxes on the property were paid by a corporation called Busty Gals, Inc.

Landers got back into his car and drove to the TBI office in Johnson City. On the way, he called the Tennessee secretary of state's office in Nashville and asked them to fax him a copy of Busty Gals, Inc.'s corporate charter. The incorporator was HighRide, Inc., a Delaware corporation not registered to do business in Tennessee. A phone call to the Delaware secretary of state's office confirmed what Landers suspected. Erlene Barlowe and her dead husband owned HighRide, Inc., which meant they also owned Busty Gals, Inc. Landers faxed the Corvette's VIN number to the National Auto Theft Bureau, an arm of the insurance industry that tracked nearly every car in the country. The Corvette was also registered to HighRide, Inc. That explained why Landers hadn't been able to get a hit from the Tennessee Department of Motor Vehicles.

Landers used all the information he'd gathered to draft an affidavit for a search warrant for the barn. He didn't mention the fact that he'd trespassed onto the property on Spivey Mountain. The way he drafted the warrant made it look as though he'd done some excellent police work, which he figured he had. He found Judge Glass in his office at 11:30, and the judge signed the warrant.

Landers was scheduled to testify in the Angel Christian case in the afternoon, but depending on what forensics found in the barn, he knew his testimony might have to change. He kept up with the radio traffic, so he knew the forensics team hit the barn a little before 1:00. He headed down to Jonesborough to talk to Deacon Baker.

JULY 24
9:00 A.M.

I found out Sarah was going to testify against Angel less than a week before the trial, when the district attorney faxed me an amended witness list and a copy of my sister's statement. I didn't believe a word of what I read. The statement had been taken by Phil Landers.

I was confident as I sat in the courtroom on the second floor in Jonesborough, but as always, I was a little nervous. The bailiff announced the entrance of Judge Len Green. The case of the State of Tennessee versus Angel Christian was about to go to trial.

Seventy-seven citizens from Washington County had been summoned. From that group, we'd choose the jury that would determine Angel's fate. I'd spend a great deal of time talking to them about being open-minded and neutral and the importance of a fair trial, but I knew the goal of jury selection was to try to make sure the trial was anything but fair. I needed to select people who were more likely to be sympathetic to Angel than to the state. The key was to talk to them as much as I could, accurately gauge their answers and reactions, and then make the right decisions.

I'd never before represented a woman accused of murder, let alone a woman who looked like Angel. Her beauty was both a blessing and a curse and presented me with a fascinating dilemma when it came to picking a jury. I knew Angel would be attractive to the prospective male jurors, especially if I chose them carefully, and I hoped the attraction would cause them to be sympathetic toward her and want to help her. At the same time, there would be evidence presented during the trial of the kind of mutilation any man would fear. If the male jurors perceived at any time during the trial that Angel might be capable of such an act, she'd be doomed.

The image Angel presented to the prospective female jurors was an even trickier issue. The average female in Washington County, Tennessee, was a God-fearing conservative. From the mouth of Agent Landers, those conservative women would hear testimony that Angel was a runaway and that she had worked, if only for a short time, in a strip club. They'd hear that Angel Christian probably wasn't her real name and that Landers had been unable to find background information on her. That alone could be enough to cause many women to vote to convict her, but my bigger concern was jealousy. If the female jurors perceived that Angel regarded herself as beautiful, or that she was somehow attempting to take advantage of her beauty to gain favor with the men, we wouldn't have a chance.

Caroline had chosen Angel's wardrobe and makeup, and when I saw my client walk into the courtroom early that morning, I was grateful for my wife's skill. The black pantsuit and cream-colored blouse were conservative but classy, loose enough to hide the curves but not frumpy. Angel's shoes were black with low heels, and her hair had been neatly tied back. Just a touch of eyeliner set off her fantastic brown eyes. There was no lip gloss, no shading around the eyes, no blush, and no jewelry. She looked like a scared, beautiful college student. It was perfect.

I nodded and smiled at the group of prospective jurors when Judge Green introduced me. I immediately scanned for Junior Tester, but he wasn't there. I introduced Angel and placed my hand on her shoulder. I wanted the jury to know I wasn't ashamed to touch her, that I felt close to her, and that I believed in her. Angel nodded her head and smiled, just as I'd told her to do.

I sat back down as Judge Green began the jury-selection process. He reached into a stack of slips and randomly pulled out a name.

"Lucille Benton," he said.

A lady wearing a denim pantsuit rose from the middle of the crowded audience.

"Here," she said, raising her hand.

"Come on down." Judge Green sounded like a game show host. "Where are you from?"

"Limestone," the woman said, walking toward the jury box.

"Ah, Limestone, wonderful little community. And how are things in Limestone this morning, Ms. Benton?"

I cringed. I was sitting next to a woman who was on trial for murder, and Judge Green was politicking as usual, pandering shamelessly to the jurors. I scribbled notes while he instructed the first thirteen to sit in the jury box and the next seven to sit on the front row of the audience, just behind the bar. Finally, after a half hour of worthless banter from the judge, I heard the words I'd been waiting for.

"Mr. Martin, you may *voir dire* the jury."

Frankie Martin rose, straightened his tie, and moved to the podium. He was about to address a jury in a murder case for the first time in his life, having spent the past four years handling misdemeanor cases in general sessions court. But he was a handsome, articulate young man and carried himself with confidence. He was also fighting for his very survival in the prosecutor's office. The fact that Deacon Baker was not in the courtroom could mean only one thing: he thought the case was a loser. Martin was Baker's sacrificial lamb. If Martin lost this trial, he'd be hustling divorce cases next week.

I whispered into Angel's ear: "I need you to watch the jurors very carefully. If anyone on the jury makes you uncomfortable for any reason, I want to know about it."

She nodded. Caroline had obviously given her some perfume. She smelled like a lilac bush.

Martin spent an hour on his initial *voir dire*. He was smooth and courteous, and he failed to make some of the mistakes that rookie lawyers tend to make at their first big trial. Judge Green didn't get a single opportunity to embarrass him.

When Martin finally sat down, I got into character. While he was speaking, I'd used the time to memorize the jurors' names. I smiled and was meticulously polite to each of them. I thanked them for performing such a valuable public service and told them if I asked a question that made them the least bit uncomfortable, they could ask the judge to allow them to answer the question in private. I encouraged them to speak openly and honestly regarding their feelings on a wide range of topics, and as they spoke, I watched them closely, looking for any sign of discontent.

Despite Tom Short's warning, a large part of my trial strategy was to deflect attention away from Angel and to put Reverend Tester on trial. If it was to succeed I needed jurors, preferably female jurors, who held sincere religious beliefs and would be deeply offended by the fact that the pastor had used donations from a church to fund a night at a strip club. It was known in legal circles as the "sumbitch-deserved-it" strategy, and under the right circumstances, it was highly effective.

I also wanted at least four males on the jury, preferably fathers. Angel had a way of engendering sympathy in men. I wanted them to feel an instinct to protect her. I wanted them to hope, perhaps to believe, that they could seek her out after the trial was over and let her know it was their vote, or their influence, that had set her free.

After three hours of questions and answers, challenges and arguments, Judge Green announced that a jury had been chosen. There were five men and seven women. I hadn't been able to get every person I wanted on the jury because Frankie kept using his challenges to kick them off, but I felt good about the group sitting in the box.

The jurors were given buttons with their names on them, and the judge swore them in. He instructed them on how they should conduct themselves during the case, then looked up at the clock on the back wall.

"It's noon. I'm hungry. We'll adjourn until one thirty for lunch."

After the jury was out of sight, the bailiffs escorted Angel back to the holding cell. Caroline had packed me a sandwich and some chips, and I spent the lunch hour going over my opening statement. At precisely 1:30, Judge Green walked back into the courtroom and ordered the bailiffs to bring the jury in.

I stood as the jury filed in and took their seats. I smiled and tried to catch the eye of each person passing the defense table.

"I trust you had a good lunch," the judge said. "Is the state ready?"

"Yes, sir."

"Is the defense ready?"

"Yes, Judge."

"Read the indictment, Mr. Martin."

Martin stood and read the indictment that charged Angel Christian with knowingly, intentionally, and with premeditation taking the life of John Paul Tester. Count Two charged her with abusing the corpse by mutilation.

"Opening statements," the judge said.

Frankie Martin stood up. "Ladies and gentlemen, the evidence in this case will show you that the defendant, Angel Christian, brutally stabbed and mutilated John Paul Tester in the early morning on April 12, 2006. Mr. Tester visited a club where the defendant worked on that same evening. The defendant flirted with Mr. Tester, she served him many drinks, and at approximately 11:30

p.m., Mr. Tester withdrew two hundred dollars from an ATM machine in the club lobby. The defendant left the establishment shortly after Mr. Tester left. A witness will testify that she saw a woman accompany Mr. Tester to his room around midnight. Mr. Tester was found at approximately 1:00 p.m. that afternoon in his hotel room. He had been drugged and stabbed nearly thirty times. His penis had been sliced off and removed from the room. His wallet was gone. His severed penis was found near Picken's Bridge that same morning."

Martin was calling Tester "Mister" instead of "Reverend." I'd take care of that soon enough.

"Among the evidence gathered during a forensic examination of Mr. Tester's hotel room were two hairs that were found on his clothing. Both hairs were tested for DNA. A hair sample was later obtained from the defendant. The DNA profile of the hairs found on Mr. Tester's body matches exactly the DNA profile of the hair sample obtained from the defendant. The chances of those hairs belonging to someone else are more than one hundred billion to one. You'll also see a photograph of the defendant taken by the police two days after the murder. The photo shows a bruise on the defendant's face, and our contention is that she received the bruise during some kind of altercation with Mr. Tester.

"But more importantly, we have a witness who will testify that the defendant confessed to this brutal crime. Our witness is an inmate at the Washington County Detention Center. Her name is Sarah Dillard. Ironically, she's Mr. Dillard's sister. She will testify that the defendant confessed during a conversation they had at the jail.

The defendant told Miss Dillard that on the night of the murder, the defendant followed Mr. Tester back to his motel room with the intention of robbing him. She'll testify that the defendant told her that she drugged Mr. Tester and killed him after he passed out on the bed.

"I wish I had a videotape to show you, or an eyewitness, but unfortunately, I don't. What I do have is a web of circumstantial evidence so tightly woven that the defendant cannot possibly escape. Everything points to her. She was at the club. She spoke to Mr. Tester. She served him drinks. She flirted with him. She invited him to leave with her. She followed him to his room, and then she drugged him, murdered him, and robbed him."

Martin turned and pointed at Angel.

"Don't let yourselves be fooled by that young woman's beauty or her youth. Don't let yourselves be taken in by her attorney's tricks or the smoke and mirrors that will be placed before you during the course of this trial. That young woman sitting over there committed a vicious murder, and we have the evidence to prove it. It will be your duty to render a verdict of guilty in this case, and to impose on her the only sentence that will give justice to John Paul Tester and his family, a sentence of death. This woman committed first-degree murder. My job is to prove it. Yours is to make her pay the price. I fully intend to hold up my end, and I hope that once you've heard all the evidence, you'll do the same. Thank you."

Martin sat down at the prosecutor's table, and I stood. Martin's argument had been passionate and persuasive, but parts of it were dishonest, and I intended to point that out immediately. I walked to the wooden lectern, picked it up, and set it down three feet to my right. I didn't want any barriers between the jurors and me. I glanced at the jurors and then out over the courtroom. Junior Tester had come in and was sitting on the front row, directly to my left. I noticed that he'd put on at least twenty pounds since I'd visited him a couple months ago. He hadn't shaved in days and looked tired and haggard. He was also staring directly at me. It unnerved me, but only for a few seconds.

"Not much point in having a trial," I said, "if you believe everything Mr. Martin just said." I smiled at the jury. "If everything he said were true, I suppose we could just go ahead and ship Miss Christian off to death row right now and save everybody all of this trouble."

I sought out eyes, looking for signs that Martin's argument had closed their minds. They weren't avoiding me. They were still receptive to what I had to say.

"But what Mr. Martin just told you isn't true. It was his interpretation of the evidence, and as every one of you knows, there are two sides to every story. Now, first things first. This young lady's name is not 'the defendant.'"

I walked over to the defense table and stood directly behind Angel. I put my hands on her shoulders.

"Her name is Angel Christian, and she's going to testify in this case. What she will tell you is this:

"On the night of April the eleventh of this year, *Reverend* John Paul Tester came into the club where she'd been a waitress for only a month. It's a strip club, a gentleman's club, whatever you want to call it. It's a place where men go to watch young ladies dance and take their clothes off. It's not the kind of place where you'd expect to find a man of God, especially if he's paying for his night out with money given to him by worshippers at the Church of the Light of Jesus, where he'd preached a sermon on the evils of fornication less than an hour before he arrived at the club."

Diane Frye had managed to get hold of a tape recording of the sermon Tester gave that night. I'd tried to get it introduced as evidence, but the judge shot me down. I wasn't even supposed to mention it, but if Frankie didn't object, I knew the judge wouldn't say a word. If he did object, he'd simply be calling more attention to it. Mentioning the tape probably bordered on being unethical, but Angel was on trial for her life. Frankie kept his mouth shut.

"Miss Christian wasn't a dancer, not a stripper, and she certainly wasn't a prostitute. She was a waitress. She arrived here in February after leaving a viciously abusive situation back home in Oklahoma. She originally intended to go to Florida, but she met a young lady on a bus in Dallas who told her she'd help Miss Christian find work here.

"Miss Christian will tell you that on the night of April the eleventh, she served Reverend Tester the drinks he ordered—six doubles, straight scotch, the equivalent of twelve drinks, in two hours. She'll tell you Reverend Tester became intoxicated and that he was aggressive, even a little abusive, toward her. She'll tell you Reverend Tester used inappropriate language and that Reverend Tester touched her inappropriately. She reported Reverend Tester's behavior to her employer, Ms. Erlene Barlowe, who will also testify in this case.

"Ms. Barlowe spoke to Reverend Tester and eventually asked the reverend to leave. Miss Christian had never seen or heard of Reverend Tester prior to his coming to the club that night, and she never saw him again after he walked out the door."

I moved back toward the jury box and stood directly in front of them.

"Now, despite what Mr. Martin said earlier, you won't hear a single witness tell you they saw Miss Christian anywhere near Reverend Tester's room that night. You won't hear a single witness tell you they saw Miss Christian leave the club at the same time Reverend Tester left. As a matter of fact, Miss Christian's employer, Erlene Barlowe, will testify that Miss Christian finished out her shift and Ms. Barlowe drove her home.

"You'll hear evidence that two hairs found on the victim's body contained DNA that matches Miss Christian's DNA. That is, by far, the most compelling piece of evidence the state will present in this case. I believe it's safe to say that were it not for those two hairs, we wouldn't be here today. But what I'll be asking you to pay particular attention to is *where* those hairs were found. Both of them were lifted off Reverend Tester's shirt. Since there will be testimony that Miss Christian had contact with Mr. Tester at the club, that she leaned over and served him drinks, and that he deliberately and obnoxiously rubbed himself against her, it's not only possible but *probable* that the hairs were transferred from Miss Christian to Reverend Tester at the club.

"That, ladies and gentlemen, is all they have, with the exception of a last-minute statement from a drug addict and thief they recruited at the jail. She's my sister, yes, and she's furious with me because I had her arrested when she stole from my family. It wasn't the first time she'd done it."

Martin stood to object. Judge Green waved him back down.

"Tone it down, Mr. Dillard," the judge said.

"They have no murder weapon. They have no eyewitnesses. They have no fingerprints, no blood evidence, and no way to place Miss Christian at the scene of the crime. They say the motive is robbery, but they didn't find any of Reverend Tester's money on Miss Christian. They have no evidence to prove it.

"In this case, the government must prove beyond a reasonable doubt that Miss Christian, acting with premeditation, stabbed the victim to death and then mutilated his body. In order for you to convict Miss Christian, you must have *virtually no doubt* that she committed this terrible crime. And beyond that, the judge will instruct you that in a case based on circumstantial evidence such as this one, you can find Miss Christian guilty only *if there is no other reasonable theory of guilt.* There are dozens of other reasonable theories as to how Reverend Tester was killed.

"When all the evidence is in, you folks will have more than a reasonable doubt. As a matter of fact, you'll probably be wondering why this young lady was arrested in the first place. Angel Christian has been living a nightmare since the day the state wrongfully accused her of murder. It's a nightmare only you can end. She is *not guilty*. She *did not do* this terrible thing."

I paused and looked at each of the jurors. I wanted the message to sink in.

"Everyone associated with this trial is doing their duty," I said. "The judge, the lawyers, the witnesses, everyone. Your duty is to determine the truth, and after you've done that, to vote your conscience. In this case, the only verdict you'll be able to return is not guilty. This is a death-penalty case. A man has been killed, and someone should pay for killing him. But none of us wants an innocent person to pay, and that beautiful young woman sitting over there is *innocent*."

JULY 24
2:15 P.M.

"**C**all your first witness," Judge Green said.

Martin called Dennis Hall, the manager of the Budget Inn, to the witness stand. Hall told the jury that Reverend Tester had checked in late in the afternoon of April 12th, said he was there to preach at a revival at a friend's church, and asked him where he could get a good burger. An hour after checkout time the next day, one of his maids told him Tester's "Do Not Disturb" sign was still on the door. Hall went to the room, opened the door, saw all the blood, and called the police.

When Martin was finished with his direct examination, I stood and straightened my tie.

"Mr. Hall, did you see Reverend Tester return to the motel at any time after he left for the restaurant you recommended—the Purple Pig, I believe it was?"

"No, sir. I got off work at seven and went home."

I touched Angel's shoulder. "Have you ever seen this young lady before?"

"No. I would have remembered her."

"Thank you."

"You can step down," Judge Green said. "Next witness."

Martin called Sheila Hunt, the clerk who was working at the Budget Inn the night of the murder. She said she saw Tester's truck pull into the parking lot around midnight, followed by a red Corvette. She said a woman got out of the Corvette and followed Tester up the stairs. Martin didn't bother to ask her whether she could identify the woman.

"Ms. Hunt," I said when it was my turn, "it was raining when you saw Reverend Tester return to the motel, wasn't it?"

"Yes, it was."

"Raining pretty hard?"

"Yes."

"And that made it difficult for you to see, didn't it?"

"Yes. The rain, and I wasn't paying that much attention. I was watching Jay Leno."

"And didn't you tell the police that the person you saw was wearing some kind of coat or cape?"

"It had a little hood. I remember thinking she looked like Little Red Riding Hood, except I don't think it was red."

"So you can't identify the person, can you?"

"No, I'm sorry."

"There's nothing to be sorry about, ma'am. You can't tell us whether this person was old or young, can you?"

"No."

"Tall or short? Heavy or slim?"

"No."

"Can't tell us whether this person was black or white or brown or yellow or red?"

"I don't *think* she was black," she said. "But that's about all I can say."

"You can't really even say with certainty that it was a woman, can you?"

"I think it was."

"But you're not certain, are you?"

"I don't know. I think it was a woman."

"You *think* it was a woman. A young lady is on trial for her life here, ma'am. You need to be certain. You're not, are you?"

"It was dark and raining."

"Thank you. Let's talk about the car for a second. You weren't able to get a tag number, were you?"

"I didn't try."

"Because there wasn't anything that alarmed you, right?"

"That's right. I wasn't alarmed."

"People come and go at the motel all the time, yes?"

"Yes."

"You didn't see the driver, did you?"

"No."

"Don't know if it was a man or a woman?"

"I didn't see the driver at all."

"Didn't see where the car went after the passenger got out?"

"I just glanced over there for a second. Then I went back to watching my show."

"Didn't see the car leave or return?"

"I told you, I went back to my show."

"Thank you."

Martin looked as confident as ever, but he had to be at least a little worried. His case wasn't exactly off to a flying start. His first witness had found a body and called the police. His second witness testified that she didn't see a thing.

I glanced over to my left and saw Deacon Baker and Phil Landers moving toward the prosecution table.

"Call your next witness," Judge Green said.

"May I have a moment to confer with Mr. Martin?" Baker said.

"Make it snappy," the judge said.

Baker leaned over and whispered something in Martin's ear. Martin nodded and whispered back. The two of them turned toward the judge.

"May we approach, Your Honor?" Baker said.

Green motioned them forward, and I got up and joined them.

"We need to speak to you in chambers," Baker said.

"We're in the middle of a murder trial, in case you haven't noticed," Judge Green said.

"I apologize," Baker said, "but something extremely important has come up. It has a direct bearing on this case."

Judge Green agreed to a fifteen-minute recess, and the judge, Baker, Landers, Martin, and I walked into his chambers. He shut the door, hung his robe on a coat tree near the window, and sat down behind his desk.

"What's going on?" he said.

"There's been an important development in this case," Baker said. "The TBI found a red Corvette in a barn up on Spivey Mountain this morning. The car belongs to Erlene Barlowe. Their forensics people are examining it now."

"I fail to see what that has to do with this trial."

"It may exculpate Mr. Dillard's client," Baker said. "Back when we made the arrest, we had a young lady who worked for Barlowe at the strip club who told us that Barlowe and Angel left the club at the same time as the victim in this case. She told us they left in Barlowe's red Corvette, and they didn't come back to the club that night."

"I remember that," the judge said. "That and the fact that Ms. Barlowe had been untruthful were the primary reasons I signed the search warrants to search her home and her club and to allow you to get hair samples from Barlowe and the girl."

"That's right," Baker said. "We've also had another witness contact us since who said he saw a woman fitting Ms. Barlowe's description standing beside a Corvette on Picken's Bridge a little after midnight on the night of the murder. He said she was alone. We think Ms. Barlowe was dumping the murder weapon and the reverend's penis. The problem we ran into was that the car disappeared. We couldn't find it anywhere, and because we couldn't find it, we believed it probably contained evidence regarding the murder. Now we've found it, and from what I understand, there are what appear to be bloodstains on the seat."

"So now you think the Barlowe woman killed Reverend Tester?" Judge Green said.

"It makes sense, especially if we can eventually prove she killed the Hayes girl, which is what we suspect."

"You people have made a mess of this investigation," the judge said. "Are you familiar with the term fiasco?"

"Please, Judge," Baker said. "Not now."

"So what do you want?" the judge said.

"I want a little time. All we're asking is that you recess the trial for a week. We should get our lab results back from Knoxville by then. If Tester's blood is in Barlowe's car or if we find a murder weapon, we're going to dismiss the charges against Mr. Dillard's client, provided she'll cooperate with us, and arrest Barlowe for Tester's murder."

Fat chance of Angel cooperating. They didn't have enough evidence to convict her in the first place, and I couldn't think of a single reason why she'd want to help them.

The judge looked at me. "Any objection, Mr. Dillard?"

"No, Judge. If there's a chance they'll dismiss against my client, I'm not opposed to giving them a week."

"All right." Judge Green pointed his finger at Baker. "I'll give you some time. But if there's still a charge pending next Monday, we're finishing this case."

JULY 24
3:00 P.M.

The judge didn't tell the jury or anyone in the courtroom why he was granting a week's recess, he just told them to come back next Monday.

Angel wanted to know what had happened. I told her I'd be over to the jail to explain it to her as soon as I could. The jurors filed out, and as the courtroom began to clear, Erlene Barlowe walked up to me. She'd been sitting outside in the hallway with the rest of the witnesses. Junior Tester hadn't moved from his seat.

"What's going on, sugar?" Erlene said.

"The police say they have some new information in Angel's case. The district attorney asked the judge for a continuance so they could develop some evidence. He gave them until next Monday."

Landers was walking out of the judge's office, where he'd apparently been holding court with Baker. When he saw Erlene, he made a beeline for us.

"Don't leave town," he said, pointing his finger at Erlene. "Your ass is mine now." He turned and walked out the door.

"What was that all about?" Erlene said.

"They don't tell me anything," I said as I started to walk away. I wasn't about to tell her she was more than likely going to be in custody sometime in the next week. With my luck, she'd disappear and I'd wind up with an obstruction charge. "I have to go over to the jail to see Angel and let her know what's going on. I'll talk to you later."

Before I left the courthouse, I took the elevator upstairs to Deacon Baker's office.

"Interesting dilemma," he said when I walked in.

"For you," I said. "I'm still in the same boat. Innocent client."

"Let's stop beating around the bush," Baker said. "Bottom line, if there's anything in that car that links it to Tester's murder, we're going to charge the redhead. I'll dismiss against your client if she'll agree to help us."

"Erlene is her only friend in this world. I doubt she'll be eager to rat her out."

"She was with her, Dillard. She knows what went on in that room."

"You can't prove that."

"Will she want to take that chance? Barlowe may have something to say about her when she finds herself facing a first-degree murder charge."

"All Erlene has ever said about Angel is that she's innocent."

"And if her lips are moving, she's lying."

"You're stuck, Deacon. The jury's been sworn in Angel's case. If you dismiss, you can't try her again because the jury's already been sworn. Double jeopardy.

If you come back and resume the trial, you're going to lose, even with my sister's testimony. Do you know what I'm going to do to her on the witness stand?"

"I was planning to make it a point to be in the courtroom for her cross-examination," Baker said with a smirk. "Wouldn't want to miss it. At least run my proposal by your client. Go over there and tell her I'm offering to dismiss a first-degree murder."

"I'll talk to her, but don't get your hopes up."

When Angel came into the attorney's room at the jail, I was surprised to see her still wearing her clothes from court.

"The guards are searching my cell block," she said. "I'm still in holding. I guess they weren't expecting me back so soon."

"Strange day, huh?" I said.

"What's going on?"

"It's good and it's bad. The TBI found a red Corvette in a barn out in Unicoi County this morning. The barn belongs to Erlene, and apparently so does the car."

Angel gasped, and I watched her closely. Her face turned pink and her bottom lip was trembling. She sat there, shaking and saying nothing. I reached into my briefcase and brought out some tissue. I'd been carrying it ever since that first visit at the jail. I handed some to her just in case, reached across the table, and put my hand over hers.

"Angel," I said, "the district attorney now thinks Erlene killed Reverend Tester. He wants to dismiss the case against you, but there's a catch. He wants you to tell him what you know about Tester's murder."

A faraway look came into her eyes, as though she wasn't really taking in what I was saying.

"Angel? Did you understand me? He wants to dismiss the case against you. They're probably going to arrest Erlene for Reverend Tester's murder."

"They can't do that!" she burst out, then laid her head on the table and started crying. I moved to the chair next to her, put my hand on her shoulders, and began to rub.

"Take it easy," I said. The door was two inches of steel and the walls were concrete block, but her sobs were loud. I didn't want the guards coming in and asking questions. "Talk to me," I said. "It's all right. Talk to me. Whatever it is that's bothering you, you can tell me. I'm on your side no matter what."

She suddenly sat up, wiped her eyes, and became very still. She looked at me pitifully.

"Can I trust you?" she said in a small voice.

"Of course you can. You know you can."

"Can I *really* trust you?"

"I've been here for you all along. Whatever you tell me, I promise I won't tell a soul. I've already explained attorney-client privilege to you."

I could see her make the decision. And having made it, she sat up straight and squared her shoulders, as if a great burden had been lifted.

"I did it, Mr. Dillard. I killed him. I can't let them blame Miss Erlene."

I'd mildly suspected it since the day I talked to Tom Short, but I hadn't wanted to believe it. Even now, even though the words had passed her lips, I didn't want to believe it. I took her hand, knowing that if I continued, if

I asked her about the details, everything about our relationship, and my entire strategy if the trial continued, would change.

"Think about what you're saying," I said. "We're winning this trial. If you tell me you killed him, it changes a lot of things."

"You want to know the truth, don't you?"

"I'm not sure."

I looked at her smooth, young face, and my heart went out to her. Something told me that if she'd killed Tester, the circumstances might justify it.

"I'm sorry, Angel. Yes, I want to know the truth. What happened?"

She bit her lip and shuddered.

"Can you tell me about it?

She nodded slowly.

"Okay, but I don't want you to get hysterical. I don't want anyone else to hear, so you have to keep control of yourself. Can you do that?"

"I think so."

"Go ahead."

She took a deep breath and squeezed my hand so hard that her fingernails dug into my skin.

"Everything I told you before was the truth except for the last part. Miss Erlene didn't just ask him to leave when he got so drunk and was bothering me and making a fool of himself. She asked me if I'd help her with something. She said she wanted to teach the preacher a lesson. She said all I'd have to do is ride with her to the man's hotel room and she'd take care of the rest. I told her I'd do it."

"What happened next?"

"Miss Erlene went over to talk to him, and he went out into the lobby for a couple minutes. When he came back, she told me to get my coat. Miss Erlene went back into her office for a couple minutes, and then we went out and got in her car. We followed him out of the parking lot to the hotel. Along the way, she told me the man thought I was coming to his room to have sex with him. Then she handed me a small bottle of scotch. She told me when we got to the motel, I was supposed to go into his room and offer him a drink first thing. Miss Erlene said she put something in the scotch so when he drank it, it would knock him out. As soon as he was passed out, I was supposed to run back to the car and get her. I think she was planning to take his money."

"Something obviously went wrong," I said.

She put a fist to her mouth and whispered, "Yes." Her eyes looked distant. It was the same expression I'd seen when she told me about the oatmeal incident.

"We got to the motel and I got out of the car and went up the steps with him. Miss Erlene waited in the parking lot. I walked into the room and he closed the door behind me. I took the bottle of scotch out of my purse and asked him if he'd like a drink. He took the bottle out of my hand, set it on a table, and when he turned back around, he said he didn't bring me there to drink. He had this awful look on his face, like he was possessed or something. Then, before I knew what was happening, he hit me in the face. He hit me so hard it knocked me onto the bed. It almost knocked me out.

"I remember him taking off all his clothes, then he pulled off my panties. ..." She paused and took a deep breath. "He rolled me over on my stomach and he put his thing in my, in my. ..." She pointed to her bottom.

"He *sodomized* you?" I said.

"What?" She didn't know what the word meant.

"Never mind. Can you keep going?"

"It was like it was happening to someone else," she said. "Like I floated to the ceiling, and I watched him do it from there. It was the same thing that used to happen when Father Thomas did things to me. I remember he was cursing and preaching at the same time, calling me names, and then he took his thing out of me and went over and grabbed the bottle of scotch and took a long drink. He started to stagger and he sat down on the bed and took all his clothes off. It was like he didn't even know I was there anymore.

"There was a knife on the table. I guess it was his. I remember watching myself walk over and pick it up. It was one of those folding knives. He was already snoring. I opened the knife and walked back to the bed and I just started stabbing him. I stabbed him until I couldn't stab him anymore, until I couldn't lift the knife. And then I think I just walked out the door. I didn't even put my panties on."

"Do you remember what Erlene did?"

"I think so," she said. "I remember she came running up to me on the stairs and she put her coat around me and took the knife out of my hand. She put me in the car and asked me what happened, and I tried to tell her. I saw her go back up to the room, but I don't know what she did in there. She took me home and took me into the backyard and washed all the blood off me with a hose. She said she didn't want any blood in her shower. Then she took me inside and said she had to leave for a little while. She was gone for a long time."

"Did you and Erlene talk about it afterwards?"

"Not much," she said. "She just told me she was sorry about everything but at least he wouldn't ever hurt another girl, and she told me never to mention what happened—any of it—to anybody. Then when the police started coming around, she told me not to talk to them. She told everyone that worked at the club not to talk to them. When they came to arrest me, she told me to tell them I wanted a lawyer."

"You didn't mention cutting off his penis, Angel. Do you remember doing that?"

"I didn't do it," she said.

"Are you sure?"

"I didn't do it. I'd tell you if I did."

I believed her.

"Telling me what happened was the right thing to do," I said.

"Am I going to have to stay in jail for the rest of my life?"

"I doubt it. This changes a few things, but it doesn't change the fact that they don't have much of a case against you."

"What about your sister? I never even talked to her."

"That's what I thought," I said. "You have to trust me. I'll figure something out. I just need a little time to think."

After the guards took her away, I sat at the table alone, unable to get up and walk out. The door buzzed twice, but I just sat there. I couldn't move.

In my mind, I kept seeing a beautiful, fragile young girl, naively walking up the steps in the rain to a motel room. She's accompanied by a man more than twice her size, twice her age. She closes the door and offers the man a drink from a bottle. He takes the bottle from her hand, sets it down, and punches her viciously in the side of the face. She sees a bright light and falls backwards onto the bed, dazed by the blow. The giant hovers over her, his drunken breathing foul and labored. He grabs the girl and rolls her like a rag doll. He's muttering, alternately calling her a slut and praising God for the opportunity to exact some righteous vengeance on a lowly whore.

I hear Sarah's voice. *"Get him off me, Joey. He's hurting me. ..."*

When I was finally able to move, I pushed the button, waited for the door to buzz, and made my way slowly down the maze of hallways and steel gates. What Angel had described to me was voluntary manslaughter, at worst. A Class C felony, maximum sentence of six years. But I couldn't bring myself to recommend to her that we go to the district attorney and tell him what had happened. I couldn't see her spending time in prison for retaliating against a man who had violated her in the most shameful of ways.

As far as I was concerned, the hypocrite got what he deserved.

JULY 24
6:05 P.M.

I drove straight home from the jail with Sarah's voice and Angel's confession alternately ringing in my ears. As soon as I got out of my truck, Rio peed on me, and instead of laughing or gently pushing him away like always, I drew my foot back to kick the crap out of him. I caught myself, but barely. For some reason, the thought of the dog pissing on me right then made me mad enough to want to hurt him. I swore at him and stepped over him as he cowered in the driveway.

I walked into the kitchen. Caroline was standing over the stove. I could smell broccoli. I hate broccoli.

"Hi, honey," she said. "I heard they continued the trial. What's going on?"

"I'm going to wring that dog's neck."

"I guess it isn't good."

"I'm sick of him pissing all over me. I'm sick of everybody pissing all over me."

"What's going on, Joe?"

"Nothing." I marched through the kitchen and into the bedroom to change my clothes. I could feel pressure, a lot of pressure, at each of my temples, and my field of vision was narrowing. I felt a hand on my shoulder, a touch that usually comforted me. It didn't.

"What's wrong, Joe? Talk to me."

"It would probably be best if you'd just leave me alone right now."

"Leave you alone? Why? What have I done?"

"Nothing," I said. "That's part of the problem."

I'd spent part of the drive home working up a healthy anger toward Caroline. I had to provide for her, which meant I had to keep working. But I was sick of busting my butt for people who neither deserved it nor appreciated it, sick of people using me and lying to me, sick of worrying about whether what I was doing was right or wrong. I was sick of everything.

"I'm not the bad guy, baby. I love you, remember?" she said.

"A lot of good it does."

"You've been under a lot of strain. How about a hot bath?"

"I don't want to take a bath. Now why don't you do what I asked you to do and leave me the hell alone?"

"How dare you talk to me like that!" Caroline said. "I know you hate your job. I know you hate yourself sometimes, but that doesn't mean you get to take it out on me. I haven't done a thing other than love you and try to help you through a difficult time, and I'm not going to stand here and listen to you degrade me. *I'm not your whipping girl, Joe!*"

All I could feel was the pressure in my head. I was losing it. I pushed past her and walked back into the kitchen.

"What are you doing?" She was right behind me. I headed for the door. "Where are you going?"

"Out," I said. "I'm going out."

And that's what I did. I drove to a bar in Johnson City called Fritter's. I sat alone at the bar and drank vodka for a while. Then I asked for a shot of Jägermeister. Then another. I was there for hours.

It was raining when I left the bar, but I didn't care. I'd convinced myself that I had somewhere I needed to go. I drove across town, holding a hand over my right eye to keep from seeing double. I pulled through the gate at the Veterans Administration campus. I turned into the cemetery toward the long rows of white grave markers and made my way slowly, drunkenly, to the section where my father was buried. I got out of the car and stumbled through the rain until I found him.

Then I lay down on his grave and passed out.

I dreamed I was lying in a thicket, above a path in the jungle in Grenada. I had somehow become separated from my squad. My face was covered in camouflage paint, and I was aiming a machine gun at the path. A group of six Cuban soldiers was moving toward me. I'd set out claymore mines in a ditch beside the path and concealed the wires carefully.

The point man moved into the kill zone. All that remained was for the rest of the group to get within range of the claymores. Once they were there, I'd open fire. When they hid in the ditch, I'd hit the clackers and detonate the mines. It would be a perfect massacre.

The last man moved in, and I started blasting away with the M-60. I sprayed them with short bursts. The Cubans melted into the ditch line. I detonated the mines, and the earth shuddered. The Cuban guns went silent, and I moved in to mop up.

I heard the sucking sound of a chest wound coming from the point man. He was lying on his stomach in the ditch; his left arm lay severed two feet away. I stuck my boot in his ribs and rolled him. He flopped onto his back, and I found myself staring into the bloodied face of a kid. He couldn't have been more than sixteen years old, and he looked just like me.

I began to scream.

JULY 25
1:00 A.M.

erry Byrd found me out there in the rain. Jerry was a
V.A. cop and army veteran I'd known for fifteen years.
His wife had gone to my high school, and his son had
played ball with Jack. We had a good deal in common,
and we'd had some good times together over the years.

When Jerry woke me up, I had absolutely no idea
where I was or how I got there. It was pouring rain and
my teeth were chattering. He helped me to my feet and
took me by the arm.

"Joe, what in the hell are you doing out here?"

"No clue."

Jerry used his cell phone to call Caroline. He told her
where I was and we could pick up my truck the next day.
Then he drove me home.

"What's going on?" Caroline said after Jerry had left.
I'd managed to down two cups of black coffee strong
enough to make my tongue curl. I could tell she'd been
crying, but I hoped she wouldn't start up again. I felt bad
enough as it was. "I've been worried sick about you."

"I'm sorry," I said. "I had a little meltdown."

I'd always kept Caroline at least a stone's throw from the worst of my work and my past. It was ugly and frightening, and Caroline was beautiful and kind. I was afraid I'd somehow contaminate her if I told her the truth, but more than that, I was afraid she might begin to think of me as weak and flawed.

"Talk to me," she said. "Please."

"You don't want me to. Believe me, you're better off if I keep it to myself."

"Joe, do you really think anything you tell me would make me love you any less?"

There was a long silence. She poured more coffee. I sat there sipping it slowly, trying to decide whether I wanted to tell my wife that for all these years, despite all the macho bravado, she'd really been married to a scared little boy trying to prove to himself he wasn't a coward.

"I don't think I *can* tell you," I said.

"Does it have anything to do with this case?"

"That's part of it. It looks like they're going to arrest Erlene Barlowe for Tester's murder." I was grateful for the opportunity to move the topic of conversation away from me.

"Do you think she killed Tester?"

"I *know* she didn't kill Tester."

"How do you know?"

"I just know."

"How?"

I looked at her, deadpan. I couldn't tell her, but Caroline was an intelligent woman. I saw the look come over her face. She got it.

"Angel told you *she* killed him?"

I nodded.

"And now you're trying to decide what to do?"

"I'm just trying to survive right now. You know I'm going to have to go after Sarah on the witness stand if the trial starts back up. I can't tell you how much I dread it."

"Why is she doing this, Joe? What's wrong with her?"

"Do you really want to know? It's not something you're going to enjoy hearing about."

"Of course I want to know. I think I've earned the right."

She had. She'd earned the right to hear about all of it. I looked at her and thought about Ma, about the regret I'd felt because she wouldn't let me into her heart and about the emptiness I felt because I'd never let her into mine. I thought about the nightmares, the anxiety, the depression, the nagging feeling that I was a pathetic coward. I looked at Caroline, saw the longing in her eyes, and knew I couldn't shut my wife out any longer. I couldn't be like my mother. It was time. It was time to open up.

I told Caroline about what Tester had done to Angel and what Uncle Raymond had done to Sarah. When she heard what had happened to Sarah, Caroline scooted next to me and held me in her arms. As I felt her breath against my skin and smelled her familiar smell, I suddenly didn't care whether she thought I was weak because at that moment, I was. I needed to lean on the only person I'd ever really trusted. For the first time in my life, I gave myself completely. There were moments I cried so hard I couldn't breathe. I was ashamed and reluctant at first, but once I started, I couldn't stop. After twenty years, I finally let Caroline all the way *in*.

I talked about the frustration of being raised without a father. I told her about the brutal things I'd done and seen in Grenada. I told her about Billy Dockery. I told her about Maynard Bush and Bonnie Tate and how I felt the day the Bowers twins died in the sunshine. I told her how I felt about my mother. I talked deep into the morning. I'd never experienced anything like it, but when it was over, I understood the power of confession.

"Do you know something?" Caroline said when I was finally too exhausted to talk anymore. She put her hands on my shoulders and looked me in the eye.

"If I was on trial, if I was in the same situation as Angel, there's nobody in this world I'd rather have on my side than you. Do you know why?"

"I'm sorry for the things I said when I came home earlier. I feel like a jackass. And I'm sorry—"

"Hush. Do you know why there's nobody in this world I'd rather have on my side than you?"

"No. Why?"

"Because you're a good man, Joe. It's as simple as that. That's why I married you and why I've loved you for all these years. That's why your children adore you. It's why you've stuck by Sarah all this time and why you went up there and sat with your mother. It's why you've spent your life trying to help people. I hope you're always just like you are now."

Her words humbled me. I didn't know what to say.

"When did Angel tell you what really happened?" she said.

"Not long before I came home."

"That's what I thought. That's what set this off. It put you back in that house with your sister. When you add it to everything else that's been going on with you lately, it isn't surprising. I'm just glad you didn't hurt yourself."

So was I.

"You're going to get through this," Caroline said. "You're a survivor. You're the strongest man I've ever met."

Caroline got up and walked over to the door that led to the garage. She opened it.

"And here's someone else that loves you," she said.

Rio trotted into the room, saw me, and stopped dead in his tracks.

"Come here, big boy," I said. His ears perked and his tail began to wag. "Come over here and take a leak on my shoe."

JULY 25
11:00 A.M.

For the first time in what seemed like forever, I slept well. There were no ambushes in the jungle to haunt me, no rapes or murders or flashes of dead children in the jungle, no raging rivers or deadly waterfalls.

I woke to the smell of coffee brewing and the sound of rain tapping steadily on the roof. I walked into the kitchen and looked outside. The sky was low and slate gray. A thin mist hung above the lake, and I knew it would be a long day of summer rain, the kind of rain that seems to cleanse the whole world.

Caroline was in the kitchen, wearing only a sports bra and a pair of biker shorts. When she hugged me, I lifted her off the floor and carried her to the bedroom. A half hour later, we were lying in bed, pleasantly exhausted.

"What are you going to do today?" she said.

"Think," I said. "I have to figure out what to do about Angel."

"What are your options?"

"The first one would be to go to Deacon and tell him we've reconsidered and we want to make a deal. But as soon as I do that, he'll know she killed Tester and he'll go hard-ass on me. He'll offer twenty years. The second option is to go back to trial on Monday and put Angel on the witness stand. If she tells the truth, I can argue self-defense or voluntary manslaughter because he sodomized her."

"What's the worst case if you go that way?"

"Worst case is they don't believe her and find her guilty of first-degree murder. That means life. I don't think there's any way she gets the death penalty under these circumstances. They could find her guilty of second-degree murder. That would mean a minimum of fifteen years. If they go with voluntary manslaughter, she'd be eligible for probation, but I doubt if Judge Green would grant it.

"The problem I have with putting her on the stand now is that I can't get any medical testimony in. Tom Short would have helped us out if she'd told me about this on the front end, but there's no way Judge Green will let me use medical testimony this late. The prosecution has the right to have her examined by their own shrink, and they're entitled to all Tom Short's reports. I didn't give them anything because I didn't intend to use him."

"What are the other options?"

"She might get on the stand and tell them she didn't do it. If she does that, I have to decide whether to tank her. The rules say that if she gets on a witness stand and lies, and I know she's lying, I can't question her and can't present a closing argument on her behalf. The jury will figure that out pretty quickly. If she lies and I don't tank her, then I'm suborning perjury and I could wind up in jail."

"You can't do that," Caroline said.

"I can't and I won't. But I swear I think I'd do it if I knew I'd get away with it. The guy sodomized her. Punched her in the head, nearly knocked her out, then rolled her over and screwed her up the butt. A man of God. I don't feel the least bit of sympathy for him. None. She should walk on this, Caroline. She should walk right out the door."

"I guess we both know where that comes from. Finally."

"I should have told you about Sarah a long time ago," I said. "I'm sorry. I was ashamed."

"It's out in the open now, and I don't think any less of you."

I kissed her on the forehead. She had no idea how much that meant to me.

"This is so unfair," I said. "The right thing would be for her to go home. Erlene set up the whole situation. She apparently intended to rob the preacher. It wasn't Angel's fault. She didn't even have a weapon with her. She killed him with his own knife."

"She didn't have to kill him," Caroline said.

"Yeah? What would you have done if a drunken redneck punched you and sodomized you?"

"I'd have killed him and cut his dick off."

"Exactly. There's really only one other thing I can do. I can try to fix things with Sarah. If I can get her to talk to me, I think I can make this turn out all right."

"What would you say to her?"

"I'm not sure. Do you know that she and I never talked about it after it happened? I guess we were both so scared and humiliated we didn't want to go near it. I really think it's the reason she's struggled all her life."

I sat up on the side of the bed and took a deep breath.

"I'm going," I said. "I'm going down to the jail. They can't keep me from talking to her. The worst thing that can happen is she'll tell me to go to hell and things will stay the same."

"Are you going to try to talk to her about the rape?"

"I have to. I have to tell her I'm sorry."

"It wasn't your fault, Joe."

"I know that now, but I still feel like I should apologize to her. I've handled this almost as badly as she has, and I wasn't the one who was raped."

"Don't expect too much," Caroline said.

I got dressed and gulped down a cup of coffee.

"Joe?" Caroline said as I was about to walk out.

"Yeah."

"Make sure you tell her you love her."

JULY 25
NOON

J ail inmates hate a lot of things. They hate the guards, they hate the food, they hate the tedium. But there are two things they hate most of all. One is a child molester, the other is a snitch.

The administration had moved Sarah to the jail's protective custody unit in case the word got out that she was snitching on Angel. Protective custody is just like maximum security. The inmates held there are completely isolated. It's an unrelenting, punitive, miserable existence.

Lawyers who want to see inmates being held in protective custody have to go to them. The guards won't bring the protective custody inmates out to the attorneys' interview room because it would mean they would encounter other inmates along the way. It took me almost an hour of wrangling to get in to see Sarah. The guards knew she was a witness against my client, and they didn't want me talking to her. But as an attorney, I had as much right to interview witnesses as the police, even star witnesses, and I wasn't going to let them keep me out. They tried to get Deacon Baker on the phone but were told he was "unavailable." Frankie Martin had taken the day off and was fishing somewhere. Finally, after I threatened to haul every one of them in front of the nearest judge, they relented.

The guard who unlocked the door to Sarah's cell walked in and announced that she didn't have to speak to me if she didn't want to. True to form, she told him to go screw himself.

He closed the door, and I heard him walk down the hall. The cell was tiny, only eight feet square, and solid gray. It contained a stainless steel platform covered by a thin mattress, a stainless steel sink, and a stainless steel toilet. That was it. There was no television, no radio, no writing or reading materials, absolutely nothing to distract or otherwise occupy the mind. Sarah, barefoot and clad in her wrinkled orange jumpsuit, was sitting on the floor in the corner beyond the sink with her knees drawn up to her chin.

"So this is the way they treat their star witness in a murder case," I said. "I wonder where they'd put you if they didn't like you."

She buried her face in her hands, and I moved toward her. I got down on my knees and put my hands on her forearms. To my surprise, she didn't flinch or draw back.

"You don't have to say a word if you don't want to," I said softly, "but I realized something last night and I want to talk to you. I want to tell you I'm sorry."

I felt tears gathering in my eyes and fought for control. I didn't know why, but even in my efforts to peel back the curtains and take an honest look at what had happened between us, I felt the need to maintain my stoic image.

"I'm sorry I let you down, Sarah. I'm sorry I didn't stop him. I'm sorry I didn't protect you. I should have killed the bastard."

As with Caroline the night before, getting it out brought down my defenses and tears began to run down my cheeks.

"Please, Sarah. I was so young. I didn't know what to do. Please forgive me."

She too began to cry, and I scooted closer to her and put my hands on her shoulders.

"If I could, I'd take you back there right now and get you out of that room, but we both know I can't. All I can do is tell you I'm sorry and I love you. I've always loved you, Sarah. I always will."

"You were too little, Joey," she said in a choked voice. "We were both too little."

She lifted her head and wrapped her arms around my neck. It was a surreal moment, a moment of desperation and honesty and, ultimately, what I hoped was love. I couldn't remember the last time I'd hugged Sarah, and I found myself content to kneel on that concrete floor and feel her breathing against my neck. We said nothing for several minutes, both embarrassed by the rare show of affection.

Finally, she spoke again.

"You're breaking my neck, Joey."

"Oh, God, I'm sorry." I sometimes forgot about my size. I let go of her and scooted back. "I have to get up. This concrete is killing my knees."

I sat on the edge of her bunk and she sat with me. We talked for an hour. The conversation was slow and stilted at first, but before long she was telling me how tormented she'd been, how the drugs seemed to be the only thing that gave her any relief, if only for a short time. We talked about growing up fatherless, and about Ma and how deeply troubled she was. We eventually got around to the future, the immediate future, and what it held for Sarah.

"So what's your agreement with the district attorney's office?" I said.

She looked at me warily. "Is that why you really came down here?"

"Please don't say that. You know why I came down here. But it's something we're going to have to deal with."

"I've agreed to testify truthfully in exchange for immediate release and probation on my sentence."

"Do you have it in writing?"

"Of course I do." She reached under the mattress and pulled out an envelope. Inside was an agreement signed by Sarah, Deacon Baker, and Judge Glass. Sarah was obligated to provide "truthful testimony" in court in the case of the State vs. Angel Christian, and upon her having provided that testimony, she was to be released immediately.

"What's your truthful testimony going to be?" I said.

She gave me a mischievous grin I hadn't seen in thirty years. "Will you make sure I get my deal?" she said.

"You bet your ass."

JULY 31
2:00 P.M.

The test results on the forensic evidence found in Erlene Barlowe's car hadn't been received from the TBI lab by 9:00 a.m. the following Monday, so Judge Green reconvened the trial. I'd spent a great deal of time explaining everything in detail to Angel during the week. She understood she couldn't get up and lie. She understood I couldn't use the doctor as a defense witness. She understood the risks. After listening intently to everything I had to say and no doubt with some input from Erlene, she decided to go for it.

Frankie Martin did his best, but ultimately he had no murder weapon, no clear motive, and no eyewitnesses. He put Landers on the stand to describe the crime scene and explain the investigation, but on cross-examination I was able to paint a picture of Tester first drinking beer at the Purple Pig, then spending the money he'd received from a church at a strip club. To top it off, I pointed out the fact that Tester was so out of control that he'd spent all the church's money and had to withdraw even more from the ATM at midnight.

The medical examiner testified that Tester died from blood loss as a result of multiple stab wounds, but on cross she also had to admit that his blood-alcohol level was off the charts. She tried to help the prosecution by pointing out that he'd ingested a date-rape drug, but she could offer no testimony as to how the drug entered his body.

An expert from the TBI lab told the jury about the hairs found on Tester's shirt and explained the DNA identification process to them. On cross he had to admit it was possible that the hairs could have passed from Angel to Tester at the club.

An elderly woman named Ina Mae described for the jury how her cat found Tester's penis and delivered it to her the morning after the murder. Her testimony provided a brief moment of levity in an otherwise deadly serious trial.

Frankie saved Sarah for last. He would have been better off going outside and shooting himself.

"Would you state your name for the record, ma'am?" Frankie began.

"My name is Sarah Dillard." She was wearing the orange jumpsuit and was cuffed and shackled. She seemed nervous but determined.

"And where do you reside, Ms. Dillard?"

"At the Washington County Detention Center."

"So you're in jail?"

"Yes. I was convicted of theft."

"Are you familiar with the defendant, Miss Dillard?"

Sarah looked at Angel and nodded. "She's in my cell block."

"And as a matter of fact, you're her lawyer's sister, are you not?"

"I am."

"And did you contact the district attorney's office and tell someone that you had information regarding the defendant that might be relevant to this case?"

"No."

"I beg your pardon?"

"I said no. I didn't contact the district attorney's office. They came to me."

"Oh, I see. And who was it that came to see you?"

"That man over there." She pointed to Landers, who was sitting at the prosecutor's table.

"And as a result of your visit with Agent Landers, what did you do?"

"Nothing." Uh-oh. Here we go.

"Nothing? You had a conversation with the defendant, didn't you?"

"No."

"This defendant confessed to you that she murdered Reverend Tester, didn't she?"

"Objection," I said. "He's leading the witness, Judge."

"Sustained. Move on, Mr. Martin. She answered your question."

"Can I have a short recess, Your Honor?" Martin said.

"Why?" the judge said.

"I need some time to sort this out. This is a complete surprise to me."

"That's quite obvious, Mr. Martin, but I'm not accustomed to stopping murder trials because prosecuting attorneys are surprised. Do you have any more questions for the witness?"

"Permission to treat the witness as hostile, Your Honor."

"She's *your* witness, Mr. Martin."

"I realize that, but her testimony is not what I was told it would be."

"You mean you haven't even interviewed her?"

"Agent Landers interviewed her. He told me what her testimony would be. She signed a statement. He showed it to me."

"Use the statement then," the judge said.

"Permission to treat her as hostile, Your Honor," Martin said.

Judge Green waved the back of his hand at Frankie as though he was shooing him away. "Go ahead," he said, "but I don't think it's going to make a difference."

Martin straightened himself and turned back to Sarah. "Isn't it true, Miss Dillard, that you entered into an agreement with the district attorney's office to provide truthful testimony in this case?"

"Yes," Sarah said, "and that's exactly what I'm doing."

"Isn't it true that you told Agent Landers that Angel Christian, the defendant in this case, confessed that she killed Reverend Tester during a conversation you had with her at the jail?"

"No, that isn't true."

"Did you not sign a statement to that effect?" Landers held up a piece of paper I assumed was Sarah's statement.

"I signed a statement Agent Landers wrote. He'd already written it before he came to see me. It was a lie. I'm sorry I signed it."

"So you're now saying you signed a false statement?"

"That's right."

"You're accusing a police officer of drafting a completely false statement that you willingly signed?"

"He drafted the statement. I signed it. He never even asked me any questions. He told me if I signed the statement and testified in court he'd see to it that I got out of jail. I've never spoken to the defendant."

Martin turned and glared at Landers. "May I have a moment, Your Honor?"

"Make it quick."

Martin moved to the prosecutor's table and began to whisper in Landers's ear. Landers shook his head emphatically and whispered back. The exchange very quickly turned into a heated argument, with both men whispering forcefully back and forth. At one point I heard Landers say, "To hell with you." I hoped the jury heard it too.

Martin went back to the lectern.

"You're lying, aren't you, Ms. Dillard? You're trying to help your brother."

"No," Sarah said. "You guys were the ones who were trying to get me to lie. The agent said it would give me a chance to get back at my brother."

"Do you expect this jury to believe you, Ms. Dillard?" Martin said. "You're a convicted thief and a drug addict, aren't you?"

"I was a convicted thief and a drug addict when Agent Landers came to the jail. That didn't seem to bother him when he was trying to get me to lie."

"This is ridiculous," Martin said. "I move to strike her testimony, Your Honor."

"On what grounds, Mr. Martin? On the grounds that she didn't testify the way you wanted her to? Your motion is denied. Do you have any more questions for her?"

"It wouldn't do any good," Martin said as he turned away from the lectern. He seemed to deflate, like a torn balloon. "She'd just lie."

He sat down. I debated for a minute whether I should ask Sarah anything. She'd already done plenty of damage, but I couldn't resist twisting the knife a little, so I stepped to the lectern.

"You are my sister, aren't you?"

"Yes, I am."

"And the truth is that you and I haven't always gotten along well, have we?"

"Not always."

"As a matter of fact, your most recent conviction was a direct result of my reporting you to the police, wasn't it?"

"It was."

"And you were angry with me for doing that, weren't you?"

"Very angry."

"How long is your sentence?"

"Six years."

"And how much of that sentence would you have had to serve if you'd testified the way Mr. Martin expected you to testify?"

"I would have been released immediately."

"Do you have a copy of the agreement?"

She produced her copy, and I asked the judge to enter it as an exhibit. Martin objected on the grounds of relevance, but the judge overruled him.

"Miss Dillard," I said, "would you explain to the jury exactly how this agreement came about?"

"Agent Landers came to see me a couple months ago and asked me if I'd help them by getting to know Miss Christian. He said he wanted me to talk to her and find out everything I could about her and then tell him everything she said. I told him I wasn't interested, and he left. Then, a few weeks ago, after I'd been sentenced to six years, he came back. He said he could offer me two things: a sentence reduced to time served and a chance to get back at you. I asked him what he wanted me to do. He said he needed me to sign a statement saying that Angel Christian confessed to the murder of Reverend Tester. He already had the statement written up when he came to the jail. It said during a conversation in the cell block, Miss Christian told me she left the Mouse's Tail strip club with Mr. Tester after she agreed to have sex with him. She went with him back to his hotel room. It said she went into his room and drugged him, then she killed him and took all his money. It said she felt no remorse because the man she killed was a pig."

"A pig? That's a nice touch. Did Miss Christian say any of those things to you?"

"No. I've never even talked to her." She pointed at Landers. "He made it all up."

"Why did you sign it?"

"Because I hated being in jail. Because I was furious at you for having me arrested. I blamed you for everything. But I realize now I was wrong. It wasn't your fault I was in jail. It was my fault." She looked directly at the jury. "I'm sorry," she said quietly. "I'm sorry for a lot of things."

"Thank you, Miss Dillard."

I thought Judge Green might grant us a judgment of acquittal at the close of the state's proof. He should have, but ultimately he didn't have the courage to let a first-degree murder defendant walk out the door without sending the case to the jury.

He looked at me and said, "Call your first witness."

I stood up. I had witnesses waiting in the hallway, including Virgil Watterson and Erlene Barlowe, but I didn't think I needed them.

"The defense rests, Your Honor."

Martin and I delivered our closing arguments, both of which were brief. The jury retired to deliberate. It took them less than an hour to come back with a verdict.

I knew Angel was guilty, but the jury didn't. They set her free.

JULY 31
4:15 P.M.

As soon as the not-guilty verdict was announced, Frankie Martin and Landers got up and walked out without saying a word. Amid the hugs and the tears and the congratulations, I watched Junior Tester walk stiffly out of the courtroom. I was sure he hated me more than ever. I'd portrayed his dead father as a drunken hypocrite who might have been killed by anyone, and the jury's verdict had given the portrayal at least some validation. As he disappeared through the doorway, I wondered how he'd feel, or what he might do, if he knew the truth about what happened in the motel room that night. I also wondered how long I'd have to keep looking over my shoulder. He hadn't made a peep during the trial.

Erlene Barlowe was flitting around the courtroom like a socialite, hugging anyone who'd stand still long enough for her to get her arms around them. She even hugged one of the bailiffs. When she came up to me, she kissed me on the cheek and whispered a sincere "Thank you" in my ear. I wanted to tell her what I knew about the Corvette and the blood, but at the time, it just didn't seem like the thing to do.

Angel hugged me for at least half a minute, then turned and walked out the door hand-in-hand with Erlene. My last image of her was of her smiling radiantly, but I knew the smile couldn't last long. Life had already been unfair, even cruel, to her. I felt sure the events of the night Tester raped her, plus the knowledge that she'd gotten away with murder, would haunt her. I wondered where she'd go, and what would become of her.

Caroline had decided to come down to watch the trial after I told her what was going to happen with Sarah. She stood just beyond the bar while I slowly packed my files into my briefcase. Besides the two bailiffs, she and I were the only people in the courtroom. I took my time. I wanted to stay there long enough to allow everyone else to leave. The last thing I needed was a confrontation with Junior Tester or Landers.

When I was ready, I closed the briefcase and turned and winked at Caroline. She stepped through the bar and kissed me without saying a word, hooked her elbow around mine, and we walked out together through a side door. We took the back steps down to the ground floor.

"Lord, it's hot," I said as we crossed a one-way street that ran parallel to the courthouse. It was almost a hundred degrees. As we walked toward the parking lot, I saw a figure step out from behind a small hedge at the corner of the building about thirty yards to my right. It was Junior Tester. He was holding his right arm tight against his side. There was something in his hand.

Tester was between us and the building. There was no way to go back inside where there were police officers and bailiffs with guns. I dropped my briefcase, grabbed Caroline's hand and began to run.

"What are you doing?" she said.

"Run, Caroline! Tester's coming. I think he has a gun."

I looked back over my shoulder and saw him. He was jogging and lifting his right arm.

The parking lot behind the courthouse was about an acre of asphalt. There was room for close to a hundred cars, and it was always full. As Caroline and I approached the first line of cars, a gunshot shattered the peacefulness of the summer afternoon in Tennessee's oldest town. I heard the bullet whiz past in front of me. It ricocheted off the fender of an old Buick and whistled away. Caroline screamed.

"My God, Joe! He's going to kill us!"

I grabbed her by the arm and pulled her between two rows of cars.

"Get down!" I yelled. "Stay low." We ran another fifty feet and I looked back. Junior had stopped. His feet were spread and he was aiming the pistol with both hands. Another shot smashed into the passenger window of the car we were running past. I stopped and crouched beside the front fender. I had to figure out a way to get Caroline out of the line of fire.

"We can't stay together," I said. I was already sweating and breathing heavily. Caroline's eyes were wild with fear. I took her face in my hands.

"Listen to me. I'm going to start running. He'll follow me—I'm the one he's after. When he does, you go in the opposite direction. They can probably hear the shots in the courthouse, but just in case, get on your phone and call the cavalry. Get me some help!"

"Joe! No—"

I didn't wait for her to finish. I came up from behind the car and started sprinting toward the west end of the courthouse. I sprinted for maybe five seconds and looked back. Junior was jogging again, but he was lagging behind me. He raised the gun and fired. High. At least Caroline was safe. I kept running.

When I came to the end of the parking lot, I stopped and crouched beside a pickup. I knew I couldn't stay still for long, but I was trapped. The parking lot ended at a concrete retaining wall at least ten feet high. I would either have to run across an open space toward Main Street or go back in the direction from which I'd come. If I went back, I could try to stay behind the cars, but Tester would have a much closer shot at me and might be able to cut me off. And I wasn't sure whether Caroline had made it out of the parking lot. If I went forward, I'd be exposed, but if I could make it to the corner of Main and get around the pharmacy. ...

I took off for the street.

I saw him in my peripheral vision as I cleared the truck. He was back in his shooting stance. The fourth shot buzzed past my ear and I started to zigzag. A group of tourists was standing on the corner outside the courthouse, pointing and shouting. I thought I saw a flash of khaki. A deputy? *Please be a deputy.* Four shots. How many bullets did he have?

I was nearing the small pharmacy on the corner of Main. I thought about ducking inside, but I didn't want to trap myself, and I didn't want to put anyone else in the line of fire. If I could get around the building, put it between Junior and me, I might be able to find cover or duck into an alley and hide long enough for the police to show up. Just as I was starting to round the corner, the fifth shot ricocheted off the brick beside me and tore into my left thigh. I didn't feel any pain, but the impact of the bullet knocked me off balance, and I went sprawling face-first onto the brick sidewalk. I lay there dazed for a second and tried to get up. My left leg wouldn't work. I started to crawl. The bricks were warm beneath my hands.

People were screaming and yelling across the street, and I knew he was getting close. I heard sirens. *Please, God, make them hurry.* There was a loose brick in the sidewalk. I pried it out with my fingers. I rolled onto my back just as Junior came around the corner, less than ten feet away. He was holding the gun at arm's length. He saw me lying on the ground and slowed. Beads of sweat were glistening on his forehead. The corners of his lips curled slightly.

I threw the brick, but it missed him by inches. He took two more steps and was standing over me, just as I'd stood over him the night I went to his house. I looked at the gun. It was a revolver, six shots. I'd counted five. He had one left.

"Therefore the fathers shall eat the sons in the midst of thee, and the sons shall eat their fathers," he said. "And I will execute judgment upon thee and the whole remnant of thee shall I scatter to the winds. ..."

I started crawling backwards on my elbows, dragging my bleeding and useless left leg. I stared at Junior, waiting for the shot and the darkness. His eyes were wild and he was still talking, but the words had become nothing more than incoherent babble. He pulled the hammer back with his thumb. His hand was trembling. I froze.

The next few seconds seemed to run in slow motion. Junior jerked forward as though something had struck him from behind. A puzzled look came over his face, and the gun roared. The bullet screamed past my left ear so close I could feel the shock wave from the velocity. The gun clattered to the bricks by my feet. Suddenly a huge, liver-spotted hand came over the top of Junior's head and covered his face. The fingers locked onto his chin and pulled straight up.

Junior went over onto his back. A man mounted him and started spraying something into his eyes. Gray-haired man in a uniform. ...

It was Sarge Hurley, the ancient courthouse security officer. I saw Sarge raise a massive fist and bring it downward toward Tester's face and heard a loud thud as fist met jaw. More uniforms, some khaki, some blue. They descended on Junior like locusts.

And then, as quickly as it began, it was over. Sarge straightened and turned toward me. He stepped over and knelt beside me.

"You all right, Dillard?"

I looked into his eyes and for the first time, I noticed they were green, just like mine. I laid my head back on the bricks and smiled. Good old Sarge, my very own geriatric guardian angel. He wasn't even sweating.

"What took you so long?" I said. "You let him shoot me."

Sarge grunted. He leaned over and picked up Junior's revolver and looked it over closely.

"I save your miserable life and all you can say is 'what took you so long?' I swear if he had another bullet, I might just finish the job."

AUGUST 2
11:00 A.M.

The Tennessee Bureau of Investigation arrested Erlene Barlowe at 7:00 a.m. on Wednesday morning, the day before Deacon Baker went up against a former prosecutor named Lee Mooney in the election. The lab results had apparently confirmed that the blood in her Corvette was Reverend Tester's. She called as soon as they finished booking her. She wanted me to come down to the jail.

The bullet that hit me had gone into my left quadriceps, grazed my femur, and exited through my groin muscle. The wound was what they called a through-and-through. It missed my femoral artery by only a few centimeters. Had it severed the artery, I'd have bled to death on the sidewalk. Instead, they cleaned out the wound at the hospital, wrapped it, and let me go home the next day. It throbbed continuously, but considering the alternative, I wasn't complaining. I took plenty of aspirin, used crutches to walk, and Caroline helped me keep the wound clean.

Junior Tester was arrested and charged with two counts of attempted first-degree murder. He'd already been shipped down to Lakeshore Mental Health Institute in Knoxville. I had mixed feelings about Junior. While it was true that he'd tried twice to kill me and had very nearly succeeded both times, I couldn't help thinking that he'd been a victim himself, a victim of a volatile mixture of fundamentalist extremism and parental hypocrisy. When he learned the circumstances of his father's murder, something deep inside him had obviously snapped. And then having to sit through the trial and listen to it all again. ... I doubted very seriously that he would be held criminally liable for his actions. Like Angel, he'd been so traumatized that he probably no longer recognized the fine line between right and wrong.

I hobbled through the maze on my crutches to the attorneys' room at the jail. Erlene Barlowe was already seated at the table. She was getting the Maynard Bush treatment—handcuffs, shackles, a chain around her waist. She made the orange jumpsuit look pretty good despite the color clash with her hair.

When I walked in, she was sitting in the same chair Angel sat in during our many talks. To my surprise, she was her usual upbeat self. It didn't look like I'd need any tissue.

"Mr. Dillard," she said as I sat down, "I can't tell you how glad I am to see you, sugar. How are you feeling?"

"Like I've been shot."

"I'm so sorry, baby doll. It must have been just awful. That man was even crazier than his daddy."

"I'm sorry to see you here, Erlene."

"You've got to get me out of this, sugar. I didn't kill that man."

How many times had I heard that? This time, though, it was different.

"I know you didn't."

"Well, I swan. Did my sweet little Angel tell you?"

"I'm sorry. I can't discuss that with you."

She clutched her hands to her heart. "Well, bust my shiny little buttons, honey. Angel told you and you got her out of it anyway. That's why I hired you, you know. I knew you were the best."

The *best*. Helping a guilty woman walk away from a murder made me the best at my profession. I wondered what I'd have to do to be the worst.

"Tell me something," I said. "Angel had an opportunity to make an excellent deal a couple weeks before the trial. She rejected it. You wouldn't have had anything to do with that, would you?"

Her smile turned from genuine to coy.

"They gave her another chance after the trial started. The district attorney was willing to dismiss the murder charge against her. All she would have had to do was tell them you committed the murder. But she wouldn't."

"That's my sweet little girl."

"Convenient for us that Julie Hayes died when she did, huh?"

"It was a terrible tragedy. I can't tell you how many times I begged that child to stay away from drugs. Turned out to be her undoing."

"You wouldn't have had anything to do with her death?"

"Why, sugar, I can't believe you'd even ask me such a thing. But I will tell you this one teeny little secret. I *may have* suggested to someone that Julie was a problem, and that someone *may have* misinterpreted what I meant. I certainly didn't mean for anyone to get killed."

I decided to leave it at that. I didn't want to take a chance on ending up as a witness against Erlene. "How do you think the cops found out about your car?"

"You know, I gave that a lot of thought myself," she said. "And I came to the conclusion that one of my girls must have called that nasty TBI agent. As a matter of fact, I'm certain of it. I believe I told her exactly what to say."

"You *what*?"

She put her hands on the table, laced her fingers, and leaned toward me.

"I probably should explain something to you, baby doll. When you run a business like mine, you meet all different kinds of people. I try to be good to every one of them, so when I need something, I usually get it. Well, this time, what I needed was some real good legal advice, but it wasn't the kind of legal advice I could get from you. So I talked to this wonderful man. He's a lawyer, but not exactly the kind of lawyer you are. He used to help my husband out with his finances. He helped me understand some things about the law. Let's see, what all were they? Things like double jeopardy, I believe is what he called it, and what was that other thing? Oh, yes, the fourth amendment."

"Who was it?"

"I couldn't betray his confidence, sugar pie. Let's just say he's a sweet, sweet man who likes to indulge in a little harmless sin on occasion. He and my Gus were real close."

I couldn't believe what I was hearing. I suspected Erlene had somehow been involved in Julie's death, but I didn't have any proof of it and doubted anybody on the planet would ever come up with any. But this was something else, something fascinating.

"Why would you want Landers to find the car?" I said.

"I couldn't let Angel spend the rest of her life in prison or get the death penalty, sugar. The whole thing with that preacher man was my fault. When he came out to the club acting a fool and pawing Angel the way he did, it just flew all over me. Do you know what he said when I asked him nicely to leave? He said, 'I want to rent your whore for the night. Who do I talk to about that?' Why, that made me mad as fire, and I just figured right then and there that I'd teach him a little lesson. All Angel was supposed to do was go into the room and give him a drink. I was going to take care of the rest all by myself."

"Didn't quite work out the way you planned, did it?"

"It was *awful*. I should've known better than to send that sweet girl up to that motel room alone. I've been around the block a few times, sweetie pie, and I knew the preacher was rotten to the core, but I swan, I was so mad I just wasn't thinking straight. I never dreamed he'd do what he did. And I never dreamed Angel would react the way she did. When she came down those steps, I thought I was going to have a stroke. I went back into the room and there was all that blood. I nearly passed out. But I told myself to calm down, and I set about trying to make things right for Angel. I picked up the bottle of scotch and her purse and the knife and his wallet and then I went—"

"Hold on a minute, Erlene. Why'd you cut his ... his ... what did you call it? His twigger or something like that?"

"His terwilliger?"

"Yeah, that. Why'd you cut it off? Angel told me she didn't do it. It must have been you."

"I saw this TV show where a man got convicted of rape because he had the girl's DNA on his terwilliger. I got to thinking that Angel's DNA might be on his terwilliger, and—well, you know, if the police *did* come around and start asking questions—I didn't want her to have to explain something like that. Besides, sugar, he didn't need it anymore."

I knew when I met Erlene that there was more to her than big boobs and batting eyes, but I never expected anything like this.

"What else did you do?" I said.

"Well, let's see. Not a whole lot. I just got sweet little Virgil to do me a favor."

"You mean he didn't see you on the bridge?"

"Nobody saw me on the bridge, honey. I can promise you that. And I thought there was no way anyone would find the terwilliger. That was just a stroke of bad luck."

It was almost brilliant. She'd managed to dupe the police into thinking she'd committed the murder to get Angel off, but she'd done such a masterful job of it, she might well be convicted.

"You've got some serious problems, Erlene. For starters, what's Virgil going to do when the state subpoenas him to testify against you? If he gets up on the stand and lies, they'll charge him with perjury."

"Don't you worry your handsome face about that, honey. I won't be going to trial."

"You—why not?"

"It's that other legal thing I was telling you about. That fourth amendment. You see, this lawyer, the one that likes to sin every now and then, he came out to the club one night and I asked him how I could lead a police officer to a piece of evidence and then make sure he couldn't use the evidence later. So he told me all about searches, and he made a *wonderful* suggestion. He said if I'd wait until the very, very last minute and then have someone make an anonymous call to that nasty old TBI agent and tell him where my car was, he'd bet anything the policeman would go tearing up there without a search warrant or anything. And you know what? He was right as rain. That TBI man climbed over a locked gate and ignored a locked door on my barn and crawled right in through a window. The car was under a tarp in the barn, sweetie. It's private property."

She'd graduated from almost brilliant to brilliant. Still, she didn't know who she was dealing with.

"Landers will lie," I said. "He'll say the gate wasn't locked, the barn door was open, he was acting on a reliable tip, and the car was in plain view."

She smiled and hunched her shoulders. "Oh, sweetie, this is the best part. I've got everything he did on video. The lawyer told me to send somebody up there in the woods with a camera. Ronnie filmed the whole thing. I'll bet I've watched it ten times."

I stared at her for a second, not quite believing what I'd just heard. I felt a chuckle making its way up through my chest. I tried to suppress it, but the more I tried, the harder it pushed. The first one made its way out of my mouth, and then another. Within a few seconds, I was laughing so hard I could barely breathe. I looked over at Erlene. She'd lost it too. It was one of the most visceral moments of my life, Erlene and I locked onto each other, laughing uncontrollably. It was almost as good as sex.

After a couple minutes, I managed to get at least a little control of myself.

"You know what this means?" I said through a chuckle. "It means they won't be able to use the car *or anything they found in it!*"

Erlene looked like a bobblehead. "That was just what I was trying to do, sweetie. Isn't it *wonderful*?"

We started cracking up again.

"They'll have less on you ... than they had on Angel."

"I know."

Finally we calmed down and Erlene turned serious.

"You'll represent me, won't you, sweetie? You'll handle it for me?"

I wiped a tear from my eye with the back of my hand. "I can't, Erlene. It's a conflict of interest."

"I don't see why. They found Angel not guilty. Her case is over, isn't it? They can't try her again no matter what. All you have to do is show them the videotape, and that should be the end of it. Don't you think?"

"I don't know. It won't be that simple. Nothing's ever that simple."

"C'mon, sweetie. This'll be a piece of cake for you. You're the best there is. Oh, and speaking of that, I meant to tell you the way you set them up with your sister was *brilliant.* When Angel told me about it, I thought I was going to wet my pants."

"I didn't exactly plan that. I'm not as smart as you are."

"Don't kid yourself, sugar. Now what do you say? Will you do the same for me as you did for Angel?"

I was thinking about the conflict. She was right about Angel. They couldn't try her again, no matter what, and since the rules prohibited me from uttering a word about Angel's confession, it wouldn't be an issue. On top of that, if Erlene really had a videotape of Landers conducting an illegal search, the car and everything in it would be out, there'd be no trial, and no risk that I'd ever have to question Angel on a witness stand. And because Angel had told me what really happened, I knew Erlene hadn't killed Tester.

My God, if I agreed, Erlene would be my innocent client. Finally.

"You're going to be locked up in here for a while," I said. "You up to it?"

"I could post a million in cash for bond if I wanted to, but I'm afraid the nosy old IRS people would wonder where I got all that money. Don't you worry about me, baby doll. I'll be fine."

"You're in for a bad run of publicity."

"Doesn't matter, sugar. The Junior League isn't ever going to ask me to join anyway."

"They'll try to paint you as an immoral madam who uses young girls and preys on horny men."

"You can clean me up. You're a sugar pie."

The woman had an almost irresistible charm about her, not to mention a fat bank account. I shook my head and grinned.

"Okay," I said. "You've got yourself a lawyer. But it's going to cost you."

Thank you for reading, and I sincerely hope you enjoyed *An Innocent Client*. As an independently published author, I rely on you, the reader, to spread the word. So if you enjoyed the book, please tell your friends and family, and if it isn't too much trouble, I would appreciate a brief review on Amazon. Thanks again. My best to you and yours.

Scott

ABOUT THE AUTHOR

Scott Pratt was born in South Haven, Michigan, and moved to Tennessee when he was thirteen years old. He is a veteran of the United States Air Force and holds a Bachelor of Arts degree in English from East Tennessee State University and a Doctor of Jurisprudence from the University of Tennessee College of Law. He lives in Northeast Tennessee with his wife, their dogs, and a parrot named JoJo.

www.scottprattfiction.com

ALSO BY SCOTT PRATT

IN GOOD FAITH

By

SCOTT PRATT

This book, along with every book I've written and every book I'll write, is dedicated to my darling Kristy, to her unconquerable spirit and to her inspirational courage. I loved her before I was born and I'll love her after I'm long gone.

PART I

WEDNESDAY, AUG. 27

Eight men and four women. A dozen citizens, filing slowly past the defense and prosecution tables beneath the stern scrutiny of a white-haired judge. All wore the dazed look of people who've been forced to sit for days in a place they've never been, listen to the words of men and women they've never seen, and pass judgment on a fellow human being.

The gallery was sadly bereft of spectators. Misty Bell, a young female newspaper reporter with short chestnut hair and curious hazel eyes, sat dutifully holding her notebook in the front row to my left. Two seats to her right sat the victim's son, an overweight, sad-looking man in his sixties with sagging jowls and receding gray hair that curled around his ears like smoke from a smoldering cotton ball. Aside from those two and me—I was sitting in the center of the back row—the gallery was empty.

The defendant, a wiry man named Billy Dockery, stood next to his lawyer at the defense table as the jury filed past. Dockery was gangly and in his mid-thirties. His dark hair snaked past his shoulders, framing a flat face that had maintained a perpetual smirk throughout the two-day trial. He wore civilized clothing—a dark gray suit, white shirt, and a navy blue tie—but I knew he was anything but civilized. Beneath the veneer was a cruel and dangerous sociopath.

His lawyer was James T. Beaumont III, a longtime practitioner of criminal defense whom I'd known casually for many years. Beaumont was in his late fifties and was somewhat of a celebrity in northeast Tennessee. He favored fringed buckskin jackets and string ties and wore a beige cowboy hat outside the courtroom. A long, light-brown mustache and goatee, heavily specked with gray, covered his upper lip and chin. With his longish hair, clear blue eyes, and a deep drawl, he reminded me very much of Wild Bill Hickok—at least the way they portrayed him in the movies.

"Call your witness," sixty-year-old Judge Leonard Green said.

Beaumont nodded and stood. "The defense calls Billy Dockery."

Dockery got up, ambled to the witness stand, and took the oath, the smirk still on his face. I'd seen the proof in the case and knew Dockery should exercise his Fifth Amendment right to keep his mouth shut. He'd be a terrible witness. But I also knew that Dockery enjoyed the spotlight almost as much as he enjoyed thumbing his nose at the prosecution and torturing defenseless, elderly women.

After a few preliminary questions, Beaumont got to the point.

"Mr. Dockery, I'll ask you this question on the front end. Did you kill Cora Wilson in the early morning hours of November seventeenth?"

Dockery leaned closer to the microphone.

"No sir, I did not. I did not have anything to do with her death. I was not nowhere near her place that night. I ain't never hurt nobody and I ain't never going to."

The sound of his voice made me cringe. Five years earlier, Dockery had been charged with murdering another elderly woman during a break-in at her home. His mother hired me to represent him, and after a trial, the jury found him not guilty and set him free. The next day, Dockery walked into my office and drunkenly confessed to me that he'd murdered the woman. He offered me a five-thousand-dollar cash bonus, money he said he'd stolen during the break-in. I threw him out of the office, along with his filthy money, but since double jeopardy prevented them from trying him again and since the rules of professional responsibility forbade me from telling anyone, I couldn't do a thing about the confession. When I read in the newspaper that he was about to go on trial for killing another woman, I wanted to be there to see his face when they sent him to the penitentiary for the rest of his life.

"Did you know the victim?" Jim Beaumont said from the podium in front of the witness stand.

"Yessir. I done yard work for her sometimes and I painted her house last year."

"Ever have any problems with her?"

"No sir. Not nary a one. Me and her got along like two peas in a pod."

"Where were you that night, Mr. Dockery?"

"I was campin' on the Nolichuckey River more'n two miles from her house."

"In November?"

"Yessir. My mamma's got a cabin down there. It's got a fireplace and all. I go there a lot."

"Anyone with you?"

"No sir. I was all by my lonesome."

"Thank you, Mr. Dockery. Please answer the prosecutor's questions."

It was the shortest direct examination of a criminal defendant I'd ever seen, and it was smart. Up to that point, the prosecution had been able to establish only that Billy Dockery had done landscaping work for eighty-six-year-old Cora Wilson. They established that Dockery had camped along the Nolichuckey River about two miles from Ms. Wilson's home the night she was beaten and tortured to death, a fact the defense did not dispute. They established that a length of nylon rope found around Ms. Wilson's neck was the same kind of rope found in the back of Billy Dockery's truck. The prosecutor's expert witness could not go so far as to say the rope was an exact match, only that it was made of the same material, of the same weave and circumference, and manufactured by the same company. Unfortunately for the prosecution, the defense subpoenaed an executive from the company that made the rope, and he testified that more than fifty thousand feet of that very same rope had been sold within a twenty-five-mile radius of the courthouse in the past five years.

The prosecution's star witness in the case, a seventeen-year-old named Tommy Treadway, had initially confessed to breaking into the house with Dockery that night but refused to sign a statement. Treadway told the police that he left when Dockery began to torture Ms. Wilson. But Treadway was released on bond after he agreed to testify against Dockery and wound up driving his car off the side of a mountain in Carter County a month before the trial. His death was ruled an accident.

The state's only other witness—besides the routine information given by the cops and the medical examiner—was a degenerate drunkard named Timmons who said he'd overheard Billy Dockery say that Cora Wilson kept cash in her house and that he "might go get it some night." Beaumont had already destroyed the witness on cross-examination, forcing him to admit that his two primary activities as an adult had been drinking whiskey and stealing other people's identities so that he could afford to drink more whiskey.

Now the assistant district attorney had his shot at the defendant. It was usually a prosecutor's dream, but Assistant District Attorney Alexander Dunn had been aloof and distracted. His case was so weak he should have dismissed it and waited to see whether any more evidence could be developed, but his ego—or his boss—had apparently driven him to trial.

Dunn, in his early thirties, was wearing a tailor-fitted brown suit over a beige shirt. A kerchief rose from the pocket of his jacket, and expensive Italian loafers covered his feet. He stood before Dockery and straightened his silk tie.

"Isn't it true, Mr. Dockery, that you and another individual broke into the victim's home around 2:00 a.m. on the morning of November seventeenth?"

"No."

It was an inauspicious beginning, to say the least, and I sank deeper into my seat. Dunn had been ordered by the judge not to mention the dead witness, and the jury was sure to wonder why, if there was a co-defendant, he wasn't on trial at the same time or testifying for the state.

"And isn't it true, Mr. Dockery, that you beat and tortured the victim in an effort to force her to tell you where her cash was hidden?"

"No, it ain't true, and you ain't got no fingerprints, no blood, no hair, no witnesses, no nothin' to prove I was there."

"But you *did* tell Mr. Timmons that the victim kept cash in her home and that you intended to steal it, didn't you?"

"I never said no such thing. Timmons ain't nothing but a drunk and a liar. He was probably just looking for some reward money so he could buy whiskey."

"And you're a model citizen, aren't you, Mr. Dockery? I'll bet you don't even drink."

Dockery's eyes flashed with righteous indignation. He leaned forward and put his hands on the rail in front of him.

"Yeah, I may drink a little, but I'll tell you what I don't do. I don't parade around in a fancy suit and put people on trial for murder when I ain't got no proof."

"I object, Your Honor," Dunn said. "The witness is being argumentative."

"Sustained. Don't argue with him, Mr. Dockery," Judge Green said. "Just answer the questions."

"Isn't it true, Mr. Dockery," Alexander continued, "that you took thousands of dollars in cash from the victim's home the night you murdered her?"

"If I did, then where is it? Y'all tore my mamma's place, her cabin, our barn, and every vehicle we own apart looking for money and didn't find a thing. And you know why you didn't find nothing? Cause I didn't *do* nothing."

Alexander Dunn's cross-examination ended shortly thereafter. It was a monumental disaster. Jim Beaumont rested his case and Judge Green read the instructions to the jury.

The judge was long rumored in the legal community to be a closet homosexual, and he lorded over his courtroom like an English nobleman. Before I stopped practicing law, I'd appeared before Green hundreds of times, and although I hadn't laid eyes on him in a year, each grandiose gesture he made, each perfectly formed syllable he spoke, reminded me of his pomposity. During lulls in the trial, I found myself imagining him prancing around the room in a white periwig, pink tutu and tights, leaping through the air like a fabulously gay ballet dancer.

As soon as Green finished, the jury retired to deliberate. I thought I'd be in for a long wait, but in less than thirty minutes, I saw the bailiffs and clerks bustling around, a sure sign the jurors had made their decision. Five minutes later, they filed back into the courtroom. Green turned his palm upward and raised his right hand as though he were a symphony conductor coaxing a crescendo from the woodwinds. The foreman rose, an uncertain look on his weathered face.

"I understand you've reached a verdict," the judge said.

"We have, Your Honor."

"Pass it to the bailiff."

A uniformed deputy crossed the courtroom to the jury box, took the folded piece of paper from the foreman's hand, and delivered it to Judge Green. The judge dramatically unfolded the paper, looked at it with raised brows, refolded it, and handed it to the bailiff. The bailiff then walked the form back across the room to the foreman.

"Mr. Foreman," the judge said, "on the first count of the indictment, premeditated first-degree murder, how does the jury find?"

"We find the defendant not guilty."

"On the second count of the indictment, felony murder, how does the jury find?"

"We find the defendant not guilty."

"On the third count of the indictment, aggravated kidnapping, how does the jury find?"

"We find the defendant not guilty."

"On the fourth count of the indictment, aggravated burglary, how does the jury find?"

"We find the defendant not guilty."

"On the fifth count of the indictment, felony theft, how does the jury find?"

"We find the defendant not guilty."

I watched Dockery pat his lawyer on the back and walk out the door arm-in-arm with his mother.

He'd gotten away with it—again.

WEDNESDAY, AUG. 27

I fumed all the way home, muttering to myself about what an idiot Alexander Dunn had been. When I pulled into the driveway, the garage door was open. Caroline, my wife, must have forgotten to close it again. I parked my truck in the driveway and walked inside. As soon as I opened the door, I heard the sound of hard nails skidding across the wood floor. Rio, my German shepherd, came barreling around the counter, headed straight for me. I was carrying a bottle of water in my hand, and when he jumped up to greet me, his snout sent the bottle flying across the kitchen floor.

"Idiot!" I said as walked toward the counter. "Why are you always so excited to see me? We're together all day every day."

The tone of my voice frightened him, and he lowered his head and slinked away. As I turned to reach for a paper towel so that I could wipe up the spilled water, I scraped my shin on the open door of the dishwasher. I reached down and slammed it closed.

"Where have you been?" Caroline said as she walked into the kitchen with her perpetual smile on her face. Caroline and I were high school sweethearts and had been married for more than twenty years. She owned and operated a dancing school where she taught jazz, tap, ballet, and acrobatics. She was leggy, athletic, and tanned, with thick auburn hair and soft brown eyes. We were still deeply in love, but at that moment, I wasn't in the mood for pleasantries.

"Caroline, why do you leave this dishwasher door open all the time?" I said as I knelt down and started wiping up the spilled water. "I just cracked my shin on it again. I've asked you at least a hundred times to close the dishwasher."

She stopped in her tracks and glared at me.

"Why don't you watch where you're stepping?" she said sarcastically. "Are you blind?"

"And why can't you close the garage door?" I said, still wiping up the spill. "Were you born in a barn? All you have to do is push a button and it closes itself."

"What difference does it make whether the garage door is closed?" she snarled.

"It keeps some of the heat out, and when we keep some of the heat out, the air conditioner doesn't have to work so hard. And when the air conditioner doesn't work so hard, it saves us money! But you don't ever think about that, do you? The money we have isn't going to last forever, especially if you keep leaving the garage door open."

"So you're saying I'm going to drive us into bankruptcy by leaving a garage door open? Sitting around the house for a year has driven you crazy, Joe."

I straightened up, wadded the paper towel, and tossed it into the wastebasket under the sink. I walked past her toward the bedroom. I grabbed a pair of shorts, some socks, a T-shirt from the dresser, and my running shoes from the closet and went back to the bathroom to change. Just as I finished tying my shoes, Caroline appeared.

"So do you want to tell me what's going on with you?" she said.

"Nothing's going on."

"You haven't been in the house five minutes and you've already terrified Rio, slammed the dishwasher, and given me hell for leaving a garage door open. Something's going on. Where have you been for the past two days?"

I looked up at her. The anger was gone from her face, and the tone of her voice told me she was genuinely concerned.

"I went to Jonesborough to watch Billy Dockery's trial," I said.

"I knew it," she said. "I've been reading about it in the newspaper. I knew you wouldn't be able to stay away. Is it still going on?"

"No. They acquitted him again. I don't think I've ever seen a prosecutor do a poorer job of trying a case."

"Come on out to the kitchen table," she said as she reached out and took my hand. "Let's talk."

I followed her out to the kitchen and sat down. She went to the refrigerator, pulled out two beers, and came back to the table.

"You're miserable," she said. "You're bored. I think you feel like you're wasting your life, and it's time to do something about it."

She popped the top on a can of Budweiser and handed it to me.

"I'm not miserable," I said. "I'm just a little upset. Seeing Dockery walk out the door today made me sick to my stomach."

"So why don't you do something about it?" she said.

"Do something? Like what?"

"Why don't you go back to work? I remember when we were young, you talked about going to work for the prosecutor's office. Why don't you give Lee Mooney a call and see if he can find a place for you?"

The suggestion took me by complete surprise. Even sitting there watching Alexander Dunn botch a trial, knowing I could do much better, going back to practicing law hadn't entered my mind. I'd quit a year earlier after spending more than a decade as a criminal defense lawyer. I made a lot of money, gained a lot of notoriety, and was good at what I did, but the profession eventually burned me out mentally, physically, and emotionally.

Friends and acquaintances had always asked me: "How can you go into court and represent someone you know is guilty?" My answer was always that my job was to make certain the government followed its own rules and to hold them to their burden of proof. It didn't have anything to do with guilt or innocence. I convinced myself for years that I was doing something honorable, that I was an important cog in the machine that called itself the criminal justice system. But over time, and especially after I realized I'd helped Billy Dockery escape punishment for murdering a defenseless elderly woman, I began to regard myself as something much less than honorable. A little over a year ago, after I'd helped a young woman walk away from a charge of murdering a preacher, the preacher's son tried to kill me in the parking lot outside the courthouse, and he nearly killed my wife in the process. That was enough.

I'd worked hard my entire life and had accumulated a fair amount of money, so I took a break, thinking I might eventually teach at a university. For the past year, I'd divided my time between watching my son play baseball for Vanderbilt University in Nashville and watching my daughter perform at football and basketball games as a member of the University of Tennessee's dance team. When I was home, I piddled around the house, worked out at the gym, ran miles and miles along the trail by the lake, and played with the dog. I enjoyed myself most of the time, but Caroline was right. I was bored, and I missed the excitement of playing such a high-stakes game.

"I don't know, Caroline," I said. "It got pretty bad there at the end. Do you really think I'm ready to go back?"

"If we were sitting here talking about going back into criminal defense, I'd say no. But I think you'd like prosecuting. You've always had a little bit of a hero complex. Putting bad guys behind bars might be right up your alley."

"You're ready to get me out of the house, aren't you?" I said. "You're tired of looking at me."

"How could I be tired of looking at you? You're gorgeous. You're big and strong, and you've got that dark hair and those beautiful green eyes. You're eye candy, baby."

"That kind of flattery will definitely get you laid."

"Seriously," she said, "I'm not tired of anything. I could live this simple little life we have now until they put me in the ground, but I know you, Joe, and you're just not happy. You have too much drive to be a professional piddler."

"So you think I should just call Mooney up and say, 'Hey, how about giving me a job?'"

"Why not? The worst he can say is no, but I think he'd be glad to have you."

I smiled at her. Caroline had a way of making me feel like I could conquer the world. She'd always had more confidence in me than I had in myself.

"Okay," I said. "If you really think it might be right for me, I'll give it a shot. I'll call Mooney first thing in the morning."

She stood and pursed her lips slightly. The next thing I knew she was pulling her shirt over her head. She slipped off her bra and turned toward the bedroom, dangling the bra from her fingertips as she looked at me over her shoulder.

"Now that's what I call eye candy," I said as I put down the beer and followed her. "Wait up. Let me help you take off the rest."

FRIDAY, AUG. 29

I felt the cool air conditioning on my face as I opened the door and stepped out of the oppressive September heat and humidity. It was a room the owner of the restaurant—a man named Tommy Hodges who fancied himself a local political insider—reserved for special customers, people he believed had power or privilege. It had its own entrance at the side of the one-story brick building. I was forty-one years old and had practiced law in the community for more than a decade, but I'd never set foot in the place.

The room was small and dimly lit, dominated by a single table, large and round with a scarred, blue Formica top. All four walls surrounding the table were decorated with autographed photos of state and local politicians. Lee Mooney, the elected attorney general of the First Judicial District, was examining a photograph of himself as I stepped through the door. Mooney was fifty years old, a lean, striking man with gray eyes, salt-and-pepper hair, and a handle bar moustache. I'd called him on Thursday morning and asked him whether he might consider hiring me, and he asked me to meet him at Tommy's place the next day. He turned his head when he heard the door open and grinned.

"Joe Dillard, in the flesh," he said, extending his hand. "It's been a long time."

At six feet five, Mooney was a couple inches taller than me. As his fingers wrapped around my hand, his white teeth flashed and his eyes locked onto mine. He held both my gaze and my hand a bit too long.

I was suspect of all politicians, but because I'd practiced criminal defense law for so long, I was especially suspect of the ego-filled megalomaniacs who typically sought the office of district attorney. A Texas A&M grad, Mooney had gone from ROTC cadet to officer training to the Judge Advocate General's office in the Marine Corps. He retired five years ago after the Marines passed on the opportunity to promote him to full colonel. His wealthy wife had persuaded him to move to northeast Tennessee, which was her childhood home, and he was immediately hired on as an assistant with the local DA's office. Before I stopped practicing law, I tried a half-dozen criminal cases against Mooney. I remembered him as a formidable adversary in the courtroom with an almost pathological fear of losing. I'd suspected him more than once of withholding evidence, but I wasn't ever able to prove it.

Mooney quit the DA's office two years ago when he smelled blood in the water. Word around the campfire was that his predecessor—a pathetic little man named Deacon Baker—had lost control of his own office and, Mooney must have sensed, the confidence of the voters. Mooney resigned and immediately announced he was running against his boss in the August election. When the last murder case I defended blew up in Deacon Baker's face just before the election, Mooney buried him.

"So what have you been up to for the past year?" Mooney said as we sat down.

"As little as possible."

"How's your wife? Is it Caroline?"

"Right. She's fine, thanks for asking."

"I've read about your son in the newspaper. He's some ballplayer."

"He's worked hard."

"Have you missed it? Practicing law I mean."

"Some," I said. There was a seductive element to defending people accused of committing crimes, especially when the stakes were at their highest. Having the fate of a man's life depend on the intensity of your commitment and the quality of your work was alluring.

Tommy Hodges, the slight and balding owner of the restaurant, showed up carrying two glasses of water and a pad.

"Don't I know you?" he said to me.

"I don't think so."

"Sure you do," Mooney said. "This is Joe Dillard, the best trial lawyer who ever set foot in a courtroom around here."

Hodges's eyes lit up.

"Oh yeah!" he said, pointing at me. "I remember you! That murder, the preacher, right? That was something. Big news."

"Yeah," I said, "big news."

"I ain't heard of you since. Where you been?"

"Sabbatical," I said.

"What?"

"Tommy," Mooney said, "how about a couple club sandwiches and a couple Cokes? Is that okay with you, Joe?"

"Sure."

He kept fiddling with a salt shaker with his right hand. After Hodges left, Mooney regarded me with a puzzled look.

"I always wondered why you were on the other side," he said as soon Hodges left the room. "I thought you would have made a great prosecutor."

"The reason isn't exactly noble. It came down to money. When I graduated from law school, I wanted to work for the DA's office. I even went for an interview. But the starting salary was less than twenty-five grand, and I already had a wife and two kids to support. I figured I could make double that practicing on my own, so I told myself I'd learn the law from the other side and then try to get on with the DA after I made some money."

"And before you knew it, your lifestyle grew into your income."

"Exactly."

"Why'd you quit?"

"A combination of things, I guess. It always bothered me that I knew my clients were lying to me, or at least most of them. And I was constantly at war with somebody—cops, prosecutors, judges, witnesses, guards at the jails, you name it. I got tired of it. But the bottom line, I think, was that I felt like I was doing something wrong."

"Wrong? How so?"

"Some of the people I helped walk out the door were guilty. They knew it, and so did I."

Mooney shifted in his chair a little and looked down at the salt shaker. "You defended Billy Dockery once, didn't you?" he said.

"He was the beginning of the end of my career as a criminal defense lawyer," I said.

"Alexander Dunn told me you were at his trial."

"I was curious."

"How'd Alexander do? It was his first big felony trial."

"The odds were against him."

There wasn't any point in telling him that Alexander was terrible and that he constantly referred to Cora Wilson as "the victim in this case" instead of by name. Even when he did mention her name, he referred to her twice as "Ms. Williams" instead of "Ms. Wilson."

"So what are you really looking for, Joe?"

"It's pretty simple. I want to do something that keeps me interested, and I want to do something that allows me to look in the mirror without throwing up."

Mooney sat back and smiled. "You looking to make amends?"

"Maybe. Something like that."

"You have to understand that Baker didn't leave me with much," he said, speaking of his predecessor. "He was so paranoid that he ran off every competent lawyer in the office. All that's left are a bunch of kids learning on the fly."

"Do you have anything open?" I said. I knew the budget in the DA's office was tight. State legislators tend to look at the criminal justice system as a necessary evil when it comes to funding.

"Not right now," Mooney said, "but I'll make room for you if you can wait a couple weeks. I was planning to fire Jack Moseley as soon as I could find someone to replace him."

"I don't want to cost anybody their job."

"Moseley's a drunk. Shows up late for work half the time, doesn't cover his cases, pinches the secretaries. Last month he disappeared for three days. We found him holed up at the Foxx Motel with a gallon of vodka and an empty sack of cocaine."

"I don't remember reading about that in the paper," I said.

Mooney winked. "Sometimes what the people don't know won't hurt them. I would've fired him months ago if I'd had another warm body. The job's yours if you want it."

"Exactly what would I be doing?"

"I've been thinking about that ever since you called. The best use for you would be to work the violent felonies, the worst ones. Murders, aggravated rapes, armed robberies. Dangerous offenders only."

I let out a low whistle. "Some job description."

"You really want to do something that makes you feel good? Here's your chance. You can make sure dangerous people wind up in jail where they belong. I'll keep your case load as light as I can so you can do it right."

"I guess it'll include death-penalty cases," I said. I'd spent a great deal of my legal career trying to ensure the state didn't kill people. If I took this job, I knew I'd soon be making some difficult choices.

"We haven't had a death-penalty case since Deacon left the office," Mooney said. "What's the point? The state's only executed one person in forty years, and there's nobody in Nashville complaining about it. I guess the legislature wants to have the death penalty in Tennessee but not have to worry about enforcing it."

"It'll change soon," I said. "People have a tendency to be bloodthirsty."

"Look at it this way. You'll be doing the same thing you did so well for all those years, practicing criminal law. The difference will be that you'll be working with the good guys, and you'll have the manpower and resources of the great state of Tennessee behind you. The pay is good, there's no overhead, and you get four weeks of vacation, state health and retirement benefits, the whole ball of wax."

I sat back and thought for a moment. The money didn't matter that much. Both of my kids had earned scholarships that paid a significant amount of their college expenses. Our house was paid for, and we had plenty of money stashed away. I'd already called both of the kids and discussed the possibility of going to work for the district attorney. Both were in favor, as was Caroline. All that was left was for me to take the plunge and see what happened.

"You make it sound like easy money," I said.

Mooney nodded his head. "There you go. Easy money. Piece of cake. Come by and see me Monday and we'll get the paperwork rolling. You start in sixteen days."

If you enjoyed the beginning of *In Good Faith*, you can purchase here via Amazon:

In Good Faith
Again, thank you for reading!

Scott

Made in the USA
Middletown, DE
02 September 2019